Gone, Kitty, Gone

EILEEN WATKINS

KENSINGTON BOOKS
www.kensingtonbooks.com

KENSINGTON BOOKS are published by

Kensington Publishing Corp.
119 West 40th Street
New York, NY 10018

All Kensington titles, imprints, and distributed lines are available at special quantity discounts for bulk purchases for sales promotion, premiums, fund-raising, educational, or institutional use.

Special book excerpts or customized printings can also be created to fit specific needs. For details, write or phone the office of the Kensington Sales Manager: Kensington Publishing Corp., 119 West 40th Street, New York, NY 10018. Attn. Sales Department. Phone: 1-800-221-2647.

Kensington and the K logo Reg. U.S. Pat. & TM Off.

ISBN-13: 978-1-4967-2300-0 (ebook)
ISBN-10: 1-4967-2300-7 (ebook)
Kensington Electronic Edition: January 2020

ISBN-13: 978-1-4967-2297-3
ISBN-10: 1-4967-2297-3
First Kensington Trade Paperback Printing: January 2020

10 9 8 7 6 5 4 3 2 1

Printed in the United States of America

Acknowledgments

Much thanks to my new critique partners, Nicki Montaperto, Lew Preschell, and Jo-Ann Lamon Reccoppa, who helped me catch any faux-*paws* in my early drafts, and to my insightful beta reader, Joanne Weck. I'm grateful, as always, for the continuing support of my fellow members of Sisters in Crime Central Jersey, my agent, Evan Marshall, and my editor, John Scognamiglio. Fellow cat lover Anne-Marie Cottone cheerfully trekked around with me to cat shows and expos to research that part of the novel. And once again, as in *The Persian Always Meows Twice*, my cousin Phil McCabe helped me understand the tech aspects—this time, how software hackers do their dirty work. Finally, thanks to Linda Bohm of the Garden State Cat Club for explaining the intricacies of competing in and judging cat shows.

Chapter 1

"Ha, looks like a crime scene out there!" The handsome stranger jokingly referred to the obstacle course of orange cones, sawhorses, and yellow tape that he'd navigated just to cross the sidewalk and enter my shop.

"Spring, and the road crews are in bloom," I volleyed back. "You're lucky they're on lunch break right now. The town's getting a new water line, and I'm told that for the next couple of months it won't be pretty."

I could not say that, however, about this newcomer, one of the best-looking guys who'd ever walked through my door. He had no cat in tow to be groomed or boarded, which told me he probably wasn't a typical customer. With a dimpled smile, he introduced himself to me and to Sarah Wilcox, my retired-schoolteacher assistant.

"Hi, I'm Perry Newton." He shook our hands and slipped me a business card with his name below the title NEW IN TOWN PROMOTIONS.

Newton . . . New in Town? Clever.

I wondered for a minute if someone had suggested my business for one of those embarrassing reality shows. Perry could have been some type of showbiz agent—his style certainly was a cut above the norm for semirural Chadwick, New Jersey. On this April afternoon, he wore a navy turtleneck with slim jeans and a distressed bomber jacket; however, I'm sure the brown leather got its vintage look courtesy of some pricey designer and not during an air battle in World War II. His short brown hair looked subtly highlighted and mussed on top. Unless some lucky lady had been running her fingers through it, the effect probably came by way of some styling product.

Now his warm cocoa eyes gazed deeply into mine and he spoke with enthusiasm and sincerity. "After the things I've heard about you, Cassie, I *had* to drop by and meet you in person. I'd say that you're a legend in this town, except you're much too young for a word like that!"

"Well . . . thanks." Smiling modestly, I decided I could sit and listen to such flattery all day. I only regretted that I'd had no idea this guy was coming—no time to change out of my goofy "Cat Wrangler" T-shirt or even comb my long, limp brown locks. Fortunately, my hot-pink sales counter probably concealed all of the fur and other feline-related untidiness that clung to my jeans.

Still, judging from Newton's business card, I suspected his interest in me wasn't all that personal. It occurred to me that we'd just passed April Fools' Day, and no one really pranked me this year. Had one of my friends decided, better late than never?

In his next breath, Perry mercifully ended my confusion. "My company is promoting the North Jersey Cat Expo, which is taking place in just a couple of weeks out at the new Bradburne Hotel and Convention Center. You've heard about it, I hope?"

This caught Sarah's attention, and she answered before I could. "Oh, sure. I've seen the posters around town."

"And the ads in the paper and online," I assured him.

Perry beamed at this. "Yes, we've marketed it pretty heavily here in Chadwick, since it's just outside of town, on the highway." After politely asking my permission, he slid onto a stool on the customer side of the sales counter and leaned on his elbows toward me. I almost worried that if my boyfriend, Mark, happened to pass by—or worse, to walk into the shop—he'd wonder what the heck was going on.

Sarah must have decided that I needed to talk business with the newcomer in private. She discreetly excused herself to go let one of the boarder cats out into the playroom.

After she had gone, Perry went back to flattering me. "From what I hear, Cassie, you've taken this niche business—very smart marketing, by the way, to identify your community's need and fill it!—and in just over a year you've made it successful. Besides that, you've built a reputation for going the extra mile for your customers and their pets. You've even been in the news a couple of times for solving some dicey cat-related problems for folks around town."

"Sounds like you've been talking to the people at FOCA." I figured he must have heard all of this from the Friends of Chadwick Animals, with whom I'd cooperated on a few occasions.

"You bet. They all think you're the cat's meow." He punctuated the old-fashioned superlative by flashing another sexy dimple.

I guessed Perry to be just a few years older than me, maybe early thirties, and wondered where he'd honed his negotiating technique. If he'd learned in the high-pressure atmosphere of Manhattan, at least he'd been smart enough to dial down his approach today for the hinterlands of northwestern Jersey.

"I've already talked to FOCA about doing something with

them for the cat expo," I told him. "That's why you're here, right?"

He chuckled. "I'm sure you're a busy lady. Sorry for beating around the bush. I just want you to understand why I think you'd be such an asset to our event. Yeah, Rebecca Newmeyer at FOCA said you might be willing to demonstrate your grooming techniques on some of their shelter cats, to help boost adoptions. She told me you even have a mobile grooming studio?"

"I do, as of just a couple of weeks ago. Want to see it?"

"Absolutely!"

I led him through a door in the screened wall that separated the sales area of my shop from the feline playroom. This central space featured cat tunnels and "trees" of many types and heights, along with a system of wall shelves that let the most athletic animals climb as high as they dared. I explained to Perry that our boarders got turned out in the playroom by rotation, so each could get at least half an hour a day of real exercise. Again, he acted impressed.

Here, we came upon Sarah using a high-pitched voice and a fishing-pole toy to coax an Abyssinian named Cinnamon down from one of the top shelves. After she succeeded, she deftly pinned the russet-colored cat against her shoulder and faced Perry. "That expo is going to be a pretty big deal, I guess."

"If I do my job right, it will be," he told her. "As far as I can tell, there's never been anything like this before in New Jersey. Some regional groups hold cat shows"—he glanced at me for confirmation, and I nodded—"and once in a while there's a big pet expo with vendors and demonstrations. But with the all the facilities at the new Bradburne Hotel and Convention Center, we want to bring together the best of both worlds: a professional, judged show, run by the Cat

Fanciers of New Jersey, plus about a hundred vendors of cat-related products."

"Sounds fantastic," I admitted.

Cinnamon had climbed onto Sarah's shoulder and now began munching on her tight salt-and-pepper curls. With a laugh, she excused herself to take him back to his closet-sized "condo."

Meanwhile, Perry continued describing to me the wonders of the planned expo. "There also will be displays to promote area shelters and rescue groups, and demonstrations by local experts—such as you, Cassie. We'll even have appearances by celebrity guests."

"Celebrity cats?" I teased.

"They exist! Some are rescues that have survived especially rough situations, like cats that are doing great with prosthetic limbs. Others have special talents, like playing the piano. Through videos on social media, they've attracted hordes of followers. But we'll have cat-loving human celebrities, too." He lowered his voice and ducked his head, as if some spy might wander in from the front of the shop and overhear. "Keep it under your hat for now, but we're negotiating for Jaki Natal."

Sarah returned from her chore in time to catch this last line. "The singer? Get real!"

Perry shook his head. "She grew up just a couple of towns away and still has family in the area. Plus, she's cat crazy."

"True," I told my assistant. "At least, she's crazy about her own cat, Gordie. She's always posting pictures and videos online of herself with him, or of Gordie alone in cute poses."

Perry pointed at me, as if I'd taken the words right out of his mouth. "By now, Jaki's cat is almost as famous as she is."

Sarah tilted her head and jutted her lower lip, assimilating this information. I'd gotten the impression that she used Facebook and Twitter mainly to communicate with her church friends and her two grown children. Though she'd probably heard Jaki Natal's music on the radio or seen her perform on TV, she wouldn't have come across any stray bits of self-promotion that the young pop star posted for her fans. I was aware of them mainly because of the cat connection, since I followed just about every thread related to feline news.

Perry assured both of us, "Really, it's almost a done deal. Jaki just has some concerns about security at the event, which I'm sure we'll be able to iron out to her satisfaction." He shifted on his feet. "So, Cassie, you were going to show me what you've done with your van."

"Right. Sarah, can you go watch the counter?"

As she left to do so, Perry and I headed toward the back of the shop. On the way, I pointed out the grooming studio, where Sarah and I tidy up our regular customers. My shop is in a converted house that goes back to the turn of the century, and the studio, in a side room, has a bay window that lets in plenty of natural light. Next, I showed Perry through a wide corridor outfitted with a dozen closet-sized cat "condos," about half occupied by boarders at the moment. I explained that some local clients brought in their longhairs every couple of weeks just to be groomed, but people going on extended vacations, moving, or having their homes remodeled came from greater distances these days to board their animals.

"Most tell me that their pets never did well boarding at the vet's, or at a kennel that also takes dogs," I explained. "For some cats, just smelling dogs or hearing loud barking makes them so nervous that they don't eat or sleep well. Here, my customers don't have to worry about any of that."

"So I see." Perry studied me with an approving glint in his eyes. I'd probably gained his respect by showing that I also could deliver a good sales pitch.

He saved his highest praise, though, for my mobile grooming van—spanking new, at least cosmetically. It had come to me as a battered-looking hulk with a black primer finish. I'd driven it that way just a few times, to transport multiple cats or bulky supplies, always fearing that I'd be pulled over by someone from Homeland Security. But after I'd used the scary van to help FOCA with a trap-neuter-return project, a couple of members had volunteered their mechanical skills to get it into better shape. That left me with enough cash to hire an outfit called YourWay Van Conversions, which had turned it into something more representative of my business.

When we stepped out into my rear parking lot, Perry planted his hands on his hips and grinned from ear to ear. "Hey, that's awesome!"

These days, the whole vehicle gleamed bright white. On each long side, a two-foot-high cartoon of a gray Persian cat, with a hot-pink nose and wearing a purple bow tie, smugly strutted his stuff. Above him, curly purple script advertised my business, CASSIE'S COMFY CATS. Toward the bottom, black print on a band of hot pink announced my shop address, website, and work phone number.

My visitor nodded approval. "This must get a lot of attention."

I rolled back the big side door and flipped on fluorescent ceiling lights. The conversion company had raised the van's top so I could easily stand while grooming, and had inserted a fan above the stainless-steel worktable. The molded-fiberglass interior surfaces, snow white except for some hot pink trim, incorporated cabinets for grooming tools, a trash can, and a coiled vacuum hose to pick up loose fur. I pointed out the rubberized flooring, which also made cleanup easier, and the small tub at the rear of the space for cats that needed bathing.

Pointing to the wall in back of the tub, I explained, "The

generator and the water tank are both behind there. If we need to get to them, we just open the rear doors."

"Fantastic!" Perry said. "Looks like you've got all the same conveniences you'd have at the shop. Have you taken it on the road yet?"

"Mostly just to do some errands, and I did make one house call to try everything out. Trouble is, I can't do that too often, because if I take Sarah with me, I have to close the shop." We stepped out of the van, and I shut the side door behind me. "That's one detail I still have to work out, regarding the expo. I'm happy to volunteer my time and help FOCA find homes for more cats. But I don't want to ask Sarah to work the expo, because she's an employee and she does have a life! She's got grown kids and grandkids, and she's very active in her church. I could pay her for her time, but she'd still be giving up a whole weekend."

He considered this. "Can you get someone else to help you for free? Maybe a family member?"

I smiled. The ironic thing was, my mother probably *would* be attending the expo, but just by coincidence. Her boyfriend, Harry Bock—the first man she'd dated seriously since my father's death three years ago—was entering his Sphynx in the CFNJ show. But besides the fact that I'm sure Mom wanted to spend her time with him, she would be a terrible choice to help me groom. The one time she'd tried it, I'd realized she had a serious cat phobia—her hands shook if she even tried to pick one up. I suspected that it took all of her courage, and a true fondness for Harry, to agree to come with him to the show at all.

"I had thought of asking one of the FOCA kids," I told Perry. Becky and Chris, two members of the group I knew pretty well, were recent college grads. I tended to think of them as "kids," even though I had only about seven years on them.

"There you go. I'm sure they'd be glad to help, since the

demo was their idea. They've got experience with animals and they're already volunteers." With another dazzling grin, Perry added, "That's what I admire about you, Cassie—you're a problem-solver!"

I thanked him, while reflecting that the trait tended to get me into situations dangerously out of my depth.

While we walked back into my shop, Perry said, "So, if you're ready to commit, I just need you to sign a paper for me."

My shields went up. "Well, maybe I should wait until I ask—"

He pulled a document, folded three ways, from his jacket pocket. "Don't worry, this doesn't lock you into anything. It's just a volunteer waiver. The Bradburne's lawyer is insisting that I get one from everybody who's going to take part, and I figure there's no time like the present."

We joined Sarah at the sales counter, where I was able to flatten out the document and scan it. She glanced sideways at me, as if wondering what I was committing to, but the waiver looked simple and straightforward. In fact, I'd signed something similar in the past when I'd helped the county Humane Society raid a backwoods cattery. That had been a challenging experience, but I strongly doubted that I would run into as many hazards while grooming strays in the comfort of my own van. True, some of the rescued cats might scratch or bite, but that was always an occupational hazard. It wouldn't provoke me to sue the convention center, FOCA, or Perry himself.

I signed the document and handed it back to him. Without even checking to see whether I'd written *Jaki Natal* instead of my own name, Perry folded it again, slipped it into his jacket pocket, and thanked me.

"Before I go, one last thing," he said. "Are there any other animal professionals in town who you think might be interested in participating? PetMart, from out on the highway, is already taking a couple of vendor tables. But I think our visitors will be most interested in local experts, like you, giving talks or demonstrations."

Again I caught a look from Sarah, plus a hint of a smile. We'd worked together so closely for the past year that by now she practically could read my mind.

"There's the Chadwick Veterinary Clinic," I said. "It's on Hamburg Road, just a few blocks from here. They're always pretty busy, so I can't promise they'd be able to make time, but . . ."

"Sounds great. Anyone in particular I should talk to?"

"Dr. Mark Coccia."

Something tipped him off, maybe the fact that Sarah's smile grew a little wider. With a twinkle in his eye, Perry asked me, "Can I drop your name?"

"It might help."

He tapped the information into his cell phone, then gave me a parting wink. "Thanks, Cassie. You've been great to give me so much of your time. When more of the details get worked out, I'll be back in touch, okay?"

"Great," I said.

Once Perry had split, taking his distinctive blend of charm and efficiency with him, Sarah could quiz me more directly. "I just knew you were going to sic him on Mark. Think he'll be jealous?"

The idea appealed to me a little, but I dismissed it. "Oh, please. For someone of Italian descent, Mark is very level-headed about such things. More often, I'm the one steaming over the women who flirt with him."

"But this guy looks like a movie star, and he sure seemed to be laying the sugar on you."

I wrinkled my nose. "Yeah, but nobody gets a tan like that

naturally in the northeast in April. And those teeth are just *too* white."

My assistant laughed. "Girl, you're funny. Glad to know, though, that you won't be throwing Mark over for Mr. Slick." She picked up and scanned the business card Perry had left behind. "New in Town, huh?"

"See, he's an event promoter. I'm sure he gives that feel-good routine to everyone he deals with, all day long." I feigned a bruised ego. "You'll notice that he got what he wanted—my signature on that waiver—and then he split."

"Just like a man, right?"

"You said it, lady, I didn't."

Sarah left for the playroom again. When I'd decided to rehab the van, she'd joked that taking my business mobile might get me into even more trouble.

Just a kind of motherly concern on her part, of course. No reason for that to be the case . . . was there?

Chapter 2

The jackhammering resumed around one-thirty and continued off and on all afternoon. Not only did it rattle the few
clients who came in off the street, but it seemed to keep our
half-dozen boarders on edge all day. A couple meowed for relief whenever Sarah or I passed their cages, and others huddled
with paws tucked in, eyes shut and ears cocked backward in
silent misery. I knew their ears were more sensitive than ours
and could only imagine how the irregular *rat-tat-tats* must be
unnerving them. I tried to soundproof their condos as much as
possible with whatever spare bath towels and fleece throws I
could find.

Sarah and I tried listening to my boom box radio to coun-
teract the noise outside, with limited success. Her taste ran
more to R&B and oldies, while I liked newer rock and pop.
Trouble was, the afternoon programming on the local rock
station included commentary and occasional celebrity interviews by Marty Blatt. Our homegrown shock jock seemed determined to outdo Howard Stern back in his younger and
more offensive days.

The two of us did smile over a couple of his wisecracks,

against our wills. But with Sarah being black and both of us being female, it didn't take us long to lose patience with his mockery of women, various ethnic and minority groups, "bleeding-heart liberals," "deadbeats on welfare," and so forth.

"Okay, enough." I reached for the keypad on my radio. "Jazz station?"

"Please!" Sarah said.

The quieter music didn't drown out the jackhammers as effectively. But at least with this compromise, Sarah and I could groom our animals and even scoop out litter pans in relative peace.

She left at five, grateful, I'm sure, to head for her home, which was two towns away and well out of the work zone.

I could at least escape to my apartment above the shop. There, my own three cats greeted me with complaints about the din, though they calmed down once they got their supper. A quick chicken stir-fry dinner and a glass of wine also helped to calm my nerves, and by seven o'clock the intrepid road crew finally quit for the day. Unfortunately, I knew they'd be waking me up the following morning, exactly twelve hours later.

The official memo that I'd gotten about the project noted that it could take weeks just to complete the work on our block. I consoled myself by figuring that this early phase, breaking up the sidewalk and pavement, should be the most annoying part.

After dinner I called my mother, who lived about forty-five minutes away in slightly more urban Morristown. She sounded thrilled to hear that I'd be taking part in the expo, since she planned to go in support of her new boyfriend, Harry. "*Ooo*, what fun, Cassie! We'll be all together, then. Just like a . . ."

When she caught herself, wisely, I took the opportunity to jump in. "Please, Mom, don't put it that way. Okay?"

I figured she'd been about to say *like a family*, and as yet I couldn't handle that image. For one thing, my father had only been dead three years; I still missed him terribly, and I knew my mom did, too. For another, if she was going to replace him, I thought she could have found a better candidate than Harry Bock. The rather fussy architect had made a bad first impression on me six months ago. After he'd boarded his Sphynx cat at my shop for a week, she'd come down with a rash; Harry had accused me of somehow causing this condition and threatened to sue me over it.

Once the cat's skin had cleared up and I'd been proven blameless, at least Harry had apologized. His having met and hit it off with my mother in the meantime also changed his feelings toward me, I'm sure. But while I didn't exactly hold a grudge, I also didn't trust him not to go off half-cocked one day on some other issue.

Mom, on the other hand, thought Harry and I should be great friends because we both liked cats.

"I only meant that it will be a shared experience, dear," she said. "Of course, Harry will be busy showing Looli, and you may be somewhere else doing your demos, but I'm sure we can check in with each other from time to time."

"We should be able to," I agreed. "I have no idea how big this new convention center is or where they'll want me to park my van. I've only seen the place from outside."

"Well, the event's still a couple weeks away. You ought to pop over there and take a look around." She paused, cogitating. "I know—why don't the three of us have lunch some day at the hotel? We can catch up, and both you and Harry can have a look at the spaces where everything's going to take place."

Even though I didn't find Bock to be the most stimulating company, I had to admit this wasn't a bad idea. The guy had designed a few municipal buildings and libraries in our part of the state, so he might have some helpful insights on how the convention center functioned.

"Harry's been to the restaurant at the Bradburne, and he says their lunch buffet is wonderful," Mom prodded me further. "Our treat, of course."

She'd said the magic words, and I laughed. "Okay, you've sold me. How about next Thursday? That'll be the day before the expo opens. We don't have any customer appointments, so Sarah can handle the shop alone for a couple of hours."

While we were talking, I got a call from Mark. As soon as I got off with Mom, I called him back, hoping he wasn't mad that I'd sent Perry Newton to see him at the clinic.

He did razz me about it and sounded doubtful about participating in the expo. "It's okay for you, Cassie, to do grooming demonstrations. But I'd feel weird, as a vet, taking a booth to promote our business. Wouldn't that be kind of crass? And our clinic already has more patients than we can handle."

I considered his point. "Don't think of it as a business promotion, Mark, think of it as a community service. You can give talks on cat-related health issues. I'm sure there's a lot of information you can share with people that's routine to you, but that the average pet owner wouldn't know."

"Hmm. I guess that's true. . . ."

I could imagine Mark as an excellent spokesman for the clinic. Not only was he smart and articulate, he was no slouch in the looks department, either, his dark hair and light olive skin contrasting nicely with electric-blue eyes. His active job kept him pretty trim, and he went for morning jogs when he had time. In short, he had almost as much going for him as Perry, without the showbiz overkill. "And you close the clinic early on Saturday, so you could do it that afternoon without missing any work."

"Or even if I want to do it in the morning, too, Maggie can probably cover for me." Mark referred to his older, even more experienced partner at the clinic, Dr. Margaret Reed. "But would people be interested in just a dry lecture? Especially at something as glammed-up as this expo?"

"Maybe you could do a demonstration of some kind, too, with live cats."

He laughed. "Oh, nothing could possibly go wrong with *that* idea. Too bad I don't have any cats of my own. Want to lend me one of yours?"

Lounging on my slipcovered living room sofa, in the apartment above my shop, I glanced around. Sleek, black Cole sat on the deep windowsill that faced the street, amidst potted plants, and gazed out at the twilight. Very strong-willed, he would definitely freak if put on display before a crowd of strangers. Tango, the orange tabby who dozed in my lap, also could be unpredictable. Normally pretty sweet, he hated being groomed so much that he'd scared the heck out of Sarah during her tryout for the assistant's job. Both cats were rescues of one kind or another, so who knew what kind of bad experiences they'd had before I'd gotten them?

My calico, Matisse, perched serenely now on the arm of the sofa, only became more quiet and passive when she was frightened. She probably would be the best candidate.

"Maybe, if you're serious," I said. "But only in a safety harness."

He sounded as if he was coming around. "Yeah, I wouldn't want to risk losing one of them in the crowd. I wonder what the setup will be at the convention center. I've never even been inside that Bradburne complex."

"Neither have I, but I understand it's massive."

"That's what Maggie said. She and her husband attended a wedding there and got a chance to roam around. She said the hotel and the convention center are linked, but they're separate wings. I gather the cat show is going to be spread through several of the hotel conference rooms, and the expo will be in the convention wing."

I'll probably be somewhere out in the parking lot, I thought, feeling a bit deflated.

"This guy Perry said they're expecting thousands," Mark went on. "They're even trying to get Jaki Natal for a guest appearance."

"Incredible, right?" So much for Perry's warning that I should keep that news under my hat. He probably was telling everybody that he was trying to recruit her for the expo, so we'd all want to bask in the star's reflected glow. "Should be a lot of excitement, for our neck of the woods."

"Sounds that way." Mark's tone sobered. "He said she's concerned about the safety of the venue, which I can kind of understand."

So could I, sort of. Chadwick and its surroundings didn't often host such an extravaganza, and although I'd lived in town just over a year, I couldn't remember any past appearance by a major celebrity. "Well, if the convention center is so huge and complex, they must have their own security staff for events like this."

"But I wonder if they've ever *had* an event like this. The place is pretty new, and this isn't your usual business conference or trade convention. Think about it, Cassie. In the one space, you'll have people bringing valuable animals to the cat show. In the other, you'll have vendors hawking their wares and people like us giving talks and demonstrations."

"And don't forget the celebrity cats!" I joked, telling him about the live appearances by pets who had scores of followers online.

"Okay, all that is crazy enough. But if you add a mob of

Jaki Natal fans, who may not even care about the cat stuff, but only want to see her . . . I'm not surprised that she wants extra precautions in place. Crowds do riot sometimes when they can't get tickets to a show. Crazy fans even jump onstage and try to grab singers while they're performing."

"But those things happen at big concert venues," I pointed out, "and there are always plenty of security guards to control the crowd."

"Exactly my point. The Bradburne isn't set up like an arena or a stadium, so it's going to be hard to police it like one. And if she's staying at the hotel, they'll also have to keep fans away from her room, probably her whole floor." I heard a pause as he mulled this issue for a second. "I guess if the job gets to be too much for the hotel's usual security staff, they could always ask for backup from the Chadwick cops."

I sniffed. "That will thrill our police chief." I knew Chief Doug Hardy didn't have enough manpower, either, for such serious crowd control.

Mark caught himself. "Guess I shouldn't be such a wet blanket. I'm sure they'll have it figured out by the time the expo opens, at least enough to satisfy Ms. Natal. If they don't, I imagine she just won't come."

A few minutes later, after we'd hung up, I remembered Perry's excitement when he'd told me about the proposed guest star. If Jaki backed out of the expo now, it would not only dash his hopes but possibly undermine his big publicity campaign.

He would have promised her anything, I suspected, to get her to appear. I just hoped he hadn't promised more than he could deliver.

Chapter 3

At work the next morning, I retreated to the grooming studio of my shop to call Becky at Friends of Chadwick Animals and ask if she'd be willing to serve as my assistant for the expo.

"I'd love to," she said. "I have to admit, though I've had a lot of basic experience in handling cats, I don't know too much about grooming them. I might need some extra training on that score."

Since I take Saturday afternoons off, she and I made plans to meet at the shelter that day. I would bring the van over at one, and Becky could practice working on some of the adoptable cats.

At least the road work stopped over the weekend, and so far, the driveway leading to my rear parking lot remained accessible. The façade of my cream-and-gray, two-story building, with the name of my business stenciled in purple across the front window, remained somewhat blockaded by orange cones and net fencing around the trench where the sidewalk used to be. I resigned myself to the idea that not many new customers would be dropping by anyhow until the water line project was completed.

Still, on Saturday I was able to nose the van out past these obstacles and drive it the half mile to FOCA's facility at the north end of Center Street, Chadwick's main drag. The non-profit, no-kill facility had taken over a low, rambling, yellow stucco building that formerly housed a luncheonette. It could accommodate up to a dozen dogs and two dozen cats at a time, in separate wings, and usually had more animals placed in foster homes around the area. All generally were strays—former pets who'd gotten lost or been surrendered by their owners— as opposed to ferals, which are born wild and are hard to domesticate.

I checked in briefly with Terry Elkins, the fiftyish woman who ran the shelter. I'd heard that she came from a business background and had spent a decade volunteering with animal groups before starting FOCA. Her thick, shagged hair needed a trim and her work outfit consisted of a button-front shirt worn loose over stretch pants, with practical running shoes. She greeted me with a big smile, and we talked a little about FOCA's involvement with the expo. Soon she had to get back to her incessantly ringing phone, but not before she pointed me in the direction of Becky.

Up to now, I hadn't spent much time touring the shelter, and, of course, the animals there changed often. While searching for Becky, I wended my way through the maze of caged critters—mostly dogs and cats, but a section tagged "Exotics" also housed a rabbit, a pair of hamsters, and a pretty gray cockatoo. Though I'd learned to handle all kinds of animals during my training and brief experience as a vet tech, I'd almost forgotten that these types of pets also could wind up in shelters.

Before long I found Becky, a pixie powerhouse, among the cages. She recently had bleached her gamine cap of hair platinum, which made her easier to spot. I knew that, since graduating from college almost a year ago, she'd been looking for a full-time position in some animal-related field, but with no luck so far. Though that meant she had to go on living with her parents a while longer, at least what money she could bring in as a pet sitter allowed her to continue as a passionate volunteer with the FOCA shelter.

I came upon her filling out a label for a cage that held a sleek, black, bright-eyed pup. "New arrival?"

"Oh, hi, Cassie! Yeah, somebody just returned this mini pinscher. Only adopted her from us a month ago, but he said she got nippy with his kids."

Meanwhile, the little dog climbed the side of the cage, wagging her tail so hard I thought it would fly off. "Looks like a real sweetheart to me."

"I know, right? Terry and I tried to talk to the guy, persuade him to try some obedience training before giving up. But you can tell when someone is just *over* a pet and doesn't want to hear it. His kids probably pulled her tail, or did something else that would make any animal snap, but parents will never admit that."

"Such a shame." I opened the cage door a few inches so I could stroke the friendly pup's dark, satiny head. She licked my hand.

"We make them sign a surrender form, which puts them on our radar in case they ever come back wanting to adopt again," Becky told me, with a note of bitter satisfaction. "We also ask if they're willing to foster or pay for the care of the animal while we find it a new home, but of course these folks had no interest in doing any of that."

"I'm sure that's the most frustrating part of your job," I said, "when you think you've placed a rescue, but the adopter brings the animal back."

Becky sniffed. "Good thing Grumpy Glenda wasn't here today, or she'd have ripped into that guy but good. She's a new volunteer and has *no* patience with people who return animals. She's really hard-core. Belongs to PETA and all that."

"A true believer, huh?"

"I think if Glenda had her way, no one would own any animal at all. Maybe she thinks they should all be running free— as if that's practical, in today's world."

I agreed. Like it or not, we lived in a human-dominated society. The best we animal lovers could do was try to ensure that all creatures, wild and domestic, were treated as humanely as possible.

Closing the door of the little dog's cage, I glanced at the label Becky had just attached. "Well, Rocket's a charmer. I'm betting she'll find a new home with a much nicer family before too long. How have you been doing with the job search, Becky?"

She straightened to her full five foot two and sighed. "Not great. Whether it's the economy or just a lot of people who want to work with animals, there aren't many openings. I've got the training to work as a pet adoption counselor, a cruelty investigator, or an animal-assisted therapist. I've seen openings in other parts of the country, but I really would like to stay in this general area."

I smiled. "At least your parents are willing to support your animal addiction."

"Yeah, they don't completely understand it, but they do like having me at home. Especially since my younger sister just went off to college in Ohio."

After she'd settled Rocket in with food and water, Becky escorted me to the cat room, which was lined with clean, well-kept cages. All were filled, some with pairs of related cats or kittens. Since their occupants were in for longer stays, these enclosures were larger than the cages at Mark's clinic, but smaller than the condos I provided for my boarders. As always happened when I visited any pet adoption center, all of those upturned, hopeful little faces tugged at my heart.

No, you've got three of your own already, I reminded myself. *With your small apartment, you're at capacity!*

"We don't get a lot of longhairs," Becky told me, "but when we do, it can be a problem. Our volunteers don't have a lot of time to spend on grooming, and as you know, if the cat isn't used to it they can give us a hard time. Many dogs actually like getting sprayed with water, soaped up, dried, and brushed . . . but the cats seem to think we're trying to kill them!"

I laughed. "Tell me about it. That's what keeps me in business."

We wandered farther down the row while, elsewhere in the shelter, a few other volunteers of assorted ages bustled about at their tasks. Most were people I recognized from my previous visits but didn't know by name.

Becky stopped by one lower cage, opened it, and lifted out a beautiful honey-colored longhair that, although he didn't have the flat face, had to be a Persian mix. "Ray here would be a good candidate. He's a senior, and they're always tough to place, but he's so mellow that he'd make a great companion for, say, an older person." She ran her fingers through the animal's dense coat. "As you can see, though, he mats like crazy. Anyone who adopts him will need to learn some grooming skills."

Becky and I brainstormed, in general, about our presentation for the expo—how to use it to promote the shelter's goals. We agreed that, while making the felines look their best, we'd also talk up pet adoption and explain the backgrounds of the individual cats during our demonstrations.

While she held Ray, I stroked his soft head; he did seem laid-back and friendly. "Hey, pal," I told him, "we're gonna glam you up, make you a star, and find you a great new home."

My comment drew a grin from Becky, and her eyes widened.

"Speaking of stars, you'll never guess who's doing a guest appearance at the expo!"

"Jaki Natal. And her cat, Gordie."

I almost regretted my guess when the girl's face folded in disappointment. "You already knew?"

"When Perry talked to me last week, he said they were trying hard to get her."

Becky gently released Ray back into his cage and shut the door. "And she's doing it for free! I guess they'll have to pay her staff—like the band, if she sings—but she's donating her own time because she's so gung-ho about cat adoption."

"That's terrific." I figured the animal-loving celebrity would set a good example for her youthful fans. "Of course, she has a purebred Scottish Fold, right? He's probably not a rescue—she must have gotten him from a breeder."

Becky laughed. "He was a gift from her ex-boyfriend, Alec MacMasters. Y'know, the actor?"

I squinted, as if that would help me scan the files of my memory. "Sounds familiar. Is he in that sci-fi TV series?"

"*Galaxy Wars*, yeah. The show is kind of meh, but Alec is really hot. Anyway, he's Scottish by birth, hence the cat. He and Jaki met when she did a real small cameo on the series, and they were a major item until last year. Then either he cheated on her or she got tired of him—guess it depends who you ask. The upshot was, Jaki kicked him to the curb." She dusted a little of Ray's caramel-colored hair from her faded green yoga pants.

"How do you know all this?" I teased Becky. "Just from social media?"

"Actually, Jaki's still got family in Sussex County, and one of her cousins, Mira, went to college with me and Chris. She's traveling with Jaki now, as her assistant, so her information is a lot more reliable than anything online or on TV gossip shows."

I couldn't argue with that. "So, Jaki dumped the hunky guy but kept his cat?"

My perky blond friend shrugged. "Maybe she had a better relationship with Gordie."

Remembering the business that had brought us together today, Becky moved a few cages down. There, a white cat with some patches of black faced away from us, tail curled defensively around her body. At least she turned her head when we approached, a positive sign.

"Now, Flo here is a different kind of challenge," Becky told me. "She's only six, but her owner died. I think on some level Flo's still mourning her. They lived in a small apartment, and unfortunately, the woman really overfed her. When Flo came to us she was very overweight and couldn't even bend enough to groom herself well. At least she's slimmed down a little since we've had her."

Becky brought out Flo and hung onto her, though this cat resisted more than Ray had. She gave a yowl of protest, and I had a sense that she'd also be tougher to groom. Her coat was only medium-long, but I could see where her back and hindquarters needed work.

"The staff here tries to do some grooming," Becky added, "but even though we're used to handling skittish animals, we don't have the same training as you."

"Okay," I said. "Want to do a dry run with these two? Let's bring them out to the van. I'll show you my layout and then we'll get to work."

We put the cats into carriers and toted them out to my showy vehicle, parked in the lot behind the shelter. Becky laughed when she saw the cartoon Persian on the side of the van and said, "I love this guy—he's got real Jersey attitude!"

She was just as impressed with the bright, clean, and efficient interior of the van. "This is so neat, Cassie, like a space capsule. What's in all the compartments?"

I opened cabinet doors to show her. "I've even got a stash of pet treats, in case any of the cats need extra purr-suasion."

Becky acknowledged my pun with a crooked smile.

We placed Ray on the worktable first, since he seemed less likely to cause trouble. That gave me a chance to introduce Becky to the array of tools I used for various problems. I also explained the different types of coats that cats might have; in dealing with mixed breeds, the FOCA volunteers might come across any and all types.

With very little stress, we worked together on Ray. I showed Becky a few techniques for pulling apart and combing out his most stubborn mats.

Meanwhile, she drifted back to the subject of Jaki's appearance at the expo. I could tell she was a pretty serious fan of the singer.

"Have you ever heard her song, 'I Need My Space'?" she asked me.

"Who hasn't? It was all over the radio last winter, and the video kept popping up online." I smiled at the memory because, although G-rated, it was a witty and scathing diatribe about a noncommittal lover.

"She wrote that about Alec," Becky assured me. "She denies it, and he won't comment, but everyone *knows* it's him. I mean, she calls the guy 'spaceman,' and Alec's in a sci-fi series! Who else could it be?"

Having no inside information myself, I just shrugged. "Guess that'll teach him to get on the bad side of a singer who writes her own material."

"Right? Bet there isn't a woman alive who hasn't known a guy she'd like to trash in a hit song—so that he'd have to hear it everywhere he went!"

I pretended to be shocked by this statement from the sweet-faced FOCA volunteer. "Got a dark side, don't you, kid?"

"C'mon. From what I've heard, you had a boyfriend, right before Mark, who deserved to have his butt kicked hard."

That was true enough. My ex Andy had a different and maybe worse set of faults than "spaceman"—at least Jaki hadn't accused her ex of physical abuse. I'd moved beyond most of my bitter feelings by now, but at one time I would've jumped at the chance to accuse and shame Andy on an international scale, if only in a song.

Speaking of catty temper tantrums, Becky and I did face a greater challenge with Flo. It gave me a chance to demonstrate my latest tool, a padded and substantial cat harness.

"I actually bought this after I agreed to do these demon-strations," I explained, as we eased the spotted cat's head and front legs into the contraption. "I figure I can't take the risk of an animal freaking out in a public space or getting away from us. This not only makes it easier to hang on to them, mechan-ically, but it also has a calming effect—or it's supposed to."

I'd already tested the harness on a couple of my customers, and it did seem to soothe Flo's nerves a little. To be on the safe side, I asked Becky to hold on to the loop behind the cat's neck as I clipped her claws. The rigid sleeves of the harness kept Flo's front legs straight, making this much easier, and because of its hugging sensation, she seemed less inclined to fight me. After that, Becky and I used a little conditioning spray and some gentle brushing to smooth out the stiff, sticky hairs on her back that Flo had neglected for too long.

"That wasn't so bad," the volunteer decided, as we released the cat back into her carrier. "I guess we'll need more than two cats for demos, though. There's a longhair mix named Lady who's being fostered right now. She's only two years old, but she's shaggy enough and usually pretty mellow."

"Sounds like another fine candidate," I agreed.

While we used the vacuum to clean up the van's interior, I asked, "So, what do you think? Could you feel at home here, at least for a few afternoons?"

Becky laughed. "It's almost as big as my dorm room was at college and probably has more closet space! Yeah, this should be fun."

We brought Flo and Ray back inside the shelter, where we met up with another volunteer, Chris Eberhardt. Slim, dark-haired, and around Becky's age, he had partnered with her on several rescue operations around the area. I suspected he and Becky were an item, or at least had been at one time. He grinned when he saw us, probably because we both looked disheveled, and asked how the practice session had gone.

"Pretty good," I said. "We just might be able to pull this thing off."

"You'd better, 'cause the pressure's really on now. Take a look at this." He turned his cell phone toward us to play a video.

A doll-faced, brunette young woman, in selfie close-up, shared the small screen with a silver tabby Scottish Fold cat. He looked bewildered, but those cats usually do because of their round eyes and flattened, forward-folding ears.

"Shout out to all you catsters!" Jaki gushed in a rich, husky voice. "Get yourselves over to the North Jersey Cat Expo, April thirteenth through fifteenth at the new Bradburne Convention Center. Gordie and I wouldn't miss it for the world, would we, sweetie?" She nuzzled the cat's furry cheek, which he tolerated patiently. "Hope to see you all there!" she told her followers, just before signing off.

"Wow, I can't believe she did that," said Becky. "How cool!"

Less naïve, Chris shook his head and chuckled darkly. "Don't know if Perry was expecting that. Supposedly he arranged for extra security just so she'd come. I hope it'll be enough to cope with the onslaught."

"Probably just one of those temperamental demands that stars like to make," I reassured him.

"No," Chris said slowly. "From what I hear, she's got good reason."

"Oh?"

Becky hesitated, as if wondering how much information to share. "Her cousin said that lately Jaki's been getting crank e-mails and texts that sound kind of crazy. The cops have even tried to trace them, but whoever's doing it has gone to a lot of trouble to hide his identity. Since no crime's actually been committed, I guess they haven't delved into it very deeply."

"That's got to be nerve-racking for Jaki. But doesn't that stuff kind of come with the territory when you're a celebrity?"

"It does, but I guess it still has her weirded out," Chris said. "Her parents and her sister still live up in Lafayette, and a couple of times printed notes and even little gifts for Jaki have been left in their mailbox. I guess the tone has been kind of ominous—like, *No one can keep us apart* and *I'm never giving up on you.* She's worried that this creep knows where her family lives and could hurt one of them."

"Wasn't there something, too," Becky asked him, "about a suspicious car accident?"

Remembering, Chris frowned. "Oh, yeah! Last fall, a mechanic who was driving Mr. Natal's Mercedes home from the garage went off the road and was killed. Nobody ever found out what happened. The car should have been in good shape, since it was just fixed, but there were skid marks, as if the guy swerved into the woods."

So the driver might have tried to avoid hitting a deer, I thought.

Or he might have been forced off the road by another car. By someone who assumed Jaki's father was behind the wheel?

And now the young celebrity had agreed to take part in a big, public event close to her home turf. Was that very brave of her, I wondered . . . or very foolish?

Chapter 4

The Bradburne Hotel had sprung up along the highway between Chadwick and Morristown a couple of years earlier, and became a popular venue for business functions, weddings, and other large gatherings. I'd always been intrigued by its exterior design, and as we pulled up in front in Harry's navy-blue BMW, I asked him what the style would be called.

He seemed pleased by my question. "Oh, I suppose it's their version of postmodernism. Those suggestions of columns and pillars are references to classical architecture, though very simplified, of course."

"I kind of like it." I felt unsure of my taste in the presence of an expert.

"Yes, it's not bad. The style's considered a bit passé now, but it's still easier on the eye than a lot of the monstrosities being built these days."

Harry parked in front of the building, and we all stepped out of the BMW. It was a perfect spring day, with a nearly cloudless sky, and I welcomed the light breeze that ruffled my bangs.

Harry, about five-eight and slim, had dressed for the occasion in chinos, polished loafers, and a gray sport coat. At least his polo shirt, almost the same butter yellow as his thinning hair, livened up his naturally pale coloring. He handed his car keys to the valet and escorted Mom and me inside. I tried to remember the last time I'd gone to a restaurant with valet parking. Probably at a family wedding, and that would have been many years ago. I knew Harry had met with clients at the Bradburne in the past, and he acted totally at home in this up-scale, businesslike environment.

Mom also had no problem blending in. As a paralegal with a Morristown law firm, she normally dressed in the kind of tailored pants, ladylike jacket, and sensible heels she wore today. That kind of wardrobe helped her get taken seriously on the job; because she was petite and colored any gray that might show up in her wavy auburn hair, she looked very young for her age. My work clothes, on the other hand, ran to jeans, sweats, and amusing T-shirts. I'd done some searching through my closet before coming up with slim ankle pants and a loose, flowered, peasanty top just dressy enough for the occasion.

We passed through a vaulted lobby, which displayed a poster for the upcoming cat expo, and made a left down a short corridor to the restaurant, The Grove. It took its name, Harry informed us, from Grove Street, a short road that had been demolished and absorbed into the hotel's footprint.

He gave his name to the hostess, a tall, cool blonde about my age, and noted that we had a reservation. She acknowledged this and handed three menus to a waiter, who led us to a table at the center of the room. While we followed him, Mom whispered to me, "Oh, this is lovely. You wouldn't have any idea you were even near the highway, would you?"

I agreed. The restaurant created a garden ambience with its light walls, whitewashed furniture, and sage-green table linens.

Natural wood planters overflowing with real ferns lined the walls, and at the center of each table, a small vase held a graceful stem of chartreuse orchids.

My mother made a decent salary at McCabe, Preston, and Rueda, but she still watched her expenses closely. Harry might turn her head if he kept treating her to these tastes of the good life. Of course, her firm had served him well during his recent divorce. Supposedly, his ex-wife, Loretta, had wanted far more than her fair share of their worldly goods for "irreconcilable differences." She'd only backed down when MP&R had informed her lawyer that Harry had proof Loretta had been running around. So he hadn't suffered too much financially. He also appeared to get a fair number of architectural commissions, so maybe he was really good at his job.

The lunch buffet left little to be desired, no matter what your taste. The cold food station featured garden greens, an array of cheeses, chopped-up vegetables, and dressings, to let guests build their own salads. Another table offered warm cheese tortellini, deli meats, and various types of seafood. In yet another spot, a young woman in a crisp, white apron concocted smoothies to order. And at the omelet station, a uniformed older man prepared eggy masterpieces with a choice of fillings.

I took a plate and wandered from one display to the next, too dazzled at first to make any decisions. Finally I settled on equal portions of salad, tortellini, and shrimp with hot sauce. Mom played it a bit safer with some greens, a mushroom omelet, and roasted potatoes, while Harry walked on the wild side with grilled vegetables and crab salad.

Once we were seated with our meals, I got the conversational ball rolling on a topic I figured would be of mutual interest to me and Harry. I asked him how he'd come to adopt Looli—Egyptian for *pearl*—the white Sphynx cat he intended to enter in the expo show. This turned out to be a smart move on my part, because apparently he could talk on this topic for hours.

"I'd seen another Sphynx at a friend's house," he said, "and was intrigued right away. Don't know why—maybe because it looked like a little space alien! Or maybe because my friend pointed out that every cat, without its fur, would more or less look like a Sphynx."

Mom gave a little surprised laugh. "That's probably true, isn't it?"

"And even though its appearance was so strange," he went on, "it was a very friendly, playful cat. So I just got it into my head that I'd like to have one." Harry's enthusiasm dipped at an unpleasant memory. "Of course, Loretta thought it was a ridiculous idea. She wasn't into pets, generally, and said she wouldn't want such an ugly creature in the house. I argued that it was half my house—and a large one—so I could keep the cat in my office and a few other rooms downstairs. Loretta wouldn't even have to see it if she didn't want to."

"And she was okay with that?" I saw a glint in my mother's eye, since she knew Harry and Loretta eventually had parted ways in a very nasty divorce. In fact, their breakup had been handled by Mom's firm.

"She was, at first. So I found a breeder in New York State and went there planning to pick out a kitten. The owner asked me a lot of questions, including whether I was interested in breeding cats myself, but I assured him I just wanted a pet. When I told him a little about our lifestyle, and that I'd never owned a cat before, he suggested getting one that was a bit past the kitten stage."

"Sounds like a very responsible guy," I said.

"I think he was. Anyway, he showed me Looli, who was about two at the time. He explained that although she had top bloodlines and was old enough to be bred, they'd had to spay her for a medical reason. He let me hold her, and she instantly climbed up on my shoulder like a monkey and purred in my ear. I just fell in love."

Even though it involved a cat, this was a romantic side of Harry I hadn't seen before. "Looli does have a great disposition."

"Even I'm not afraid of her," said Mom. "And Cassie can tell you what a coward I usually am where cats are concerned."

"So I brought Looli home," Harry continued, "but for Loretta, it was *hate* at first sight. She kept calling her names like Goblin and Mutant, and even when Looli would rub against her leg, Loretta would shudder. Frankly, I think that was the beginning of the end for our marriage. We already had other problems, but the fact that she couldn't tolerate even that sweet little creature was the last straw for me."

"On the other hand, Harry, it's probably a good thing she didn't like the cat," Mom pointed out. "Looli is about the only thing she didn't try to take away from you in the divorce!"

"Too true. It's only thanks to your firm that I held on to as much as I did. I still pay her alimony, but . . ." He shrugged as if it was worth the price to be rid of Loretta.

I decided to steer the conversation back in a less litigious direction. "So I guess you'll be entering Looli in the purebred altered classes at the expo?"

Harry nodded. "As you know, she did very well at several regional shows over the past couple of years. I'm not so intense about campaigning her for a championship anymore—not going to make either of us travel those long distances. But I can hardly pass up a show that's practically in my own backyard."

It was my mother, amazingly enough, who encouraged this train of conversation by asking him what was involved in showing a cat. I also was curious, because even though I had customers who occasionally entered their cats in shows, and I'd dropped in to spectate at a few, I didn't really understand how the judging worked. Harry regaled us for the next twenty minutes or so with the standard show rules and categories, how to register with the sponsoring organizations, studying up on what traits judges will be looking for in your breed or category, et cetera. If he had begun this as a hobby while he was still married, he seemed to have thrown himself even more deeply into it after his divorce.

While we wound up our meal with coffee, I tried to draw my mother out a bit on the subject of her book club, an interest she'd recently taken up again. She admitted, with blushes, that the latest novel they'd opted to read was a popular erotic romance of dubious literary value. "Not my choice, but I was outvoted."

Harry smiled thinly. "Yes . . . I don't usually read fiction anyway, but I've heard that one is pure trash."

"I guess at least it will make for a lively discussion," said my mother, with a shake of her head, "but give me a good Louise Penny or John Grisham mystery anytime."

I laughed. "Right with you there, Mom!"

Harry grabbed the check and treated us, waving away her mild protest. We left the restaurant and strolled back through the atrium, past four sets of double doors marked as ballrooms A, B, C, and D. He explained that this was where the cat show would be held, with "benching" for all the competitors' cages and five or six judging rings. Judging for a few different categories would take place simultaneously, Harry said. "In a big show like this, if your cat does well, you can end up competing several times over the weekend until they choose a Best in Show. This is going to be a three-day show, which is unusual. Most of them run only Saturday and Sunday, but this one kicks off Friday afternoon."

Mom got a wary look in her eye. "Not sure how long I'm going to last, though, being in a space this big with all of those cats running around!"

I laughed. "Don't worry, they won't be running around. They'll mostly be in cages. It's fun, really, to walk around and look at them all. The cages need to have curtains to keep the cats calm, and beds or shelves they can lie on, so the owners decorate them in all kinds of different motifs. The Bengals and Ocicats usually have drapery with leopard spots, the Persians tend to get very froufrou, princessy cages, and a black Bombay might get kind of a punk or gothic theme."

Harry chuckled. "Some people do go a little crazy dressing up their cages. I have to admit, when I first started with Looli, I went all out, too, and had a professional dress her cage. So it has gray satin drapery with a kind of Egyptian trim, and a little chaise for her to lie on—y'know, like Cleopatra."

There was a time when my mother probably would have found this idea laughable. But now she sounded sincere when she told Harry, "I can't wait to see it!"

Maybe because of my psychology background, I suspected that Harry was projecting some frustrated instincts onto his cat. Mom had told me that he and his ex-wife, Loretta, had no children together. She had one son from a previous marriage, and initially the teenager had gotten along well enough with Harry, but after the divorce he'd naturally sided with his mother. Was Looli the child Harry had never been able to take to baseball practice or dance recitals, to show off and spoil? Being hairless, the Sphynx even required a sort of doll-like wardrobe.

Of course, many cats basked in extravagantly decorated cages when they went to shows, and I imagined that silver satin would show off the white Sphynx beautifully. At the same time, I began to understand why Harry's ex-wife might have grown a bit impatient with his hobby. I doubted that Loretta had such a lavish, satin-draped boudoir!

Lastly, we followed a glass-enclosed walkway from the hotel to the new convention center. Harry apparently had followed the news of its construction closely, because he was able to explain how the vast structure was organized to accommodate large crowds, for maximum efficiency and security. This, I knew, was where most of the vendors would set up displays and experts would give live demonstrations.

Above the indoor entrance to the convention center hung a horizontal banner that proclaimed, WELCOME NORTH JERSEY CAT EXPO, APRIL 13-15, with a blown-up portrait of a lovely Siamese. Below it, a couple of workers in jeans and gray Bradburne Hotel polo shirts were adding a strip that announced, SPECIAL GUEST STARS, JAKI NATAL AND GORDIE! Clearly, the young celebrity had left the marketing team in suspense about her appearance until the last minute.

Other folks in similar clothing hustled about, adjusting smaller posters and directional signs and shifting furniture. The clang of an occasional tool and the shout of one worker to another echoed through the vaulted space. The structure muted sounds from the nearby highway, though. The air smelled fresh, clean, and just a little cool, probably thanks to some state-of-the-art filtration system.

We strolled a little way down the commercial concourse, where a real estate convention appeared to be wrapping up. I asked Harry, "Just how big is this whole place, do you know?"

"The hotel plus the convention center? I think about a hundred fifty-thousand square feet. They haven't even finished it all yet. I understand there's a whole catering kitchen somewhere that won't be completed until the fall. I guess the idea is to take some strain off the hotel facilities."

We passed another closed set of double doors, identified by

a permanent sign as a theater. Harry cracked the doors open and we stuck our heads inside to admire the vast space, which had tiered seats and a sizable stage at the front.

"This," he explained, "will be for really important guest speakers that are expected to draw a large crowd."

Or someone like Jaki Natal, I thought.

When I wondered aloud where I'd be parking my van, Harry cocked his head toward the deep, street-facing windows. "There's supposed to be some kind of pedestrian mall on the side street. Maybe they'll put you there."

"Sounds better than the parking lot, anyway," Mom said. "Where do you think that would be, from here?"

"I don't know. Wish I had a map!" Harry frowned. "Damned place is so big, I'm not even sure which way we're facing now."

Near the entrance to the main concourse, a young guy in jeans and a dark windbreaker emerged through a door marked STAIRS. He paused there to make some notation on an iPad that he carried.

"Ask him," I suggested.

Harry approached the curly-haired, bespectacled younger man. "Excuse me—would you know if Perry Newton is here today?"

The stranger looked a bit startled by the question, as if he'd been working out some problem in his head and we'd broken his concentration. "Who? Oh, that promoter guy? Yeah, I think I did see him. Out there." He pointed to his left.

Harry thanked him, and we made the turn. Outside, I spotted Perry and, I suspected, also the answer to my question. The sliding glass doors opened onto a wide plaza; a curb cut at one spot suggested you might be able to drive a food truck—or a cat-grooming van—right up onto the pavers. It even featured an overhang that would keep me, and any audience I might attract, dry on a rainy day.

Perry stood beneath the overhang, speaking rapidly into his cell phone. His voice sounded far tenser than when he'd first smooth-talked me into participating in the expo. "We'll need security in the hallway outside the Presidential Suite. . . . Yeah, 'round the clock, starting when she arrives. The garage should be well covered, too—we've asked for extra cops all weekend. The other hot spots will be Conference Room D, where she does her interview on Friday, and the theater in the convention center for the concert Saturday night." He paused to listen, then barked a response. "Sure, she's got her own bodyguards, but this is a special situation. Listen, she's doing this as a *favor* for us, for *free*. So don't gimme grief, okay? Just get it all done. And any hitches, call me right away!"

Perry disconnected the call with such a deep frown that I hesitated to approach him. When he glanced up and spotted me, though, his anger evaporated and the polished charm returned. "Cassie, great to see you again. Scoping the place out?"

"Thought it might be a good idea." I introduced Mom and Harry and explained about Looli taking part in the upcoming cat show. "I guess the pressure's ramped up now that Jaki's definitely coming."

"Oh, sure, sure," Perry said. "But at least sales of tickets and of vendor spaces have ramped up, too. I'm delighted to say, we should make quite a bit of money for the animal charities that are taking part."

I imagined they would. As a volunteer, I hadn't checked the prices for commercial vendor spaces, but it cost ten dollars just to come to the cat show as a spectator and thirty-five to enter a cat. Admission to the expo on the concourse ran another twenty. The Friday afternoon interview with Jaki that Perry had just mentioned cost fifty dollars a ticket, and her Saturday evening mini concert was three hundred a head. Seating was limited, of course, for the last two events.

"I was just wondering what time I should come tomorrow," I told him, "and where I should set up."

Perry looked aghast. "Nobody got in touch with you about that? I'm sorry. I'd suggest you get here pretty early, maybe eight-thirty, because the other vendors will be loading in and it will probably be a zoo. At least you can bypass the garage, though, because you'll be right here on the plaza." He spread his arms to indicate the same space I'd pictured. "Should be a prime, high-traffic area. Just stay to one side of the entrance so you don't block the doors. We'll have some signage out here for you, too." He swung toward Harry. "Cassie said you're showing a cat. Do you have a room? We set aside a block just for the cat owners, but I'm afraid they're probably all filled by now."

"Thanks, but I don't need one." Harry smiled. "I live close enough to drive back and forth."

"I'll bet the tickets to Jaki's interview on Friday are sold out, too," I said, hoping I might be wrong.

Perry hesitated, then dropped his voice to a whisper. "They are, but between you and me, if you want to sneak in the door and stand along the back, I'll see to it that nobody stops you. Have your volunteer ID?" When I shook my head, he beckoned to an assistant, who fetched a file case the size of a large shoe box. Perry searched through the *M*'s and pulled out a tag on a lanyard. My name and the name of my business appeared on the lower half, with the word VOLUNTEER printed across the top in dark blue.

Mom beamed as if it were a prize I'd won. "That certainly looks official."

"Got one for my assistant, too?" I asked Perry. "Becky Newmeyer?"

He found a second tag among the *N*'s and handed that to me, also. Some of the tension crept back into his tone as he added, "We're trying to keep everything running as smoothly as possible, making sure everyone's accounted for and has proper ID. Jaki's taking a leap of faith for us, stepping a bit out of her comfort zone. My reputation's on the line, and so is the reputation of the Bradburne."

"Well," said Harry with a smile, "it looks like you're on track to have a very successful event. And as for your guest star, I'm sure you'll do everything in your power to make her comfortable."

With a nod, Perry added, almost under his breath, "And to keep her safe."

Chapter 5

At least the road crew didn't take me by surprise on Friday morning when they started up at seven, and the jackhammering phase seemed to be over. Now a backhoe began scooping up the chunks of broken sidewalk and pavement and dropping them into a Dumpster. Compared to the machine-gun assaults of the previous week, I found the drone of the digger's powerful engine and the crash of the stony pieces into the container a little easier on my ears and nerves, though not much.

By the time the work had started, I'd already been up for half an hour, anyway—eating breakfast, showering, dressing, and putting my shop in order so Sarah could let herself in at nine and take right over. I felt almost guilty, leaving her to work in such noisy conditions, as I set off for the day in my van. During the drive, I wondered if the expo might offer me a bit more peace and quiet.

Not likely. I turned into the Bradburne's parking lot to see vendors' trucks queued up at the rear entrance of the convention center to unload their goods. A freight elevator located back there could bring their larger display pieces and equipment right up to the concourse. Meanwhile, a line of passenger cars and SUVs waited, engines idling, to enter the hotel's multilevel parking garage. I glimpsed pet carriers in a couple of the hatches and figured these were cat owners who, like Harry, lived near enough to commute back and forth to the show.

All of this made me glad I had that parking space all to myself on the plaza. I drew a sharp glance from a beefy security guard when I climbed the curb cut with my van and pulled right across the pavers, stopping under the overhang. But true to his word, Perry had marked the spot with a small stand-up sign that said, RESERVED FOR CASSIE'S COMFY CATS. Once the guard realized that this matched up with the name flamboyantly displayed on the side of my vehicle, he gave me no trouble.

Becky, bless her, already waited on the plaza with a large tan pet carrier. She wore a short thermal jacket and a beanie against the morning chill, but like me, she'd left her official ID tag hanging in plain sight. When she saw me pull in, she brought the molded-plastic carrier containing Flo over to my van.

I peered through the wire-grid door at the black-and-white semi-longhair. "How's our girl today?"

"A little grumpy, but who can blame her?"

"Get her into the van so she can at least keep warm," I suggested.

There, we moved Flo into the roomy cage that was designed for blow-drying cats who had been bathed. Today I'd stocked it with dishes of food and water and a small litter pan, for the ones we'd be using in our demonstration. I also sprayed the interior with a special pheromone formula designed to calm nervous felines.

"Speaking of grumpy," Becky said, "at least one person isn't too thrilled that I'm assisting you this weekend. I had planned to help Chris staff the FOCA table, but because I'm tied up, the director drafted Glenda to do it instead."

"Sorry about that. I guess that means both Glenda *and*

Chris will be grumpy, since she's not the most congenial company."

"You'd think she'd be happy to help, right? But she doesn't approve of the whole cat show aspect, or even of breeding purebred animals, so she's participating under duress. I hope she doesn't drive Chris too crazy—he's liable to lose his temper and tell her off. Then Glenda might quit the shelter, and we need all the volunteers we can get."

Once we had settled Flo, Becky and I took turns running into the convention hall, to use the restroom and to check out how things were progressing on the main concourse. On my turn, I spotted an electronic schedule that listed the day's presentations. Perry had slotted us in for one demo from nine to ten and another from two to three. I was sure if our programs ran a little longer no one would mind, but ideally, we could use that midday break to switch cats. We'd bring in Ray for the afternoon, and tomorrow we'd plan to groom Lady.

The electronic sign also said Dr. Mark Coccia would be speaking about veterinary care for cats from eleven a.m. to noon. He hadn't needed to borrow any of my personal pets after all. Dave, one of the clinic's young techs, had volunteered to bring his rescued cat for the occasion. Mark's session and mine didn't overlap, so I hoped I could catch some of his presentation. It would be nice if we could even grab lunch together.

Along the convention center's vast concourse, most of the vendors already had set up and had begun doing business. I had expected that a lot of them would be selling catnip mice and feather toys, cat beds and climbing towers, carrier covers and other supplies, but they also offered a ton of goodies for cat-crazy humans. I passed displays of feline-themed artworks, home furnishings, fashion accessories, books, and children's toys.

If that wasn't enough to help you meld with your favorite species, a caricaturist would draw you as the cat breed of your choice, another booth would sell you furry pointed ears on a headband, and a face painter would give you the finishing touches of slanted eyes, a cat muzzle, and whiskers.

I even saw the occasional adult walking around in a full-body cat costume, complete with head, like a sports mascot. Couldn't imagine what those folks were promoting and was afraid to ask.

Taking time to browse, I came across one table that offered images of various breeds on small items like mugs, coasters, and accent pillows. A gift for Sarah came to mind, but I was sure that with her grown children and grandchildren she probably had more than enough mugs. I hesitated to buy kitty décor for her home, in case she wasn't into that kind of thing.

I was about to move on when I spotted the cell phone covers. Sarah's had come with her phone, it was getting shabby, and I knew she had no particular attachment to it. I asked the vendor if he had any covers depicting a light-toned Persian. Sarah had acquired Harpo, a cream-colored purebred, when his owner had died and none of the guy's friends or relatives wanted the cat. She often told me how much she appreciated his company now that her children were busy with jobs and families of their own.

The accommodating vendor came up with a phone cover featuring a lovely white Persian, close enough. After I'd purchased the gift, he also gave me a free North Jersey Cat Expo tote bag. It was more than I needed for one small item, but who could say what more shopping I might do?

At another booth with plenty of feline-themed jewelry, I found a cute, polished-brass hair clip in the outline of a cat's face. It was about three inches wide and would be perfect for Dawn Tischler, my friend who owned Nature's Way, the health food store a couple of blocks from my place. She'd had no interest in cats until a stray kitten had taken up residence in her storeroom about a year ago and had stolen her heart. Since falling for Tigger, she had become a true feline fanatic.

Dawn used creative braiding techniques and accessories to control her abundant auburn locks. Guessing that she'd get a kick out of the hair ornament, I bought that and dropped it into my tote bag, too. A few booths farther down, I also found a fat, striped catnip mouse that would make a perfect souvenir of the expo for Dawn's pet.

My own three had more stuff than they needed or even played with, but maybe I'd still pick up a few fresh catnip toys for them before I left.

At a booth draped with a banner for the Chadwick Veterinary Clinic, I found sturdy, freckled Dave unfolding a portable steel examining table for the morning demo. Several rolling cases that probably held medical equipment or other supplies were stacked behind him. Nearby, on the floor, an orange tabby complained from inside a carrier. When I stopped to say hello, Dave explained that the cat was Ginger, his own pet, and he and Mark would be using her for the day's demos.

"Mark went to deal with some sign-in paperwork," Dave told me. "He'll be back in a little while."

I thanked the tech for this information and moved on. No need to bother Mark now with a phone call; I'd catch up with him later.

At the hotel's snack shop, I picked up coffees for myself and Becky and brought them back to the van. My flashy vehicle already had begun to attract passersby, so she chatted with them about the work of the FOCA shelter, and I about my business. Toward ten, when a photographer from the regional newspaper showed up wanting to take a picture, we brought out Flo and began our formal demonstration.

Luckily, the side panels of my van opened wide, and if

spectators crowded close, they could watch the grooming process. Even though Flo had been lounging in the cage treated
with pheromone spray, the crowd of strangers still agitated her,
so I got to demonstrate the advantages of the grooming harness.
Again, it not only restrained Flo but also seemed to soothe her
while I demonstrated how to clip claws and tidy up a cat's coat.
I explained why regular grooming was important not just for a
cat's looks but even for its health.

"Because they have thin skin," I said, "matted hair can become very uncomfortable for them. Over time, it can cause ir-
ritation and even infection. On the other hand, you have to
groom carefully, because it's easy to cut or tear a cat's skin by
accident."

Projecting my voice over the street noises and crowd conversation proved more challenging than I'd expected, and I almost wished we'd brought along some kind of microphone
setup. This got worse during the course of our demo as the
foot traffic on the plaza grew. More people arrived with their
own cats, probably for the show. Besides toting carriers, some
pulled them like wheeled baggage or even pushed their animals in strollers.

It surprised me to see a knot of protestors on the fringe of
the crowd carrying signs that read RESCUED IS MY FAVORITE
BREED and ADOPT, DON'T BREED OR BUY! I wondered if they
were aware that proceeds from the expo were going to benefit
several local animal-welfare groups. Maybe they thought that
was contradictory, and to an extent, I could see their point. Cat
shows promoted the desirability of purebreds, which didn't
help reduce the vast numbers of mixed-breed but lovable felines that languished in shelters. Those that stayed too long
without attracting any adopters, even if they were healthy and
good-tempered, often ended up euthanized.

As the morning wore on, I started to recognize a new contingent infiltrating the crowd—clusters of teenage girls, most with trendy haircuts and sexy makeup. They wore short skirts or skinny jeans, with tops a little too dressy and heels a little too high for the occasion, and waved and shouted to each other. One quartet wore matching snug, pink T-shirts with purple letters that, when they stood together in the right order, spelled out *J-A-K-I*. The tallest, blondest member recruited a passerby to take a video with her camera while all four sang what I assumed was a Jaki Natal song, accentuated by a few hip-hop dance steps. They sounded a bit off-key to me, and their steps didn't quite sync up. Still, once they finished and struck various vampy poses, people near them on the plaza chuckled and applauded.

Besides the female wannabes, I spotted at least one male wanna-have—a tall, skinny guy with lank, shoulder-length hair and a ratty beard. His T-shirt bore a sultry portrait of Jaki Natal framed within a heart. Below was printed the plea, *Marry me!*

Becky also noticed all of this, and during a lull in our demo, she muttered to me, "Uh-oh, heeere they come."

I grinned. "I thought you were a Jaki fan, too."

"I am, but I wouldn't go being an idiot about it."

At eleven, we thanked our latest audience and put Flo back in her kennel to chill. I gave Becky my blessing to go off for a stroll inside the convention center.

I phoned Sarah to see how things were going at the shop. She told me she'd come equipped with earplugs today, and they made the racket from the street demolition more bearable.

"No new customers," she told me, "but your neighbor stopped in. Mrs. Kryznansky, right?"

"Yeah, she lives next door, over the insurance office." The

older woman and I rarely spoke except to wave and say hello, unless there was some kind of trouble at my place. "What did she want?"

"To gripe about the road work, of course. Said she gets migraines and the noise and vibrations are making them worse. She called the cops, but they told her the work's necessary and there's nothing they can do."

"And she thinks there's something we can do?"

"She was hoping you could 'use your influence' with the Chadwick PD. To do what, I don't know. Put mufflers on the jackhammers?"

"Oh, for heaven's sake." Adele Kryznansky must have read in the paper that I'd worked with the cops on a couple of local cases, and now she thought I could perform miracles. "Tell her it's driving us crazy, too—not to mention our customers' cats—and I only wish I had enough 'influence' to stop it."

"I did tell her some version of that. Anyway, how are things going at the expo?"

I managed to give Sarah a brief summary before she had to hang up and tend to the owner of the Abyssinian boarder, who had come by to pick him up. Not for the first time, I felt grateful that I could leave my shop in the hands of such a capable assistant while I occasionally took my business on the road.

I then answered a call from my mother, who by now ought to be smack in the middle of the cat show down in the hotel ballroom area. "How are you holding up?" I asked her.

A quavering laugh. "Oh, I'm okay. After a couple of hours *surrounded* by cats on all sides, I'm gradually getting used to it. You studied psychology—what's that called?"

"Desensitization," I told her, with a chuckle of my own. It was hard for me to imagine anyone, much less my own mother, having such a fear of the species that I loved and handled all day long, every day. But then, if I started dating a herpetologist, I might have some adjustment issues myself.

"Going around looking at the different breeds and cages *is* interesting," she admitted. "It's just when I see a cat that's loose—like when someone walks by with one slung over his shoulder—that I still flinch a little."

"I give you credit, Mom. Plunging yourself into a show this big is a real trial by fire."

"Anyhow, Looli did very well in her first class, so Harry was pleased." She handed the phone to him, briefly, so he could crow about his pet's first ribbon of the day.

"She got Best Color for her breed," Harry told me. "Of course, there were only two other Sphynxes, and her color always does get attention."

"Still, she's off to a good start," I said. "Congratulations to both of you!"

Shortly after I hung up, Chris from FOCA arrived to pick up Flo and leave Ray with me for the afternoon demo. The golden Persian was more relaxed, and I gave him a quick cuddle as I moved him from his carrier to the drying cage inside the van. Becky returned, at that point, and shot the breeze for a few minutes with me and Chris about the swelling crowd inside the convention hall and the obvious infusion of Jaki Natal fans.

"Becky, if you can hold things down here for a few minutes, I'd like to see a little of Mark's program," I said.

"Sure, go," she told me.

Inside, the main concourse was jumping, the vendor booths along the walls now fully staffed and doing a brisk business. In addition to the ones selling products and services, a couple advertised appearances by the "celebrity cats" Perry had mentioned. His handler persuaded Liberace, the piano-playing Maltese, to strike a string of harmonious notes on an electronic keyboard. At another booth, a veterinarian encouraged several cats to demonstrate how well they got around, and even chased toys, with one or more prosthetic limbs.

The FOCA display consisted of two long tables with literature for the organization and four large cages featuring rescue cats. One held an adult calico, and the next housed her three kittens, just a few months old. A pretty black shorthair watched everything alertly from another cage while a gray-and-white cat dozed in the last one.

Chris, cute enough with his longish dark hair to audition for a boy band, cheerfully chatted up anyone who stopped to look at the rescues and even some passersby. His helper, no doubt the one dubbed Grumpy Glenda, put forth less effort. The tall, athletically built woman wore faded jeans and a caution-yellow T-shirt emblazoned with the protestors' motto, ADOPT, DON'T SHOP! I wondered if that was such a wise move, considering that she and Chris were surrounded by vendors with goods for sale.

A neatly dressed man with a receding hairline, who'd been admiring the kittens, asked Glenda about her shirt.

"People should get their animal companions from shelters like ours, not from pet stores or breeders," she clarified. "FOCA is no-kill, but millions of healthy cats like these are destroyed in shelters every year because there's just no more room for them. And cats in pet stores often come from kitten mills that breed them in horrendous conditions."

Her mature listener decided to play devil's advocate. "That may be true, but I don't see the harm in someone buying a purebred from a reputable cattery. Some people are interested in perpetuating and refining a certain breed."

Glenda tossed her single long, hay-colored braid back over her shoulder in a gesture of disdain. "They also breed certain weaknesses into the animals, so that they're born with physical problems they'll have for their whole lives. All just for a particular look that wins ribbons in a show."

The man smiled slightly, and by now I guessed that he must be associated with the cat show in some way. "There are classes for household pets, who don't have to be pedigreed or purebred."

Glenda sniffed. "Still a beauty contest."

"You are aware, I'm sure, that the show taking place this weekend is raising money to help organizations such as yours?"

"We're glad for the assistance, but it's pretty ironic, isn't it? And of all people to sign on as a guest celebrity, they get Jaki Natal!"

"Do you also have some issue with her?" the man asked mildly.

"She carries her poor cat with her everywhere, just to attract media attention. These spoiled celebrities who treat their animals like fashion accessories make me sick."

A young couple who had picked up some FOCA literature seemed unnerved by this heated exchange. Chris also overheard and decided to intervene. "Glenda, these people want to sign the mailing list, but I can't find it. Didn't you have it last?"

When she disengaged to hunt for the list—which I suspected Chris had purposely mislaid—he apologized to the older man. "As you can see, some of our volunteers are extremely devoted to the cause. I hope she didn't offend you."

The well-groomed fellow smiled. "I have a thick skin. And the lady did make a few valid points. Now I'd better get back to the hotel—I'm judging the Premier Longhairs this afternoon."

As the man walked away, Chris winced.

"I suspected as much," I told him.

"You see what I mean about Glenda," he whispered to me.

"I do. Hope she doesn't lose you too many customers."

Moving on down the concourse, I passed exhibits by several other local humane and rescue organizations. They all offered a few caged animals that were available for adoption—cats only, since that was the theme of the expo—along with literature on rescue, providing for pets in a will, feral management, and other issues. All had set out cans or boxes for donations. I hoped the folks browsing at the tables would be generous. Even if each person only gave a couple of dollars, over three days it ought to add up nicely.

When I made another pass by the veterinary clinic's booth, Mark had returned. His demo already had drawn a respectable crowd, and I'm sure his dark, clean-cut good looks—even in drab, dusty-blue medical scrubs—didn't hurt. Neither did his clear baritone voice and his obvious intelligence. Using Ginger as a willing prop, he spoke about how to determine if your cat needs to go to the vet, what exams and shots a cat should have regularly, and the importance of spaying and neutering.

Stroking the orange tabby's head to keep her calm on the table, Mark asked his listeners, "Does anybody want to guess how many kittens one female cat can have in a year?"

A middle-aged blond woman in a peasant dress raised her hand. "Eight."

Mark shook his head with a sad smile. "A female cat can give birth to as many as eight kittens *at one time*, and can have up to three litters a year. So if Ginger here hadn't been spayed, over her lifespan she could produce about a hundred kittens. If all of those kittens went out and made more . . . in seven years, she could be responsible for 420,000 new cats. Is it any wonder that we end up with so many unwanted animals in shelters?"

I'd never heard Mark speak before an audience, and his ease and professionalism impressed me. He continued to answer questions about such things as how a vet safely examines a difficult cat, using Ginger to demonstrate some techniques. He switched to a life-sized feline dummy to demonstrate performing CPR in certain emergency situations. Just past noon, when Mark thanked his listeners and reminded them he'd be doing another session at three, they applauded warmly. Several lingered after the demo to ask him more specific questions.

I waited my turn, then congratulated him. "Great presentation! I think these folks probably learned a lot."

"Thanks. I've had some practice. Maggie and I both have given workshops for the techs and even for veterinary students from the college. I just tried to adapt the material to pet owners who may not have any medical background at all." He glanced at his watch. "Now I'm starving—haven't had anything but coffee since about six-thirty. What's there to eat out on the concourse?"

"There's a pizza stand, of course," I reported. "I also saw gyros, tacos, wraps, and regular ol' hamburgers. In typical Jersey fashion, it's a multicultural buffet."

"Haven't had tacos in a while. You game?"

I seconded the motion and offered to bring lunch back for him and Dave so they wouldn't have to leave their booth. While I waited in line at the concession, I texted Becky, who was still with my van; she said Chris was getting some food for her. I guessed that Glenda would be staffing the FOCA table alone for a while, giving her even more to be grumpy about.

I sat with Mark and Dave on the hard-sided equipment cases, and we ate with paper napkins spread on our laps. Over tacos and sodas, we all marveled at the size of the expo and the vast assortment of paraphernalia offered for sale. A human disguised as an extremely tall tuxedo cat strolled past us, stopping now and then to pose for pictures with strangers like Pluto does at Disneyland.

I already had told Mark about the weird notes Jaki had received and the mechanic who'd mysteriously crashed while driving her father's car. Now, spotting the costumed figure, he huffed in mild suspicion. "With all the extra security they hired for this weekend, I hope they checked that guy out."

Dave's mouth twisted in a cynical smile. "Yeah, he could be wired with explosives underneath that thing."

"Now guys," I muffled my own similar concerns, "he's probably just promoting one of the animal shelters."

We were finishing up our hasty meal when I noticed a din building outside—horns honking, people shouting and even screaming. My first thought was that something had gone wrong. Maybe a traffic accident?

Mark must have seen my worried expression, because he offered another explanation. "Bet our celebrity guest has arrived."

"Gosh, you're probably right. Wanna go see?"

We glanced at Dave, who, being a good sport, promised he'd stay behind to keep an eye on the clinic's booth and Ginger.

Mark and I reached the outdoor plaza just as the black stretch SUV turned under the overhang, making for the garage. A crowd of people, mostly young, flowed after it until they ran into a barrier of sawhorses and uniformed police. No rough stuff, fortunately. The cops simply announced that Ms. Natal would make a brief appearance on the concourse before she checked in, and only those holding tickets to the expo would be admitted. A video cameraman and a woman with a microphone, both wearing the logo of *New Jersey News*, pushed close enough to capture the action.

Meanwhile, I noticed that the limo cruised around to the most remote corner of the parking garage. No doubt they planned to spirit Jaki into the hotel by a rear entrance.

"Boy, not even a wave to her fans!" Mark grumbled in mock disappointment.

"Guess they can't take any chances, in case one of those fans is the stalker." As we strolled back inside, I told him, "Don't worry. Perry said we volunteers can sneak into her interview later on today without paying the fifty bucks."

"Oh, Perry said so, did he?" Mark slipped an arm around my waist and gave me a firm squeeze. "He seems to be doing you a lot of special favors."

I grinned. "Ha, Sarah said you'd be jealous. I'll have to tell her that she was right. Perry's a decent guy—I think—but a little too 'Mad Ave' for my taste. You have nothing to worry about."

"I'd better not, because two can play that game," Mark warned me. "I understand Ms. Natal is back on the market these days."

I glanced out through the building's deep windows at the jostling throng of fans. "Yeah, right, babe. Get in line."

He laughed.

Chapter 6

Mark and I went back to our separate posts to prepare for our afternoon presentations.

I crossed the sunny plaza and noticed that the protestors had grown to a half dozen by now. While I watched, a couple of police officers attempted to move them elsewhere so they couldn't block people from entering the hotel and convention center. The activists didn't go quietly, and the shouts and scuffling drew looks of alarm from people passing by. I suspect they played up even more when they spotted the *New Jersey News* team.

Finally the cops managed to corral them into a pocket park across the street from the hotel. From a few gestures made with nightsticks, I assumed the marchers got a stern warning to stay there and not invade the plaza again.

When I reached my van, Becky already had Ray ready to go. I'd expected that the Persian mix with the luxuriant coat would be a hit with our audiences, and I was right. As people murmured about how pretty he was, I stressed that anyone getting a similar cat must either learn to comb him themselves or take him to a professional groomer as often as every other week. I explained that various longhaired cats could have different types of coats, and a Persian would need a different approach from, say, a Maine Coon. Luckily, my listeners seemed to find this information new and interesting.

Most of them, at least.

Partway through, the four young women in the *J-A-K-I* T-shirts joined our crowd and giggled among themselves. Of course, the TV reporter *had* to talk to them, and they preened for the video cameraman. They were so distracting that a few listeners crowded closer to the van just to be able to hear our demo. Finally, during a lull in my talk, the taller of the two blondes called out to me, "What about Scottish Folds? Do they need special grooming?"

Of course, she would ask about Gordie's breed, but at least this shifted the attention back to my demo. Even the *New Jersey News* guy swung his camera toward me and Becky for a few minutes.

"Actually, I've only had one Scottish Fold as a customer," I admitted. "I do know they have very dense coats and come in both shorthaired and longhaired types. For the shorthairs, probably just an occasional brushing at home would be fine. Longhairs would need grooming a couple of times a week, but I understand they're not as hard to keep up with as, say, a Persian."

I'd never yet seen Gordie in person, but I could tell from Jaki's online videos that he was a shorthair.

After our demo wound up and the TV news duo moved on, the four girls still lingered on the fringes of the crowd. I pointed to their T-shirts. "Diehard fans, I see."

One of the blondes linked arms with a slightly chunkier brunette, and the two others also fell in line to spell out their idol's name. "We're the Jak-ettes!" they announced. They obviously expected someone to take a picture, so Becky and I grabbed our phones and obliged. The taller blonde introduced herself as Dria, and the others sounded off as Ashley, Tiff, and Lexi.

I said to Dria, "I guess you have a Scottish Fold cat."

She looked surprised. "No. . . . ?"

"Because you wanted to know about grooming one."

She creased her narrow nose. "My family's got a cat, but just a dumb old one from a shelter."

Though her tone made me feel sorry for her family's pet, I stayed upbeat. "Well, good for you, adopting a shelter cat. There are so many in places like FOCA that need good homes." I glanced toward Ashley, her brunette companion. "What about you?"

"I've got a couple cats, but they're just regular, too. You said you wanted a Scottish Fold, though, didn't you, Lexi?"

The redhead colored a little. "Yeah, but my dad says we can't afford one."

"Oh, please," Ashley muttered. "How much could it cost?"

"Aaashley!" Dria reprimanded her.

"Well, we already have one cat and a couple of dogs," Lexi admitted.

"Not to mention your beast of a brother," Ashley teased her.

"I'll get one, though," the redhead vowed with quiet determination. "I've got a plan. . . ."

Meanwhile Tiff, the shorter blonde, glanced at her phone. "Hey, you guys, let's move. It's almost time."

Spinning in unison—a minor miracle, on those precarious heels—the quartet sprinted for the hotel's main entrance. Over her shoulder, Ashley called back to me and Becky, " 'Bye, guys! Good luck with your . . . uh . . . grooming."

Once the Jak-ettes had gone, I checked my own phone for

the time and realized they must be headed to the singer's four o'clock interview. It was only three thirty—our question-and-answer session had run a bit longer this time—but they probably intended to claim the best possible seats.

Becky and I both wanted to see the interview, too, she out of hero worship and I out of sheer curiosity. By then the temperature had warmed to a mild seventy degrees, so we left Ray in the van with food and water, locked up securely. I figured that, coming right off the plane from California, Jaki might talk for an hour at most. Possibly, she'd take questions from the audience and reporters and pose for pictures with a few fans afterward.

The conference room was on the second floor of the hotel opposite a wing of guest rooms, so Becky and I entered the lobby and took the main escalator upward. That gave us a panoramic view of the many people with pet carriers and related equipment shuttling back and forth from the show that occupied the first-floor ballrooms. I wondered if everyone lined up at the registration counter also was involved with the expo; anyone who wasn't must have been startled to find themselves surrounded on all sides by felines and their handlers. I hoped the hotel staff had warned off any potential guests with severe cat allergies.

The hubbub from the lobby receded as Becky and I stepped off the moving stairway into the carpeted, civilized atmosphere of the second floor. This wing held several conference rooms, and the double doors to Room A stood open, with a hotel staffer checking tickets.

We met up with Chris and Mark in the hallway, where they marveled at the number of people who had come through the convention center that day, even during work hours. Up ahead, a stern-faced security guard was screening everyone for tickets.

When the four of us reached the door, I swallowed my apprehension and pointed to my volunteer badge. "Mr. Newton said that we—"

"Volunteers, okay." He quickly hustled us through the door, as if not to raise any questions among the folks who had paid. "You can stand in the back."

We'd have had to, anyway. The conference room probably accommodated only about two hundred people, and by the time we got there, every seat was filled. Still, the stage was well lit. There, two armless, white upholstered chairs flanked a small table with two glasses of water and a microphone on a stand.

Perry himself stepped onto the stage to welcome all of us. Since meeting him, I'd checked his bio online. Although it seemed his main focus always had been marketing, he'd done a bit of acting on the side, appearing in commercials and one soap opera. Not surprising, with his dimpled, boyish good looks. The businessman in him must have decided that promotion was a much more lucrative field, but Perry still seemed at home playing the emcee.

He drew some chuckles by saying that the enthusiastic crowd packed into the conference room just demonstrated the passion and loyalty of cat lovers. "But seriously," he went on, "I know that all of you are really here to meet, in person, a bright new media star whose looks and charm have captured everyone's hearts. So without further ado, I'm honored to present . . . Gordie!"

Laughter turned to wild applause as Jaki strolled onto the stage, her silver tabby comfortably cradled in her arms. She looked stunning in skinny black pants, high-heeled sandals, and a loose-fitting, white lace blouse that contrasted with her long, dark, wavy hair. Her face still showed a girlish softness in spite of smoky eye makeup and vivid red lipstick. From her broad grin, I guessed that having Perry introduce the cat instead of her might have been Jaki's idea . . . or, at the very least, she'd been happy to go along with it.

She and Perry sat in the white chairs, which were angled toward each other and the audience. Gordie settled calmly in his mistress's lap. Even from where I stood, I could easily make out the silver cat's black tabby stripes and folded ears. He also seemed to have some type of collar with a bow around his neck, partly hidden by his short, thick fur.

I realized now that Perry intended to do the interview himself. He started out in the same wry tone, implying that Jaki would graciously serve as a spokesperson for her "famous" pet. He asked if she always had liked cats.

"Yes and no," the singer admitted. "My family had a small farm a little west of here. We had indoor-outdoor cats that mainly hunted the mice, so growing up I bonded more with our dogs. But after I moved to LA to do the TV series—"

"That was *Too Cool for School*, right?" Perry asked.

A few in the audience clapped, and with a sweet smile, Jaki thanked them for remembering her show.

"Anyhow, out on the coast I lived in an apartment and kept crazy hours, so I figured a cat would be easier to take care of. I got a shelter rescue, and she made me appreciate how cool cats are. I loved her a lot and was really upset when she got very sick and finally had to be put to sleep."

"I can imagine," said Perry, respectfully. "How did Gordie come into your life?"

"He was a gift from a friend who knew that I'd just lost Samantha."

Behind me, Becky whispered, "We know who *that* was." From the murmurs in the audience, I imagined others were making similar comments.

If Jaki heard, it didn't bother her. She just stroked her pet's plush coat and smiled down at him. "I never thought another cat could replace Samantha, but Gordie has his own personality. He's so much fun . . . a real clown. He loves posing for pictures!"

"And you take a lot of pictures of him," Perry pointed out. "I like the ones where he's on a sofa with you, sitting up like a person."

"Isn't that crazy?" Jaki laughed. "It's just a weird thing that Scottish Fold cats tend to do."

"Did you particularly want a Scottish Fold?"

"No, that was the choice of . . . the person who gave him to me," Jaki responded, and skillfully steered the conversation back to the cat. "But Gordie's such a love, and nothing rattles him. I can take him anywhere. It's great because if I'm on the road and get stressed-out, he calms me down. He even sleeps in bed with me at night. . . ."

Chris chuckled. "She'll never get away with that!"

I also figured, from the impish look on Perry's face, that he wouldn't pass up the straight line. "We're still talking about Gordie, right? Not your 'friend' who gave him to you?"

Even from a distance, I could detect a blush creep up Jaki's cheeks, but ever the good sport, she still smiled. "That's right. I don't see that friend anymore, but I'd never part with Gordie!"

"Gotta give her credit," Mark muttered to me. "She's not letting him throw her."

"He's just trying for a laugh," I said. "He figures all her fans know about her and Alec."

Perry gave his guest star a break at that point, and asked her what else was special about Scottish Fold cats.

"Well, I *have* found out a lot about them," Jaki said. "The main thing, of course, is that the tips of their ears fold forward, the way they do on some dogs. It's a genetic thing. They only started breeding these cats in the 1960s, and the first one came from Scotland."

Perry encouraged her to hold Gordie facing the audience so everyone could see his ears. "And are they all this silver color, or—"

The overhead and stage lights flickered. Then the whole room went black.

Without a working microphone, Perry still made himself heard above the anxious rumblings of the audience. "It's okay, folks. Please stay in your seats. I'm sure it's just a temporary glitch."

My eyes adjusted to the murky darkness, lit by only the red EXIT signs over the doors and some dim cove lighting in the ceiling. Most people stayed seated for a minute or two, expecting the problem to be resolved.

The fire alarm sounded, repeating three shrill blasts.

Now the crowd stirred nervously, and some began to leave their seats. In the gloom, I could see Perry and Jaki glancing around in panic, too. A couple of figures who looked like support staff ran onto the stage to assist them.

Meanwhile, Mark, Becky, Chris, looked at one another. In wordless agreement, we left through the back doors.

In the hall, we could see our way by the late-afternoon glow through the windows along the outer wall. The sconces and other lights in the upper corridor also appeared to be knocked out. The nearby escalator was working, though, and so was the ultramodern chandelier that hung over it. I pointed this out to my friends.

"Might just be a minor bug in the system," Chris said. "But they'll probably pull the plug on her interview anyway, until they check it out."

"What a bummer," groused Becky.

Along with most of the audience members, we took the

escalator down to the hotel lobby. There we waited with dozens of other confused folks until someone finally silenced the piercing alarm.

An announcement followed in a calm, female voice: "Ladies and gentlemen, one of the hotel's fire alarms has been triggered, and we are investigating the cause. Please evacuate all upper floors and proceed to the lobby until we can be sure that it's safe for you to return to your rooms. Do not use the elevators. Cat show participants can remain in place in the ballrooms for now. Thanks for your cooperation."

"Think it's an electrical problem?" I asked Mark. "First the lights, then the fire alarm?"

"Does seem like a weird coincidence," he said.

The crowd in the lobby swelled as overnight guests evacuated their rooms, many with their cats in tow. Through the tall windows we saw one fire truck roll up outside with no apparent urgency. However, two black-and-white Chadwick PD patrol cars already stood near the hotel's entrance with their emergency lights flashing.

A uniformed, female cop strode past me at a brisk clip, talking into her radio. I caught just a few words: "Need ambulance . . . security guard down, in stairwell . . . unresponsive."

What did *that* mean? An accident, maybe? Someone electrocuted?

A knot of panic-stricken hotel guests had jammed up at the lobby's automatic front doors, trying to get out to the plaza.

"C'mon," said Mark, "there's another exit from the concourse."

We followed him out that way and ended up in the parking garage. From the back corner I could hear raised voices. Two of them belonged to Perry and Jaki.

"Sweetheart, I'm sure he's okay. We'll find him. Just calm down."

"*Don't* tell me to calm down, and *don't* call me sweetheart!" The lady did have a set of lungs, for sure. "Mira said some random guy grabbed the carrier from her. She thought he was a hotel employee, but no one's seen him since." I heard hysterical tears in her voice. "Oh my *God*, somebody took him! They stole Gordie!"

Chapter 7

The young pop star sounded so distraught that I wanted to do or say something to help her. I rounded the blind corner of the parking garage and saw her sagging against the shoulder of a tall, elegant black woman in a businesslike beige pantsuit. Nearby stood Perry and another man, a bit thick around the middle, with graying temples and a black mustache. When the older guy noticed me and my friends approaching, he stalked over to intercept us. His forbidding glare stopped me in my tracks.

"Nobody comes back here!" he barked with a faint accent. "Who are you and what do you want?"

I felt Mark's hand on my shoulder, warning me not to get involved. But the knowledge that he had my back also bolstered my courage. I introduced myself and showed my ID tag. "I'm a volunteer with the expo, and I was in the audience for Jaki's interview just now. Is it true? Is Gordie missing?"

Since the guest star continued to reject his help, Perry left her and came to my rescue. "These folks are okay, Hector."

"How do we know that?" the other man demanded.

For whatever good it might do, I fished a business card out of my shoulder bag and handed it to him.

"C'mon, Cassie." Mark tugged at my elbow. "We don't want to intrude...."

"Of course not," I told Perry and Hector, whoever he was, "but if I can do anything to help ... maybe keep my eyes open for the cat ..."

Perry's cell phone rang, and he stepped to one side to take the call.

"Keep your eyes open for it." Hector snorted. "And then maybe you'll want a reward for returning it, eh?"

"No, no. Nothing like that."

By now, Mark, Becky, and Chris all were urging me to step away from the situation, and I knew I ought to. But when Perry ended his phone call, his stunned expression froze me in my tracks.

"What's wrong?" I asked.

"A security guard went to find out what made the conference room black out. They found him dead in a stairwell. They're not sure yet what killed him, but—"

Hector threw up his hands, though he kept his voice low enough that Jaki wouldn't overhear. "Someone got *murdered*? That's it, we are out of here. My daughter isn't staying in this place one minute longer!"

Okay, that solved one mystery. Becky had mentioned that Jaki's father acted as her manager.

Blanching beneath his tan, Perry shook his head. "I'm afraid Jaki *is* staying here, at least a while longer. We all are. The cops don't want anyone to leave until they have a better idea of what happened."

We heard a chime, and the doors of the garage's rear elevator opened. Out sprang a young woman dressed all in stretchy black; she had Jaki's coloring, but tomboyish angles where the sexy singer had curves. She threw her arms around the star and said, "Cuz, I'm so sorry!"

"He's not upstairs, either?"

The newcomer shook her head. "I should never have handed him over to a stranger."

"It's not all on you, Mira," Jaki told her. "I should have been paying more attention, too. Right after you put Gordie in his carrier, the fire alarm went off and Perry tugged at my arm, said we had to evacuate."

Mira nodded. "I swear, the guy looked like hotel security, and he said he'd take Gordie someplace safe. I tried to ask you if it was okay, but you were facing away . . . and by the time I looked back, they were gone!"

The woman in the pantsuit tried to reassure Jaki that her pet's disappearance probably was just a misunderstanding. "He could have thought there was a fire and taken the cat out of the hotel, some back way. Gordie will turn up soon, you'll see."

An announcement told us that the fire siren had been a false alarm, and it was safe for guests to return to their rooms. Mira and the older woman persuaded their tearful young star to go back up to her suite while they checked into the situation with her missing cat. Hector yanked out his phone again and stabbed at numbers on the keypad, making another desperate call.

Mark and I backed off then and followed our FOCA friends toward the concourse. Perry caught up with us to deliver one last message: "Please, guys, keep this quiet! The police are going to say that they're investigating an incident at the hotel, but without any details."

"But if people are in danger . . ." Becky began.

"From what I heard, there's no obvious sign of foul play," Perry told us. "The guard might just have fallen down the stairs when the lights went out. Any rumor that it was murder could cause a panic, and we can't have all of these people going into a frenzy!"

"We understand," Mark said.

"And," I added, "I guess if we even say that the cat's gone missing, whoever took Gordie might turn him loose to avoid being caught."

"Well, yeah. That, too." I'm sure, after the news of the dead security guard, Perry had temporarily forgotten about the kidnapped cat. But I suspected that Gordie still would be topmost in Jaki's mind.

As the four of us passed back through the double glass doors into the convention center, Chris muttered, "What a freakin' mess, eh?"

"Crazy," I agreed. "So, Hector is Jaki's father and manager?"

Becky nodded. "They worked out that arrangement when she was just a kid doing the TV series. Probably to keep her from being exploited by sleazy showbiz types."

"The lady in the pantsuit is Rose Davidson," Chris told us, "and the girl in black who just came down in the elevator is Mira, Jaki's cousin and personal assistant. I went to college with her."

Aha, I thought. His reliable source for all the inside-showbiz gossip.

As we walked back down the concourse, Mark shook his head. "The missing cat has to be a simple mistake. It probably has nothing to do with the dead guard."

I disagreed. "Or it could have everything to do with it. Maybe somebody *caused* the room to black out, and the fire alarm to go off, while Jaki was doing the interview. The confusion gave him a chance to steal the cat."

"And to kill a man in the process?" Becky challenged me.

"Like Perry said, that could've been accidental," Mark reminded her, "if the stairwell also went dark, and the guy was taking a step at the wrong time."

I had a sudden inspiration, but one I thought I should keep to myself. "'Scuse me for a second, guys. I'd better check on my mom and Harry. They're over at the cat show and probably don't know anything about all this."

"And you shouldn't tell them." With a glint in his eye, Mark added, "Remember, *Perry* said not to."

I ignored the ribbing. "I wouldn't, anyway, unless it was really necessary. How about we meet back here in half an hour at the food court?"

Everybody else agreed to this, and I headed toward the hotel. At least no cops or guards barred people from entering that part of the complex any longer.

As Harry had predicted, the cat show extended throughout four merged first-floor ballrooms. The doors of the two center rooms stood open to the corridor, with a banner for the event stretched across the top. I could have found my way without signage, though, just by following the intermittent mews and the mingled odors of cat litter and dry kibble.

To the right I passed six partially curtained booths, called rings, where cats were being judged. Two currently stood empty, the wire cages along the back unoccupied. In one ring, handlers were picking up animals from the last round and the judge was wiping down the raised table with disinfectant. In the other three, judges tried to entice a massive Maine Coon to chase a feather toy, or checked the stubby tail on a red-and-white Manx, or stretched a Siamese full length as if he were airborne. I had to wonder what the cats thought of all this strange behavior, but most had been handled this way all of their lives and were used to it.

I made my way to the benching area, where the competitors waited between judgings in their fairly roomy, comfortable cages. I had no idea where Harry and Mom had set up, but that gave me an excuse to wander down all of the rows and admire the variety among the animals and their cage decorations. Most cats had at least one person keeping watch over them, and some owners had taken their restless pets out to cuddle or play with them.

They were not grouped by breed, so I kept my eyes peeled for any Scottish Folds. I spotted only four, and just one silver tabby. According to the info on the cage, she was a female, and her markings were much lighter than Gordie's.

That didn't convince me that he had not somehow been smuggled down here to the show floor. Many of the cages were heavily draped to protect their inhabitants from sensory overload, and some openings even were screened with a fine black mesh that made it hard to tell if they were occupied at all. It would be so easy for someone to bring Gordie's carrier in here, transfer the cat to a heavily swathed cage, and hide him until the coast was clear to spirit him away.

Mom hailed me before I saw her, and I gathered from her bright smile that she was having a decent time. I wound my way toward her, through the other seated owners and handlers. Harry turned his lean, professorial face toward me, with Looli lounging in his arms like an elegant, bat-eared E.T. I reflected that Harry had made a pet of the only living creature paler than he was.

"Look!" Mom pointed to a row of three small, shiny ribbons in assorted shades on the Sphynx's cage.

"Way to go Looli, Harry!" I congratulated him, as I read the title of a blue one: Best of Color. "Guess she's still got it."

"Well, her coloring always gets attention," he said proudly. "But she should have a good shot at Best of Division, too, because she has such a great temperament. When the judge handles her she's always relaxed, but when he swishes that feather toy she's also ready to play."

"Aww, such a good girl." I held out my arms so Harry could pass me the leggy little creature.

He went on to explain, or try to, the whole judging process. I gathered that Looli competed as a Premiere, or adult altered cat, and as a Specialty Shorthair. In some rings she'd go up against other exotic shorthair types, and sometimes only against other Sphynxes. How many points she would accumulate toward a Premiereship would depend on how many other cats she'd beaten for a certain title. Oh, and the top prize, or "final," wasn't always a blue ribbon—depending on the category, it might be brown or even black. But a rosette, a multi-ribbon award with a medallion at the top, always meant some type of major prize. Looli would get one of those if she won a significant number of finals.

Though all of these technicalities set my head spinning, I nodded and pretended to absorb them. Meanwhile, I enjoyed the simpler, quirky charms of Looli's wrinkled little face, huge ears, and wide, curious yellow eyes. I will always prefer my cats with a bit more fur, but had to admit that petting a Sphynx was an interesting sensation—like stroking warm suede. And she purred as sweetly as any other cat.

I flashed back on Glenda's complaint, that cats bred for special traits also tend to inherit special problems. I knew Sphynxes got oily skin, lacking the fur to absorb it, and when Harry had boarded Looli with me, I had instructions to bathe her every other day. "Do you give her a lot of baths to prepare for a show?"

"I was up early this morning doing just that," he said, "before I picked up Barbara to bring her to the hotel."

Okay, so he and my mom hadn't spent the night together. Not that it was any business of mine. Why did knowing that make me feel better? Was I really such a sulky child?

"It amazes me, how much work these people go through to get their cats ready for a show," Mom said. "We were talking to Nancy Whyte, down the row here, who has these huge, fluffy cats. . . ."

"Maine Coons," Harry put in.

My mother nodded. "And she was telling us— Oh, here she is now!"

A plump woman with a full head of blond curls—giving her a silhouette not unlike one of her cats—was just returning to her seat. Her rather short arms struggled to support a massive brown tabby with white underparts. The animal gave her no trouble, but his sheer size would have challenged Vin Diesel.

Mom eagerly introduced the two of us. "This is my daughter, the professional groomer. I was just telling her how much you went through to get King here ready for the show."

Settling in a chair with her boy—who apparently had just scored his second final, in Longhair Specialty—Nancy sighed. "It's a production, all right. I wash and condition and dry and fluff and powder. Of course it pays off, because by the time he goes into the ring, he looks spectacular. But he's a big fella, I'm kind of a little woman, and sometimes I think I'm just getting too old for all this."

Harry explained that I was doing public grooming demonstrations out on the plaza. "Cassie's got a van now, so she can make house calls."

"Mom, Harry, please!" I said, embarrassed by their naked attempt to drum up business for me. And I wasn't even sure I wanted the gig. King was indeed a lot of cat, and his prep routine sounded way beyond what I usually provided for my customers. Besides, if Nancy was a breeder, she might have plenty more Coons at home.

At least she didn't seem to mind the sales pitch. "There's an idea. And you're in Chadwick? I'm in Sparta, not that far. Maybe you could groom for me sometime."

"How often do you show your cat?" I didn't want to make such a big commitment that I wouldn't be able to deal with my other customers.

"I have two, King and his sister Jessy, but I only show them a few times a year. I have a sister who comes along when I go out of state, but maybe you could help me with the Jersey shows."

We exchanged cards and agreed to talk further after the expo was over. Then a couple of admirers stopped by to ask her about King, and she turned her attention to them.

Mom whispered to me, "You could do that stuff for Nancy's cats the same as she does, couldn't you, Cassie?"

"Thank God, most of my customers don't ask for all that. They just want their pets clean, neat, and free of any mats or tangles. I only helped someone prep a cat for a show one time, and like you say, it was much more work."

"I'll bet they paid you more, though," Harry put in, with a shrewd smile. "You could probably hire yourself out at a show like this and name your own price."

Mom apparently had grown bored with the cat chat, because she asked me, in a quiet tone, "Cassie, maybe you can tell us—is there something strange going on? An official came through here a few minutes ago and said all people leaving today with their cats—not staying over at the hotel—would have to be cleared by a security guard at the exit. I can understand why they'd inspect us when we come into a big event, but when we're leaving?"

I felt Harry's eyes on me, too, as they both waited for my answer.

"I did hear they were going to be checking people, but I don't really know what's up," I fibbed, as I'd been told to. "Could be that a cat's gone missing, and they want to be sure no one is leaving with more than they came with."

Mom glanced at Harry. "Does that happen often?"

"Never heard of such a thing before," he said. "These cats all have microchips and paperwork. Be crazy to steal one—you couldn't breed or show it. Not legitimately."

"Guess there *are* some crazy people out there." Fondly, I handed Looli back to him. "Well, I'm meeting Mark, Becky, and Chris back at the food court to grab a quick dinner. Can I bring you two anything?"

Mom shook her head. "We'll probably stop somewhere in town after we wrap up here."

"Providing we pass the security check," Harry added, with a frown.

I met up with my friends at a concession stand that sold light food, and we got wrap sandwiches and soft drinks. Chris arrived last, explaining that he had to wait for Glenda to come back to watch the FOCA table.

"She keeps making excuses to leave for, like, fifteen or twenty minutes at a stretch," he complained. "I don't get that lady. If she's so darned devoted to her job, why doesn't she spend more time doing it?"

"You should ask her that," Becky said.

"I did, tactfully, but she just makes one lame excuse after another. I don't want to give her too hard a time, because I don't want to get slugged." He chuckled darkly. "That chick must have a good twenty pounds on me, and it's all muscle."

Mark, not having met Glenda, just raised an eyebrow, but Becky and I laughed.

The four of us pulled up chairs around one of the metal café tables provided. While we ate, we tried, in hushed tones, to make sense of what had happened with the death of the security guard and the theft of Jaki's cat.

I told them I'd done some sleuthing around at the cat show, but it was impossible for me to tell if the missing Gordie might be stashed anywhere among the entries.

Mark played the skeptic. "Jaki seemed convinced that something bad was going to happen even before she came here today, and I'm sure the blackout and fire alarm fed right into those fears. She probably freaked out over nothing. I'll bet her cat was already in her room by the time she went back up there."

Chris nodded. "I'd be a lot more worried about whether somebody actually offed that security guard."

"But what if the two incidents are connected?" I chewed a mouthful of my turkey wrap, thoughtfully, before telling the others what Perry had confided to me. "Jaki's been getting threats. That was the reason for all of the extra security this weekend. She seemed to feel that she had at least one serious stalker. Now she probably thinks that person has taken her cat to gain leverage over her. And she could be right."

"Or somebody might be planning to hold Gordie for ransom," Becky suggested. "Everyone who follows Jaki on social media knows how attached she is to him."

"Alec gave her the cat," I recalled. "Now that they've split and Jaki wrote that snarky song about him, maybe he's taking Gordie back to punish her."

Chris scoffed. "Alec MacMasters is in California, probably busy shooting another season of *Galaxy Wars*."

"Well, he wouldn't do it himself, of course. He'd hire somebody."

Still, Mark sounded doubtful. "Somebody hard-core enough to kill a guard who got in the way?"

"That would be pretty extreme," I admitted. "But maybe something went wrong. Apparently the ME couldn't tell exactly how the guard died. Maybe somebody shoved him aside and he fell down some stairs . . . and landed the wrong way."

Becky lifted her eyes to gaze over my shoulder. "Well, if there's anybody who's got better information, Cassie, she's standing right over there."

I looked around to see Detective Angela Bonelli, of the Chadwick PD, about twenty feet from us and conferring with one of her officers. I hesitated and asked Mark, "Should I?"

He knew my track record of sticking my nose into Chadwick police business and that I was almost pals with Bonelli. "Might as well. If she doesn't want you involved, I'm sure she'll tell you flat out."

I stood up near my chair, far enough away not to eavesdrop on Bonelli's conversation with the balding, uniformed cop whom I recognized as Officer Mel Jacoby of the Chadwick force. The fortyish detective looked a bit preppier than usual today, in chinos, loafers, and a teal-striped blouse along with her regulation navy blazer. But her dark, bobbed hair and strong-featured profile communicated all business, as usual.

After Officer Jacoby gave a brisk nod and strode purposefully away, Bonelli paused to jot a note in the small vinyl-covered pad that she seemed to carry everywhere. I approached, but before I could speak, she glanced up and favored me with a crooked smile. "Ah, Cassie. I've been looking for you."

"You have?" I couldn't possibly be a suspect, could I?

"We've been trying to talk to people who were in the conference room audience today when the excitement occurred. Perry Newton, the promoter of this extravaganza, said you and your friends were present, too."

"Yes, we were." I glanced toward the small table where my group still sat. "Though we were standing all the way in the back."

"Might've been a good place to observe things. Did you notice anyone in the crowd behaving suspiciously?"

Tough question. "Not really, under the circumstances. There were a lot of Jaki fans whispering to each other, taking pictures with their phones, and probably sending them to friends. Nobody skulking around like a terrorist. Perry told me they found a security guard dead. Do they know yet how he died?"

"It's still under investigation. The full autopsy might take a couple of days. Meanwhile, we'd appreciate it if you didn't spread that information around."

"We won't, but . . . Do you think it had anything to do with the blackout and the fire alarm?"

"As I said, we're still looking into it."

"Someone said he was found in a stairwell. Do those areas have security cameras?"

"Unfortunately, no. Most hotels put them in the elevators, but there are so many stairwells that they usually don't think it's cost-effective. Would be helpful to us if they did."

Bonelli always played it close to the vest, even with me, this early in an investigation. Still, I felt sure the incidents must be connected, if only because the cat had been whisked away. "Did Gordie turn up?"

The detective looked blank. "Who?"

"Jaki's cat. She said that, during all the chaos in the dark, he vanished along with his carrier. Mom told me hotel security plans to check everybody leaving the show today."

"Riiight, Newton did mention that someone took off with the cat—I guess he also told the hotel to keep an eye out for it. Probably was just a hotel staffer, trying to be helpful. Jaki may even have the cat back by now."

I could see that, sharp as Bonelli usually was, she had not connected the disruption of the interview with the cat's disappearance. "Jaki really loves Gordie, and she was extremely upset when we saw her in the parking garage. It's possible the whole thing was staged so somebody could steal him. Somebody who knew it would send her into a tailspin."

Bonelli's features went through a sequence of expressions I had seen in the past—she wanted to dismiss my theory, then realized it had some merit. She tapped a series of numbers on her cell phone and waited. "This is Detective Angela Bonelli. I'm downstairs on the concourse, and someone just reminded me that Jaki's cat went missing during the blackout. Has it been located yet?"

I glanced again toward the table where my friends sat, and Mark caught my eye. He must have overheard, because he gave me a half smile and a thumbs-up.

"Uh-huh . . . uh-huh . . ." said Bonelli. "Yes, I'm sure she is. Yes, we definitely will. I'll be in touch." She ended the call. "Still no sign of the cat."

"That's it," I said, aware that I might irritate her if I sounded too cocky. "That's got to be the motive. Find Gordie, and you'll have the person who blacked out the ballroom and triggered the false alarm. And maybe killed the security guard."

Bonelli hesitated. "I shouldn't be telling you this, but if it'll help to squelch any rumors . . . There's no indication that it was murder. We didn't find any weapon, just a bruise on the guy's throat. He could have been walking down the stairs when the lights went out, took a tumble, and fell against something . . . maybe the handrail."

I considered this. "But why would he be in the stairwell in the first place? Maybe he saw someone acting suspicious who ran in there, and he was chasing them. Even if the guard did fall, maybe he had some help."

"That's always possible, which is why we're still investigating. At any rate, we can't be sure yet that his death had anything to do with the disappearance of the cat. This case seems to have a lot of moving parts—I'm not expecting any simple answers."

"You can start by checking out the cat show entries," I suggested. "I was down there a little while ago, looking in cages, but I had to be discreet. The cops could—"

"Yes, we can, though I don't know how much good it will do." Bonelli frowned. "If this person is as smart as you seem to think—figured out how to hack into the hotel's lighting and alarm systems, and how to kill a man with no evidence of a struggle—they won't be sitting around the ballroom with the cat in a carrier. They'd have left the hotel before we even had a chance to put out the alert. Which means they could be anywhere . . . and anyone."

Chapter 8

Becky and Chris headed back to FOCA to return Ray, my afternoon demo cat, and Mark and Dave took Ginger back to the veterinary clinic. Before splitting up, we all speculated as to whether we'd be expected to do our demos again tomorrow. We decided we'd stick to the agreed schedule unless someone called and told us the programs were canceled.

On my way out of the hotel, I observed a long line of people with pet carriers at the main exit. It reminded me of an airport security checkpoint, as a Bradburne staffer in the standard gray polo and black pants peered closely at each feline and perused its papers before letting it leave the building. I wondered how long my mother and Harry would get hung up by this inspection, yet outside on the plaza, before I'd even reached my van, I saw Harry's BMW glide out of the parking garage.

I waved him over to the curb, and my mother rolled down the passenger side window. "You two must have been the first ones out of there," I teased.

"We bent the rules a little," Mom said with a wink. "One of the hotel staffers showed us a back way out to the garage."

"Really? Should he have done that?" I worried that someone less honorable than Mom and Harry might get the same idea.

"Oh, he knew we were just leaving with the same cat we came in with. Maybe he felt sorry for us because we're old codgers."

"Barbara!" said Harry, sounding shocked.

I laughed. "You're hardly that. Anyway, as long as you got a break, I won't hold you up. Have a good evening."

"You, too, honey," Mom said, before they cruised away.

I pondered the idea that even the hotel guys on the floor at the cat show didn't seem to know any type of serious crime had been committed. Maybe that was intentional on the part of the cops. I was glad I hadn't told my mother and Harry the whole story.

Before I could drive off the property, I had to let a female guard check the inside of my van, including all the built-in compartments. She was vague about the reason for the search. I could have gotten huffy and told her to call Perry Newton, who I'm sure would have let me off the hook, but I really didn't mind. I was glad to see them making some effort to find Gordie.

When I reached my shop, I was way more tired than I should have been at seven p.m. At least the road crew seemed to have quit on time and even made an effort to leave the driveway clear for me to get into my rear parking lot. They must have assumed I'd only be driving the tidy little CR-V parked back there. They either didn't notice, or forgot, that I'd left that morning in the monster van.

I pulled the van's nose right up to the available opening, parked there, and got out to assess my chances. A hair too far left or right and I'd scrape either the shovel of their massive backhoe or the equally massive elm tree at the edge of my neighbor's property.

I gritted my teeth. So far I'd been able to avoid leaving the flashy vehicle parked on the street overnight. I don't know what I was afraid of—it had a secure lock and an alarm, and there wasn't really anything of value inside it to steal, but maybe someone would *think* there was. A greater threat might be a driver who'd been drinking or dozing behind the wheel, who might slam into it and then drive away. After all the money I'd spent customizing the thing, I dreaded not only paying for the repair but patching up the fancy paint job.

On the other hand, a thief or a drunk driver was a remote danger. Scraping the paint by trying to get in the driveway, under the present circumstances, was almost inevitable. If I didn't do it on the way in tonight, I surely would when I drove out tomorrow. And even if I made it into the lot now, the road crew could start work before I left tomorrow and block me in.

That decided it. My flashy vehicle with its prancing Persian on the side would have to spend tonight parked in front of the house two doors down . . . which had been spared any construction activity so far. The resident was an older guy who mostly kept to himself and didn't seem to go out much; I doubted that he would complain. At any rate, I made sure not to encroach at all on *his* driveway.

Sarah had left by now. She had her own set of keys, so she'd been able to let herself into the shop at nine and lock up when she left at five. I hadn't scheduled any customers for grooming over this weekend, because I didn't want Sarah to have to handle those jobs alone. Most cats fussed at least a little and needed two sets of hands to manage them.

In the early days, when I'd been grooming solo, I'd had to use a harness much more often. I'd tried out several other assistants—some younger and supposedly with training and experience—before Sarah had come along. Her unflappable temperament, from decades of teaching math at an inner-city high school, qualified her more than anything else to work at Cassie's Comfy Cats. Our typical customer came with four sets of claws, sharp teeth, and lightning reflexes, and could twist himself around in your hands like a Slinky. Sarah had needed those steely nerves of hers, especially while she was still learning the job.

At this stage, she probably could deal with a more compliant feline on her own, but if anything did go wrong, a cranky owner might take issue with the fact that Sarah wasn't certified as a groomer, which I am. No sense setting her up for any type of trouble—she'd have plenty to keep her busy, dealing with the boarders and any drop-in customers. Though we'd been having fewer of those, too, since the road work had started.

Once inside the shop, I found a message on my front counter phone from my neighbor Mrs. Kryznansky. That didn't surprise me much, since Sarah had prepared me for the woman's complaints.

"Ms. McGlone, I know you have contacts with the local police. Can you get them to stop this awful noise and disruption on our street? I actually had a picture fall off my wall the other day from that terrible drilling! I asked the head man how long it's supposed to go on, and he said they'll be working on our street all month. How is that allowed? I'm hoping there's something you can do. . . . Thanks!"

I shook my head over the message. The jackhammers were done, anyway, so her pictures should stay in place from now on. And annoyed as Adele Kryznansky might have been, at least she didn't have cats from four paying customers staying on her ground floor and getting agitated by the din. Plus, I knew all too well that the Chadwick police had more urgent problems to deal with right now. I didn't look forward to the road work stretching out all month, either, but removing and replacing a mile or so of deteriorated sewer line *was* a big job. Afterward, I supposed they'd also be rebuilding the curbs and the sidewalks, though at least that should be less noisy.

On the sales counter next to the phone, I found a handwritten note from Sarah—her graceful, legible schoolteacher penmanship put mine to shame. She told me everything had gone smoothly that day, and a repeat customer wanted to bring his cat in the following Monday to board. She also hoped I'd had a fun, "star-studded" experience at the expo.

Poor Sarah's doing her usual half shift for me tomorrow, with all the disruption outside and the complaints from Mrs. K. I'll make it up to her and pay her for a whole day. And just maybe, if I can talk to Bonelli at a less-than-frantic moment, I'll ask if anything at all can be done about the road work noise.

Perry nailed it, didn't he? I always end up being the problem solver.

I hated to disappoint Sarah by telling her how badly the "star-studded" part of the expo had gone. At any rate, I wasn't free to do that.

Reporters from both the local paper and a TV station had attended the opening of the expo. What would they report, or not report, by tomorrow? Maybe just that Jaki's interview had to be cut short because of technical problems? There would be no suppressing that part—the whole audience had seen it. But the guard's death probably could be kept under wraps for a while if the cops wanted it that way.

I ran a quick check on my boarders. Sarah had promised to let each of them out in the playroom for half an hour during the day and had fed them just before she left. Now that things outside were quiet, they seemed calm enough. The only sign I found that the day's noise had disturbed them was a hairball coughed up by Mia, the Siamese. I cleaned it out of her cage, then soothed her with a stroke and a little more dry food.

All those tasks done, I climbed the stairs to my apartment and called to my three cats. Black Cole and calico Matisse came trotting to the top of the stairs, while orange Tango galloped up like a Shetland pony, his version of sarcasm. I'm always amused by the way the same cat can slink around soundlessly when he wants to keep a low profile, or thunder across a room when he wants attention. At various pitches, they all voiced complaints along the lines of, *It's about* time *you got home!*

After feeding them, I wandered around the apartment checking for signs of stress and boredom. All I came across were teeth marks on the corner of a magazine I'd left on the trunk/coffee table and a few new snags in my vintage chenille bedspread. The first mischief I probably could blame on Cole, since he liked to gnaw; the spread damage looked like Tango's work. Not too bad, though, when you considered how I'd neglected them, while pampering other cats, over the past few days.

As a child living in a suburban home, I'd had a variety of pets: turtles, fish, birds, and often both a dog and a cat who always coexisted fairly well. It was Cassie's Peaceable Kingdom, you could say, and my parents just lived in it. My dad had tolerated all of the creatures about equally, but I knew my mom abhorred anything in the reptile family. I didn't find out until last year that she also had a mild phobia about felines.

My first cat, Candy, had been a calico like Matisse and an equally good sport. When I'd been too young to know better, I'd dressed her in doll hats and sweaters, and she'd sat still for that indignity long enough for me to snap pictures. My felines lived a long time—Candy had made it to twenty—so although I always had owned at least one, overall I hadn't had that many. And the three living with me now represented the most I've ever shared my space with at once. I've seen victims of animal-hoarding situations, and know too well what can happen when you take on more pets than you can decently care for.

Sarah helped with the feeding and litter pan duty in the shop, but upstairs, those chores all fell to me. After doing them tonight, I finally got to relax. The wrap sandwich I'd eaten before I left the expo seemed like a distant memory, so I grabbed a yogurt from the refrigerator. Organic vanilla with little bits of the beans in it, very tasty. From Nature's Way, Dawn's shop. Since I'm not fond of cooking, being tight with someone who ran a health-food store had greatly improved my eating habits.

Dawn had been my best friend in high school. We'd gone to different colleges but reconnected a few years after graduation. That she and I now owned businesses within blocks of each other was no coincidence. Her success running a shop in Chadwick actually had inspired me to take the entrepreneurial plunge.

I always enjoyed visiting Nature's Way. The building had started life at the turn of the century as a feed store, and Dawn had preserved as much of that atmosphere as possible. She'd kept the vaulted ceiling with its exposed beams, given the rough plank walls just a light wash of pale green paint, repurposed the built-in shelving, and installed a beautiful oak-and-glass display counter from an old pharmacy. Along with health foods, Nature's Way sold related goods such as natural cleaning products and toiletries, and New Age trinkets and jewelry.

I hadn't spoken to Dawn in a couple of days, which was unusual, and I felt the need to connect with her now. She'd always helped me to make sense of stressful, overwhelming situations. But how much should I tell her about the craziness happening at the expo?

I didn't need to worry about that. When Dawn answered the phone, we instantly got off on a different subject.

"Oh, Cassie," she said, an edge of pain to her voice, "I'm so sorry I haven't been in touch sooner. I spent most of this morning at the doctor's."

"You did? Why, what's going on?"

"Nothing *too* serious, but I broke a bone in my foot. So dumb! I was carrying a case of canned goods in from the store-room, tripped on the hem of my skirt . . . and dropped the case on my foot! Of course, it *would* have been a day when I was wearing sandals instead of shoes or boots."

Tall and willowy, Dawn affected a neo-Bohemian style of ethnic, ankle-length skirts and dresses that went well with the theme of her store. I'd never known her fashion choices to cause her injury before, but I guessed there was always a first time. "You poor thing! You should have called me."

"I knew you were busy with the expo, and Keith was coming by anyhow. So I just limped to one of the chairs by the wood stove and sat with my foot up until he got here. He took me to an urgent care clinic. The doctor there took an X-ray, put me in one of those big Frankenstein-monster boots, and told me not to walk on it."

I winced. "That's got to be a drag. Will you need surgery or anything?"

"Fortunately, no. The doctor said it should heal okay in the boot. But I've still got to stay off the foot for at least six weeks."

"I'll bet it hurts, too. Did he give you something for pain?"

She sniffed. "You know me, I won't take anything too strong. Right now I'm on regular Tylenol. I can still feel a throb, but I'd rather at least be able to function."

"Can you still run the shop like that?"

"Not very well, but Keith's helping me. He brought me some crutches he had left over from a hiking accident, and once we adjusted the height, they worked pretty well. Still, I'm not much use except to sit behind the sales counter. We opened late today and will probably close early. When things are slow, he can even do some work at the counter on his laptop."

Dawn's significant other, Keith Garrett, was a freelance commercial artist. Although he had a studio in his loft apartment across town, I supposed he could create his designs electronically anywhere.

"Well, that's lucky." I still felt unreasonably guilty that I hadn't known about Dawn's accident sooner. "I wish I could help you, but I'm committed to this expo for the whole weekend."

"I know you are. I'm just disappointed that I can't get over there to see one of your grooming demos and to stroll around. I thought I'd go on Sunday, but now I'd never be up to all that walking. I couldn't even climb the stairs from the shop to my apartment—I had to use the old freight elevator."

"Oh, gosh. Lucky that's still operating." Usually, Dawn reached her second floor via a winding wrought-iron staircase toward the back of her sales area; that would never work with crutches and the padded boot. The elevator, reconditioned by our favorite local handyman, Nick Janos, was a relic from the days when the store had sold large bags and bales of animal feed.

"Anyway," she said, "I'm lounging around in the apartment, bingeing on British murder mysteries on cable, and waiting for Keith to come by with Thai takeout for dinner. How about you? Did the road-work racket finally let up outside your place?"

"At seven, thank God. Tonight they had my driveway partly blocked, so I had to leave the van on the street. Hope it's still there in the morning."

She laughed. "I'm sure it will be. Who'd try to make off

with something that has a huge cartoon of a cat on the side?" Dawn said this with a touch of pride, because Keith had designed that preening Persian for me. "And how's the big expo going?"

I hesitated, wondering if I should burden her with the whole messy story. But we'd worked on so many intrigues before that she'd probably want to know and might even be able to help. So I told her everything, even about the disappearance of Gordie and the death of the security guard. If I ask Dawn not to repeat something, I know it's locked in the vault until I give her the all-clear.

"And you don't think the missing cat could have been just a mix-up?" she asked.

"By the time I left, around six-thirty, he still hadn't been returned. If one of Jaki's people or someone on the hotel staff had taken him, they certainly would have known how to get him back to her room."

"Maybe he got loose somehow, and the person who was in charge of him is afraid to admit it."

"I guess that's possible, though Jaki's assistant already had put Gordie into his carrier. From what I overheard in the parking garage, Jaki is half-hysterical over losing him. She'd just been saying during the interview that she takes him everywhere. That when she's stressed by performing or touring, he's a big comfort to her."

"That's rotten. Why would someone steal her pet? Is he valuable?"

"I doubt that he's able to breed, and Harry Bock said there's not much point in stealing any cat to show because you need their paperwork."

"Still . . ." Dawn reflected a minute. "People have stolen famous artworks that they could never resell to a museum, just to be able to hang them in their homes and look at them."

"But anybody could get a nice-looking Scottish Fold cat without going to the trouble of stealing one that's so high-profile." And certainly, I thought, without killing someone in the process. "I think he was taken specifically because he was Jaki's cat."

"*Mmm.* She's had pictures of him all over the Internet, hasn't she?"

"She has. I guess a crazy fan could have taken him just to be able to say they now owned the famous Gordie—to have a link to Jaki. But also, she and her family have been getting weird, stalker-type messages lately. I'm guessing this person wants leverage. Maybe they're holding Gordie for ransom, or maybe they want something else from Jaki."

In my mind, I couldn't help picturing the tall, gawky guy who'd watched my demo while wearing the T-shirt with Jaki's photo and the message, *Marry me!* Then I felt bad about suspecting the singer's fans, including the Jak-ettes, just because they acted a bit too enthusiastic.

Over the phone, I heard the freight elevator clunk to a stop just outside Dawn's apartment. Keith shouted a hello.

"C'mon in. I'm on the phone with Cassie," Dawn shouted back.

"Hi, Cassie," said Keith into the phone. "I hear you've got the road-work blues."

"I shouldn't complain, compared to what Dawn's going through. So glad you're at least able to help her out! Listen, I'll let you two enjoy your dinner. I have some research to get back to."

"Ah," said Dawn, who caught my meaning. "Good luck!"

Setting aside my phone for the rest of the evening, I brought my laptop into the bedroom to pursue a new angle in my investigation.

This delighted the cats, who followed me. I never allowed them in the bedroom while I was sleeping, because among the three of them, someone was sure to cause mischief that would wake me up. While awake, though, I enjoyed their company, and my mishmash of bedclothes in assorted floral and striped patterns were all easily washable. I'd done the room in my personal take on cheap country chic—this was Chadwick, after all. The space was just large enough to accommodate a queen-sized iron bed, an old trunk at the foot for extra linens, and a few pieces of secondhand furniture. The dresser, nightstand, and chest of drawers all had seen better days, but looked pretty cool after I'd painted them all pale green. The rag rug camouflaged any cat accidents and could go in the washer.

By the light of my bedside lamp, wired by Nick from an old lantern, I began my high-tech search on the Internet.

The stalker was someone obsessed with Jaki, though probably he didn't know her very well. It might help to study just what kind of image she was putting out there. I had heard a couple of her hits on the radio, had seen her perform on an awards show, and had once come across a video for "I Need My Space" online. When I searched the web, though, I found many other videos that included clips from her first TV series, cameo appearances acting on other shows (most notably, *Galaxy Wars*), concert footage, and interviews. And of course there were promotional videos for at least half a dozen of her best-known songs, which supposedly Jaki penned herself.

I checked out the last group first. These were artsy compositions, keyed to the song lyrics, that spun fantasies ranging from romantic to rebellious. For Jaki's wistful ballad of loneliness and frustration "Free Me," the lovely brunette ran and danced in slow motion across a field beneath an overcast sky, sometimes glancing behind as if something were chasing her. To the tune of her sultry rocker "Vicious Circle," she swaggered around in a black crop top, leather mini, and stiletto boots, and at one point grabbed her anonymous partner forcefully by his tie. In the hip-hop number "Bits and Pieces," she performed in front of a wall of colorful graffiti, abetted by four equally limber male dancers. I recognized this song as the one the Jak-ettes had been singing and dancing to back on the plaza at the hotel.

While this research was entertaining, it didn't help me pin down what kind of stranger might be drawn to Jaki, or why. Her image shifted like a chameleon's, from sweet and vulnerable to boldly sexual to hip and sassy. It was smart marketing, of course, designed to appeal to a wide spectrum. The really young girls and their parents could view her as an acceptable role model, while the older teens, especially boys, might prefer the tougher, hotter Jaki. Well, she *had* trained as an actress. No doubt she saw these different faces simply as roles she needed to play.

YouTube also offered some concert footage that showed the petite brunette commanding a stage in front of a vast audience, bantering with the band or her backup singers, and again performing both a sweet, vulnerable love song and a streetwise, sexy dance number. For an interview at her California apartment, Jaki shot the breeze with a writer from an e-zine (unseen behind the camera) and tossed off glib answers to all of his questions, as if nothing could throw her. I could see why girls her own age and younger would look up to her as the epitome of cool, totally in charge of her own life.

But was that really true?

And which side of her persona appealed the most to her

troublesome stalker? The brazen vamp? The fun-loving hip-hop chick? Or the lonely, frightened girl running blindly from a threat that could come from anywhere, at any time?

Around eight-thirty, when I just wanted to watch some silly TV and forget the whole issue, I got a call from Perry. Maybe the rest of our demos had been canceled, after all?

"Hi," I said. "Are we still on for tomorrow?"

"You are, Cassie . . . as long as you still feel safe coming to the expo."

"I think so. It's not as if you've got a sniper on the loose who's picking off people at random . . . do you?"

A tight chuckle. "The cops don't seem concerned about that, and if they were, you can be sure we'd shut the whole event down. As long as you're willing to come back, though, I do have a special favor to ask. I've rescheduled your first grooming session tomorrow for ten instead of nine."

"Sounds as if you're the one doing me a favor. What's up?"

He hesitated. "At nine, can you come up to Jaki Natal's suite? She wants to meet you."

It was my turn to laugh nervously. "Of course she does, seeing as we're both such big celebrities! Seriously, though, why—"

"You gave your card to her father, and Jaki noticed that we talked with you in the parking garage. I mentioned that you deal with cats professionally and have even helped solve some cat-related crimes around town. . . ." He sighed, as if in apology for getting me involved. "She figures you might have some special insight."

A year ago, I might have pooh-poohed this idea. But a few times since then, I'd worked closely with the police, or other official organizations, to check out angles they didn't have the time or manpower to investigate. And after all, when I'd given Hector my card, I *had* offered to help in any way I could.

"All right," I told Perry. "Nine it is. Just tell me where to go."

He gave me directions, saying the security staff would be told to expect me. "Come alone," he added.

Had I suddenly graduated from police informant to undercover agent?

Chapter 9

True to Dawn's prediction, I found my van still out front and unharmed the next morning and drove to the convention center. I had called Becky and told her that our morning demonstration had been postponed by an hour, so she didn't need to join me on the plaza until just before ten. She sounded a bit sulky, probably because I would be meeting Jaki, who after all was Becky's idol, not mine.

After parking in my assigned spot on the plaza, I entered the Bradburne and took the elevator up to the fourth-floor Presidential Suite. A swarthy bodyguard, well over six feet tall, checked my volunteer tag and driver's license before ushering me toward the door. At my knock, Mira opened it only as far as the swing bar would allow. When she recognized me, she smiled faintly, unfastened the bar, and introduced herself. She still wore black, as if in mourning, but I suspected it was more of an artsy affectation, like her trendy, angled-bob haircut.

"Thanks so much for agreeing to meet with Jaki," she said in a soft voice. "I think it will mean a lot to her."

That sounded ironic to me, as if I were the celebrity and

Jaki were some young fan, maybe wasting away from a horrible disease. "Glad to help."

I stepped into the suite's living/dining room, almost as large as the whole first floor of my shop. It featured sleek, contemporary furniture—light earth tones, gender-neutral—but in upscale materials like leather and tufted velvet. One alcove near the door held the components of a full kitchenette, including sink and microwave. A round, glossy dining table stood near the window beneath a modern, drum-shaped chandelier of hanging crystals. A short hallway probably led to the master suite. I guessed these must be the standard accommodations for hotel guests in Jaki's income bracket.

Hector Natal stepped forward to shake my hand, with a much more genial attitude than he'd shown in the parking garage. I still didn't think he was convinced I could be of much help, but if his daughter thought so, he seemed willing to go along with the idea.

Jaki rose from the low, cream-colored sofa to welcome me. Though far from wasting away, she bore little resemblance to the charismatic star who'd handled yesterday's interview with such professional poise. She'd muffled her curves under a baggy gray sweater and fashionably ripped and faded jeans. Without makeup, her slightly tawny complexion—I'd read that her father was mostly Cuban and her mother half-Lebanese—looked faded. Her big, long-lashed eyes had a puffiness to them, I guessed either from lack of sleep or from crying. Anyone would have thought someone close to her had died.

She shook my hand and said in a low voice, "Cassie, thanks so much for coming."

"Not at all. I'll be happy to do whatever I can." She radiated such a deep sadness that I felt my own eyes tearing up, and fought to control the reflex.

The two of us sat on the sofa. It faced a large, horizontal abstract painting, which I bet concealed a wall-mounted TV. While Hector and Mira hovered on the fringes, they mainly left us alone to talk.

"When Perry told me about some of the things you've done here in Chadwick, I felt you might understand what I'm going through," Jaki said. "The police are concentrating on the security guard who died, trying to figure out if it was foul play, and of course I understand that. But in the meantime, I can't be sure anyone is really trying to find Gordie."

I nodded. "And the thing is, the two incidents could be connected. Whoever blacked out the conference room might have *intended* to steal him and only attacked the guard because he got in the way. So Gordie could be the key to the whole incident."

Jaki's wan face brightened. "You do understand! Everybody's been asking why I'm so worried about a cat, when a man is dead and I might be the next target. But I don't see it that way. Someone took Gordie to get to me. I don't think that person is out to hurt me—not physically, anyway—but they might hurt Gordie. Especially if they actually killed a human being."

My estimation of the singer's intelligence shot upward—Jaki was more than just a great voice and a pretty face. "Do they know yet how the guard died? I got the impression that it wasn't anything obvious."

Fear crept back into her eyes. "We're not supposed to 'speculate' about it, but it wasn't an obvious killing, like a stabbing or a shooting. The guard was in his fifties, and he did fall down some stairs afterward, but I overheard one cop saying he also had a weird bruise on his neck. So if someone did kill him, they might have done it with their bare hands! That's seriously *bent*, isn't it?"

If there had been an attacker, I wondered if he had left behind any helpful fingerprints. But if the same person had sabotaged the lights and the fire alarm, he might have been smart enough to wear gloves.

Bonelli probably would know.

Jaki wrapped her arms around her body, looking childish and vulnerable in the oversized sweater. "It creeps me out to think it was probably the same person who talked to Mira onstage and took Gordie away in the carrier."

"Yes, how exactly did that go? What can you remember?"

She drew a deep breath, as if she'd already told the painful story several times. "You said you were there for the interview, so you know that I had Gordie on my lap with my arms around him. I left his carrier at the back of the stage. He's very chill in front of an audience, 'cause I take him out in public all the time, so I wasn't worried that he'd try to get away. Anyhow, when the lights went out, at first I didn't move. I thought it was just a glitch and they'd be back on in a minute. But after the fire alarm went off, I started to panic. If it was for real, we'd have to leave the building, and I knew somehow I'd need to take Gordie with me.

"A few emergency lights came on at that point, and I could see well enough to stand up. Perry was tugging at my elbow, trying to get me out, but I was still worried about the cat. Then Mira came up behind me and said, 'You get to safety, Jaki. I'll take care of Gordie.' I handed him to her and she put him in the carrier."

It occurred to me that it might be helpful to know what the carrier looked like, and I asked Jaki.

"It's aqua blue. Almost looks like a big purse, except for the mesh openings," she said. "Anyway, Mira handles Gordie for me all the time, so after that, I figured he'd be safe, and I followed Perry out into the hall."

Jaki's cousin, hearing her name mentioned, edged over to join us. She still looked utterly ashamed at having failed in her responsibilities.

"What happened after that?" I asked Mira.

She lighted on the arm of the sofa. "I started to leave, but the back of the room was still dark, and people were kind of stumbling around. I wasn't familiar with the layout and wasn't sure how to get out. This guy came up with a small flashlight and started talking fast. He said there was a fire and we had to evacuate. Just then my foot caught on something, and I tripped. I set Gordie down for a second to steady myself, and this guy picked up the carrier."

"Did you see what he looked like?" I asked.

Mira shook her head. "The flashlight in my eyes made it hard to see his face. I just had the impression he was medium height and wearing dark clothes, like a uniform. And had some kind of tag around his neck, like one of the hotel staff."

"So you trusted him."

A tear rolled down her face. "I thought he must be with security! He sounded so take-charge and confident. He pointed me toward a rear staircase, where some other people were walking down, and said, 'You go on ahead, I'll take the cat.' I figured this guy would be right behind me, with Gordie. But when I got to the first-floor landing, where we finally had lights, I didn't see him anywhere." Mira twisted her slender hands in her lap and stole a miserable look at her cousin. "I feel so stupid! I never should have let Gordie out of my sight."

"Mira, don't blame yourself," Jaki told her gently. "I probably should have stayed behind, too, except Perry was hustling me out. I can understand why you would have trusted the guy. I might have, too, in your place." But her lovely face crumpled once more.

At this sight, Jaki's father crossed the room and put his arm around her shoulders. "*Mija*, don't worry. I'm sure the cat's okay. Can I get you something to calm you down? The doctor left some pills. . . ."

"No," the singer snapped. "Not going down that road again, ever. I'm fine."

Hector startled a little at this response, then asked her, "Want some of your tea?"

Jaki drew a deep breath. "Maybe. The chamomile?"

Mira went to heat some water in the small coffee maker on the room's corner bar. Meanwhile, I commented to Jaki, "I like that stuff myself. My best friend runs a health food store, and she got me into all sorts of herbal teas."

She managed a smile and called over to her cousin, "Cassie will have a tea, too."

Mira brought us both white ceramic mugs branded with the words BRADBURNE HOTEL in burgundy letters, with tea bags steeping in them. Then she discreetly left me and Jaki alone again. From this exchange, I got a brief glimpse of the slightly spoiled celebrity who felt free to give orders even to her relatives.

While we both sipped the calming brew, I tried to reassure Jaki that she and Mira didn't need to feel stupid for handing Gordie over to the stranger with the flashlight. "Whoever's got him obviously planned out this whole stunt. I'll bet the guard surprised him, but other than that, he thought of everything and was very clever."

"I guess that's true," Jaki admitted. "Still, I should've been more careful. Y'see, I've known for a while that some creep out there was stalking me. That was the reason we requested extra security at the expo."

I nodded. "Perry did mention something about that. You've gotten threats?"

"It's hard to say if they're threats, exactly. I guess all celebrities get nutty calls, letters, e-mails, and tweets these days. Most come from fans who say how much they love you and your music, but even those can get a little creepy. I hardly ever give out my cell phone number, and Mira opens most of my actual mail so she can flag anything too weird. But lately it's gotten really disturbing."

"How?"

"There have been several, probably all from the same person, saying we were meant to be together, someday soon we will be, and nothing can stop it. He quotes lines from my songs, especially 'Free Me,' and seems to think I'm writing to him."

Returning with sugar and sweetener for our teas, Mira overheard this. "Yeah, he interprets the words as if Jaki is being held prisoner, like we're all exploiting her and making her work too hard or something. He thinks it's up to him to save her."

"He also blames Alec for breaking my heart," Jaki added, with a tilted smile, "but I think he also was glad when Alec got out of the picture, 'cause he thinks it clears the field for him."

Sounded pretty bizarre, all right. "And you've never met this person?"

"Not as far as I know. He's obviously been to some of my concerts, because he'll mention things that happened onstage at different places I played, little details that weren't on any official videos. All on the East Coast." She took a sip of her tea before continuing. "There's been some more hostile stuff, too. Like he said he tried to get backstage a few times and the security staff wouldn't let him. He sounded pretty angry at that, really cursing out the security guys."

Could be, I thought, that her stalker finally took all of that frustration out on the poor guard at the Bradburne. "I guess no one's been able to trace these e-mails?"

Hector joined in. "The cops in LA tried but couldn't. They

said the guy probably sends them from disposable phones, using some kind of fake identity."

"That's not even the part that spooks me the most." Jaki glanced toward her father and Mira. "My folks still live around here. They've had notes left in their mailbox, warning them not to come between him and me, and threatening them if they interfere with our 'destiny.' So this creep is probably from somewhere around here—northern Jersey—and he definitely knows where my family lives! I've got a younger sister still at home and a brother in college, and now I'm afraid for their safety, too."

I remembered what Chris had told me about the garage mechanic who'd been killed a year ago while driving Hector's car. Could that have been an early salvo? Did the stalker think Jaki's father was keeping them apart?

"No one's ever seen who left the notes?" I asked.

Mira shook her head. "For a while we asked the local cops to watch the house, but they never caught anyone—he probably was smart enough to avoid them. The Natals' house is on a couple of acres, and the mailbox is out by the road. Anyone could drive up there quietly, maybe in the middle of the night, and slip a note into it. The messages came from a common model of electronic printer. The police tested a couple of them but didn't find any fingerprints."

"Some of them have been signed, 'Your last, best hope,' " Jaki added. "That's a reference, I guess, to my song 'Free Me.' It's got a line, 'Are you my last, best hope for love?' That phrase is actually from a speech by Abraham Lincoln that I learned about in school and always liked. Kind of sickening, though, to see it turned around and used against me."

This stalker did seem to know how to get into Jaki's head and manipulate her emotions, I thought. "So you're thinking

this person might have snatched Gordie to get your attention
and force you to meet with him?"

"I think it's possible, yeah," Jaki said.

Hector frowned. "I don't know . . . these kooky fans are
usually just talk. I don't think he'd have the guts to actually pull
off something like this."

"You have someone else in mind?" I asked him.

"That no-good Alec, the space cadet. He gave her the cat,
and now that she broke up with him, he wants it back. He
couldn't steal it back himself, o' course, but he probably hired
some thug."

"And gave him the okay to kill whoever got in his way?"
Mira made a skeptical face.

Hector shrugged. "The guard wasn't shot or stabbed, so it
might not have been planned. Maybe the goon panicked and
pushed him, and it just happened to be fatal. That could be
why Alec isn't owning up to the stunt—it turned out worse
than he expected."

Silently, I gave Hector credit for putting together another
valid theory.

But Jaki couldn't accept this. "Alec is a horndog and a
cheat, but he's not crazy. I don't think he'd do anything so extreme. Though, in one way, I wish he *was* behind it all. At least
I think he'd take good care of Gordie."

Hector snorted. "He's an *anguila*. He gave you a sick cat to
begin with. . . ."

"Gordie's sick?" I asked her.

She waved a hand. "Not exactly, but he has a couple of
chronic issues. Even though he's only four, he's got some arthritis
and the beginnings of kidney disease. I give him some mild pain
medication if he seems to need it."

"Also, he gets a special diet and lots of water," Mira added.

"He goes to a vet for checkups every four months," said Jaki. "I told Alec about all that, so at least he knows. But I've kept it quiet otherwise. Even if my stalker has read everything I ever tweeted, or said in an interview, *he* won't know how to care for Gordie. Plus, with the stress of being stolen like that and taken God knows where . . ." She choked up again.

I felt pressure to help her solve the crisis. "Any chance that someone just stole him to get a ransom from you?"

"Nobody's asked for money so far," said Hector. "It's too bad, really. At least that might give us some chance to trace whoever took him."

"I asked the police detective if I should go on Twitter and offer a reward," Jaki said, "but she thought that might just bring more crazies out of the woodwork."

"Probably true." I turned back to Hector. "I agree that the thief probably didn't intend to kill the guard. And like you said, even if he originally planned to contact you, he could be afraid to now. If it were just a matter of getting the cat back, he'd figure you might be willing to negotiate with him. But now he may have committed murder."

I felt Jaki watching me closely as I spoke to her father. Whether she reacted to my words or just the chamomile tea, by the time I faced her again, she'd gotten some healthy color back and looked almost excited. "Perry told me that you've worked with the SPCA and the police to rescue cats and even solve murders. If you can help me get Gordie back, I'll pay whatever you ask!"

This flustered me, especially after we'd just been discussing ransom, and I heard Hector clear his throat.

"Jaki, I've never taken money in any of those situations, and I couldn't take it from you," I said. "I'm not a professional investigator, and I may not be able to do anything more than the cops can, but at least I can make Gordie my highest priority. I'll be working at the expo through tomorrow, and my mother is involved in the show at the hotel, helping a friend with his cat. So we all can keep an eye out for anyone who's acting suspicious, and I can ask some questions."

Hector shuffled restlessly again. "I just want to get Jaki out of this hotel, now that this maniac has targeted her."

"She's got a contract," Mira pointed out tactfully. "She *has* to perform tonight. They've sold out the concert."

Jaki ran both hands back through her thick, wavy hair, leaving it disheveled. "Oh, *Dios* . . . I can't imagine going on-stage like this. Maybe if it was just one song . . . but doing a whole show?"

"I won't allow it," her father insisted. "The guy could take a shot at you."

"There won't be anyone in the room except official staff and ticket holders. . . ." said Mira.

"How well did that work last time, for the interview? And how do we know this *bastardo* might not plunk down the three hundred bucks just for the chance to hurt her?"

I checked the time and realized I needed to get back to my van for my ten o'clock demo. "I'm so sorry, folks . . . I'm supposed to be someplace else now. Jaki, I'll be in touch as soon as I have any information. Just let me know if you do decide to cancel the concert and leave early."

She thanked me and saw me to the door of the suite. There she confided, "I wish I could go looking for this creep myself! Maybe I could wear a disguise or something, and snoop around. But you can see"—she nodded toward her father and her cousin—"they'd never let me take that chance, and I guess they're right."

"They absolutely are," I warned her. "Even if you found this person, there's no telling what he, or she, might do to you."

Jaki nodded in surrender. "Anyhow, no matter what we decide about the concert, Cassie, I don't see how I can bear to leave the hotel, at least not before Sunday. Whoever took Gordie probably has him stashed somewhere nearby. Until I know I can get him back . . . I've *got* to stay here."

Chapter 10

Still in a daze, and wondering how I'd ended up volunteering to do crowd surveillance for Jaki Natal and her handlers, I got myself back down to my van by ten.

Becky knew I'd spent the past hour in the presence of one of her idols and eyed me with intense curiosity. I didn't know how much I should tell her about the meeting, though. At any rate, we needed to get on with our grooming demonstration.

For today we'd be using Lady, a gray-and-white longhair being fostered by a family in the area. The shelter had said Lady was generally laid-back but didn't especially take to grooming. That, we found, was an understatement. Her initial yowls and hisses at least drew a crowd to our van, but from the frowns on some of the onlookers, I worried that we might be accused of animal cruelty.

Time to call the pheromone spray and the special grooming harness back into action.

When things seemed under control, we fully opened the side panel door so people could watch us work. The harness didn't quiet Lady completely, but at least it kept her from breaking free and reassured the audience that we weren't hurting her in any way. Becky steadied the cat while I gave my usual spiel about coat texture and very gently coaxed some knots out of Lady's plumy white tail.

An older man in the crowd muttered, "If I tried to do that with my cat, he'd claw my eyes out!"

I smiled. "Most cats adjust to being brushed and combed by their owners over time, but some never do. For the really resistant ones, you do need a professional groomer."

Dria and Ashley loitered at the back of the crowd, and as it started to disperse, I waved them nearer. Today Ashley wore a tee featuring a punked-out white cat with tattoos and a nose ring—probably what Looli would look like if she fell in with a bad crowd. Dria's shirt commanded, *Get outta my space!* which I recognized as a line from Jaki's famous song that sliced and diced her ex-boyfriend.

"Hi again," I said. "You guys enjoying the expo?"

"It is pretty rad," Ashley said, with a grin. "Have you been inside? I never in my life imagined people could buy so much stuff for their cats."

"I guess if there's a market for it, someone will make it . . . and sell it," I said. "Did you see those people walking around in, like, cat mascot costumes? I have no idea what that's all about."

"They're putting on some kind of kid's show about adopting animals," Dria told me, her tone more blasé than her friend's. "We saw part of their skit."

Okay, that eased some of my suspicions. Jaki's stalker probably was not strolling around the expo disguised as a man-sized tabby; those costumes would be expensive to rent and pretty cumbersome if he had to make a quick escape. Still, I didn't completely discard the notion.

Faced with only two of the Jak-ettes, my thoughts traveled back to Lexi, who coveted a Scottish Fold. "Your other friends didn't come today?"

"Oh, yeah," said Ashley. "We just got separated. They're around somewhere."

"Lexi ought to check out the cat show in the hotel," I recommended. "All the purebred breeders are in there. If she really wants a Scottish Fold, she might be able to find someone who'd sell her one."

"Hey, that's a good idea. I'll have to mention . . ."

Dria clutched her friend's arm. "Y'know, Ash, maybe that's where they are. We should go look!"

"Huh? Oh, right." Being pulled away, the brunette hung back long enough to tell me, "Nice talking to you again, Cassie. Cool demo."

By that time, all of our other listeners had dispersed, and I rejoined Becky inside the van. I told her that I'd tried to probe the subject of Lexi wanting a Scottish Fold cat, but Dria had found an excuse to cut the conversation short.

"That's a little strange, though it doesn't prove anything." As we removed Lady's harness and released her into the drying cage, my helper added, "I guess Gordie's still missing."

I nodded and drew a deep breath. "I'm going to tell you some things, Becky, but you have to keep them quiet. Maybe share with Chris, because he might be able to help us, but swear him to secrecy, too."

"No problem."

"The cat hasn't been returned, and I've been asked to keep an eye out for anyone who could be responsible." I nodded in the direction of the departing duo. "We know those girls are major fans, and apparently one of them told the rest that she really wanted a Scottish Fold cat."

"That doesn't mean she stole Gordie."

"Of course it doesn't. Still, the cat *could* have been taken for that stupid a reason. A crazy fan wanted to have something of Jaki's, to brag about, or to feel more like a star herself. Mira thinks the person who took Gordie was a man, but she barely glimpsed them or heard their voice. Could have been a tall woman with a low pitch."

"And you think that same person could've killed the security guard?"

I pictured Dria's tall, athletic build and hard-edged Jersey attitude. "I'm just saying, we need to consider every possibility."

Becky had packed Lady away in the roomy cage normally used for blow-drying. Now the cat lounged happily on a cushion with food, water, and a shallow litter tray nearby.

"For someone who kicked up such a fuss, she's calmed down pretty fast," Becky observed. "Think we can use her again for the afternoon demo?"

"Should be okay. She might be over the shock by now and take it more in stride." The fluffy gray-and-white animal's queenly pose reminded me of the show cats in the hotel ballroom, so dignified in their similar, large cages.

"And it's cool again today," Becky added. "Will it be safe to just lock her in here while we go meet Chris and Mark for lunch?"

"I think so." I glanced at my watch—quarter after twelve. I had thought Dria's sudden departure seemed suspicious, but maybe she and Ashley just had plans for lunch. "First, though, I'm going to pop back over to the hotel and see how Mom and Harry are doing. Meet you guys at the gyro stand?"

"Sounds like a plan. Hope Looli's crushing the competition!"

The pearl-white Sphynx *was* beating all comers so far and had taken another first-place ribbon, Best in Division. Harry sat cradling her against his chest, and Mom held up the cat's two most prestigious ribbons, blue and black, as a hotel staffer snapped a photo with Harry's camera. I noticed that, while my mother leaned close enough to be included in the shot, she did not make contact with Looli.

"Thanks for all your help, Steve." Harry reached into his jacket pocket and handed the young man a folded bill.

"Oh, no, sir, that's not necessary." The staffer declined the tip with a smile as he passed the camera back to Harry. I recognized him as the same employee we'd run into at the conference center the week before—the one who'd told us where to find Perry out on the plaza. Average in height and build, he wore the informal Bradburne uniform of black tailored pants and a gray polo shirt. His short, curly hair gave his face a rectangular look, echoed by the shape of his dark-rimmed glasses.

Mom introduced me by name and profession, and explained that I gave grooming demonstrations outside the expo. She told me, "If it hadn't been for Steve, here, we'd have gotten stuck yesterday in that mess leaving the parking lot. I heard Security was checking all the cars and carriers. Do you know what all that was about? When we were driving away, we saw a couple of police cars outside the hotel, too."

I hesitated, unsure how much I should tell them. In the meantime, Harry chimed in, "Steve heard there was a power failure while Jaki Natal was doing her interview."

Well, if even the staff was spreading that information, I saw no reason to deny it. "That's right. I was at the back of the conference room when it happened—the room went dark and a fire alarm went off. But emergency lights came on right away, and as far as I know, everybody got out okay."

"I think a guard got hurt." Steve sounded eager to spread the gossip. "I saw him carried out on a stretcher. Maybe he fell over something when the lights went out?"

"Maybe." I wasn't about to feed Steve more fodder for rumors. If he didn't even know the guard had died, the hotel's management still must be playing it close to the vest.

"Well, I'd better get back to work," he said, with a shy smile and a wave. "Nice talking to you folks, and good luck!"

Harry thanked him again for taking the photos and tucked Looli back into her silver satin, Egyptian-themed boudoir . . . complete, of course, with covered litter pan. Mom scrolled back through the shots of the three of them, trying to decide which was best to post on her Facebook page.

"Your friends and family are going to have hysterics when they see you that close to a cat and actually smiling," I told her.

"Oh, she's made a lot of progress with her phobia," Harry assured me, settling back into his metal folding chair beside Mom's.

I pulled up an extra chair, reassured myself that there was no one close enough to overhear me, and confided, "I'm going to tell you guys something, but you have to keep it to yourselves. I mean, it's something the police might not even want me telling you."

That made them both sit up straight. "The police?" Mom asked. "Are you in some kind of trouble?"

"Not me! Just getting recruited, again, to help with an investigation." I told them about the missing cat and my meeting a couple of hours earlier with Jaki and her people.

"I told them you two were down here on the show floor," I said, "and maybe you could keep your eyes open. For what, I'm not sure, but this would be the perfect place to hide Gordie in plain sight. Maybe there's someone who has a Scottish Fold that's not accounted for, or who's acting suspiciously."

"I wouldn't even know what one looks like!" Mom protested.

While Harry launched into a long-winded description of

the breed type, I searched briefly on my cell phone and came up with a nice, clear photo of Gordie himself.

While Mom studied this, Harry's lean features folded in a frown. "I can't imagine why anyone in this crowd would want to steal a celebrity's cat. They couldn't breed it or show it."

"I'm sure Gordie's neutered, anyway, and yeah, they'd need his papers to enter him in a show." I wouldn't go into the background of the singer possibly having an obsessed stalker or about someone holding the cat for ransom—that was police business. "Jaki's concerned that maybe someone took him just because of the connection to her."

"In that case, they *might* have plans to sell him on the underground market," Harry suggested ominously. "Someone might pay a lot to own a celebrity's cat, even if they never told anyone but their closest friends where they got him. Kind of like a James Bond villain who steals the *Mona Lisa* and hides it away in some top-secret vault."

And Gordie would be less likely to arouse suspicion, I thought, because he was far less unique. There were a lot more silver tabby Scottish Folds in the world than *Mona Lisa*s.

Mom looked spooked now, probably worried about what kind of criminal mastermind could be hanging around the expo. "Do you think this person had something to do with the guard who was injured?"

I didn't tell her that I knew the guard to be dead. "The police are looking into that possibility."

Harry's narrow cheeks actually flushed with a tinge of pink, as if it excited him to be helping with the investigation. "So, if we do see something odd, we should call you?"

"Yes, right away. And if it sounds at all suspicious, I'll tell the cops."

"Good," Mom said, worry lines corrugating her brow. "Cassie, please don't go chasing down this character yourself!"

"I don't plan to. Angela Bonelli is already on the case, so I'll just pass along anything I learn to her." I glanced at my phone and saw it was quarter to one. "Right now, I'm going to chase down lunch. Can I bring you anything from the concourse?"

"We brown-bagged it today," Mom said, "but thanks anyway."

"Stop by and see us later," Harry told me, with a glint in his eye. "We should have a good shot at Best of Breed, too."

I knew that, rather than bragging, he was actually being modest. Looli should have a lock on the next award. She was up against only two other Sphynx cats and had already beaten them in every category so far.

On my way out of the show area, I found myself distracted by the Feline Agility class. Here, pedigree and even appearance didn't matter much. Unlike the other competitions, where owners left their cats in the hands of a judge, for agility, the animal's owner or trainer coaxed him around an obstacle course. I'd seen some balk in the past, but at the moment, a little spotted guy, probably an Ocicat, streaked around in pursuit of a feather toy. He easily leaped over hurdles, dashed through a couple of long fabric tunnels, charged up and down steps, and swerved in and out of a row of closely set poles until his handler finally let him catch the "bird." Whether judged on speed, obedience, or sheer coordination, he looked like a winner to me. From the applause and whistles when his young female handler scooped him up in a hug, the crowd of onlookers agreed.

Moving along, I headed up to the gyro stand on the main concourse, scanning passersby all the while. At least I saw no one toting anything aqua blue that looked like a big purse with mesh openings.

Mark sat at a café table with Becky and Chris. The FOCA folks already munched on gyros, but being a gentleman, Mark had waited for me to join him. Fortunately, gyros are easily slapped together, and soon we had our lunches, too.

"Who's minding the store?" I asked Chris.

"Grumpy Glenda, and she's not happy about it. When she's there, she harangues anyone who stops by about adopting a shelter cat instead of buying from a pet store or a breeder. Which is a valid point, except she's too abrasive about it. Then whenever there's a lull in the foot traffic, she disappears for, like, ten minutes at a stretch. I don't get her."

"Yeah, that's weird," Becky agreed. "If she's so passionate about the cause, why does she spend so little time at the table? Maybe she's got attention-deficit."

"She's got a deficit of something!" With a resigned air, Chris took another bite of his gyro.

While we all ate, I told him and Mark about my morning meeting with Jaki and her "people," and officially deputized them.

"Becky and I are stuck outside," I explained, "but you two are here on the concourse, where hordes of people pass by."

"I'll gladly keep my eyes open," said Chris. Lightly, he added, "Hey, how about that guy?"

I followed his pointing finger to the tall, skinny, and scruffy dude in the *Marry me!* T-shirt. Was he wearing it for the second day straight . . . or did he have more than one? His faded jeans and dirty sneakers looked the same as the day before, too.

Unlike the quartet of giggly female fans, this character always seemed to be wandering around by himself. Seeing him for the second time, I realized he must be pushing forty, pretty old for a Jaki Natal groupie. As Chris and I watched, a young couple—apparently strangers—grinned over the man's shirt, and the woman stood next to him while her companion took a quick photo. The bearded guy posed willingly enough but never cracked a smile. When the couple moved along, he also continued on his way.

I told Chris, "You might laugh, but he's already on my personal radar. I definitely will mention him to Bonelli."

"Seems like a serious stalker would know better than to advertise it," Chris suggested.

"You're thinking like a sane person. We don't know just how unbalanced this creep is."

"Remember, the stalker *could* be female," Becky insisted. "Any physically strong and tech-savvy woman could have sabotaged the lights and killed the guard, or a woman could have hired a guy to do it. Has Jaki made enemies of any other female singers?"

I tilted my head. "No one has mentioned that. But you're right, it's worth checking out."

Mark frowned. "Whoever took Gordie, I hope they at least know something about caring for him. The cat's got to be upset, being dragged away from his owner like that. I hope he's not stuck in some dark, airless closet with no food or water."

That's why I love this guy, I thought. *Jaki would love him, too. Maybe it would be best—for me—if the two of them never actually meet!*

Becky said, "I wonder if the police have searched the guest rooms."

"I don't know if they can, unless there's a direct connection to the crime," I told her. "If they did, they probably would have been looking for someone who might have killed the guard, not for the missing cat."

But if they opened closets and checked under beds, and Gordie was there, they would have found him. And, I'm sure, they'd have told Jaki immediately.

Of course, the cat could have turned up already since my

meeting with her that morning, and maybe no one had thought to tell me.

Chris and Becky cleaned up their lunch trash and went off to staff the FOCA table for a while. She promised to return to my van by three for our afternoon demo.

Left alone with Mark, I recalled his caring statement about the kidnapped cat's welfare, and it reminded me of something else. "Jaki said Gordie's got some health problems, too. Arthritis and kidney issues . . ."

Mark's deep-blue gaze locked on mine like a laser. "Cartilage abnormalities and polycystic kidney disease. Those are both hereditary in some Scottish Folds."

"She knows. She's been giving him special food and medication to keep him healthy, but a stranger isn't going to know or care enough to do that."

"Which makes it even more of a race against the clock to find him. She's supposed to do that concert in the theater tonight, isn't she?"

I nodded. "I wonder if it'll even come off. When we talked this morning, she was a basket case, crying her eyes out—as bad as if someone had kidnapped her little sister or brother. Hard to believe she'll be able to pull herself together by showtime."

Mark had to start his two o'clock demo then, and I hung around on the concourse to watch. He'd just begun his spiel about the most common feline health complaints when my cell phone rang. It surprised me to see Angela Bonelli's mobile number.

"Hi, what's up?" I asked.

"You busy with anything right now?"

"I've got nothing until three. Why?"

I heard weariness in Bonelli's tone, though it didn't seem directed at me. "I understand that you already know your way to the Presidential Suite. Could you join us up here again for a few minutes?"

"Sure. Something happen?"

"There's been a possible development. And once more, Ms. Natal is asking for you."

Chapter 11

I took the elevator back up to the hotel's elite suite and once again passed muster with the hall bodyguard. This time, Detective Angela Bonelli opened the door. Beyond her, the living/dining room, already designed to double as a meeting area, had taken on a more serious and utilitarian atmosphere. Papers lay spread out on the round, contemporary dining table, and a uniformed cop with a solid build and a flat Marine haircut sat typing on a laptop, as if copying information from some of the documents.

The bar on the other side of the room held remnants of a light lunch buffet, with fruit, cheese, and small sandwiches. Those present appeared to have eaten little of it, though.

Jaki still wore the same shapeless sweater and depressed air as she had that morning, though now at least she appeared dry-eyed. She huddled on the ivory sofa next to her father, who kept his arm loosely around her shoulders. Perry slumped in one of the elegant beige-suede side chairs, his clasped hands dangling between his knees. He still looked natty, in a deep blue open-collared shirt, a checked sports jacket, and gray slacks. Now, though, his eyes had a haunted expression—like those of a proud, free-roaming animal whose spirit had been broken. Was it just because the extravaganza he'd worked hard to promote seemed to be going off the rails so badly? Or, in the past three hours, had something even more dreadful happened?

I asked Bonelli, "What's going on? You said there was a development."

Her full lips quirked in grim amusement. "We've gotten a couple of what you might call ransom notes. Apparently, word has started to get around that Jaki's cat is missing."

In the corner of my eye, I caught an accusatory glance from the young singer. I assured her and the detective, "I only told five trusted people: Mark, Becky, and Chris . . . and just a little while ago, my mother and her friend Harry. They all know better than to tell anyone else. But they're all watching for any suspicious activity on the cat show floor and the vendor concourse."

"To be fair," Perry said, "when Jaki and the rest of us met up in the parking garage, right after the blackout, none of us were keeping our voices down. We all were wondering out loud where the cat had gone. If Cassie and her friends overheard us, other people might have, too."

"At any rate," said Bonelli, "we've determined that it's too risky for Jaki to go on tonight. Perry has notified everyone who bought tickets to her performance that it's tentatively rescheduled for seven p.m. tomorrow."

"If they can't make it then, or if that show also has to be canceled, their money will be refunded," Perry added.

Now I understood at least part of the reason why he looked like he was going to his own funeral. Proceeds from the mini concert would have gone a long way, no doubt, toward putting the whole expo in the black. If it had to be scrapped entirely, they might actually lose money.

"You think she's in that much danger?" I asked him.

"Like the detective said, we've gotten ransom notes. About an hour ago, I got a message via my company e-mail demanding a million dollars for Gordie's safe return. Shortly after that, Jaki got a text from some aspiring songwriter who wants her to give his songs to her agent. The second note didn't mention the cat, per se, but promised to trade Jaki 'something of value' in return for this favor."

"Can the first message be traced?"

"Not easily," Bonelli told me. "It's from an anonymous account."

I dropped into another side chair, opposite Perry's. "Unless they're working together, doesn't seem likely that *both* of those people could have Gordie."

"No, it doesn't," the detective agreed. "That's why I think the rumor has spread far enough that a few people are trying to exploit the situation to further their own interests. They've tried to conceal their identities, but not very expertly—we should track them both down before too long." With a weary air, the detective sat on the sofa next to the brooding celebrity. "She got another series of texts on her own phone, about fifteen minutes ago, that concern me more. Jaki, you want to explain?"

The younger woman swallowed hard before speaking. "This person claimed to have Gordie and said he, or she, didn't want to hurt him. Of course, that just planted the idea in my head, like it was a threat. I texted back that Gordie meant a lot to me and I was willing to pay anything to get him back."

Her father grimaced. "I wish you'd asked me before you said such a thing. This idiot probably thinks you're made of money! What if they'd asked for more than we could afford?"

Jaki ignored the rebuke. "Doesn't matter, because this person said they weren't interested in money. They just wanted to talk with me. Someplace alone, so we could 'really get to know each other.' So we could 'become friends.' "

Hector threw an agitated look at Bonelli. "We can't let her do that! This is probably a guy, and he could do anything to her. . . ."

"Of course we can't," Perry agreed, his face grave.

"This person said we 'have a history together,' that we've met before," Jaki said. "He even said that he'd been very close to me recently and wanted to touch me, but 'the timing was wrong.' "

"Sick stuff," said her father. "You're sure this couldn't be MacMasters?"

"It wouldn't make sense, Pop. As soon as this all happened, I called him, and he swears he had nothing to do with it. He even sounded upset at me that I'd neglected Gordie and let some stranger make off with him."

"Nice," I muttered.

Bonelli was still trying to interpret the text message. "It could just be a fan you said hello to once. Somebody who asked you for an autograph."

"I know." Jaki shut her eyes and massaged her forehead with one hand, as if trying to activate her memory. "But I meet so many people, especially on the road. I can't think who. . . ."

"Of course not." Hector patted her shoulder. "You wouldn't remember, it's not your fault. This is a crazy person!"

"Trouble is, he described Gordie's carrier in detail," Jaki recalled miserably. "So *he's* the one who's really got my cat."

I ached with sympathy, knowing the young woman was frightened for both her pet and herself. "Was the last message signed in any way?"

She nodded. " 'LBH,' which I guess is an abbreviation for

'Last, best hope.' It's got to be the same creep who left all of those notes in the mailbox at my family's house."

Hector scowled, mustache drooping. "We should leave right now, forget the damned cat."

The mere suggestion started Jaki sniffling again.

"That might not solve the problem, anyway," said Bonelli. "Her cat is just the bait . . . this time. If this person knows where her family lives, her brother or sister or mother could be taken hostage next. I think we should try to find this guy and stop him, here and now."

The young star dried her eyes and nodded emphatically. "I do, too."

"The other troubling thing," Bonelli went on, "is that this person somehow got Jaki's unlisted cell phone number and is texting her from a fake number, possibly also using burner phones. So these texts will be even harder to trace than the e-mails—maybe impossible."

"Which suggests this person really knows what he's doing," I guessed.

The detective nodded grimly. "We figured that stealing the cat might be linked somehow to the conference room black-out. We also were thinking that the guard might have been killed because he blocked access to an electrical panel that operated those features."

"Right, that makes sense," I said.

The cop at the table had finished his typing and now listened to his boss intently, like the rest of us.

"But the Bradburne is state-of-the-art, so the lighting, the smoke alarm, and other security features are all computerized," Bonelli explained. "Lights can be preprogrammed to go on and off at certain times without anyone having to manually operate them. About half an hour ago, I talked to the hotel's IT manager. He thinks someone hacked into the computer yesterday to black out the room and trigger the alarm remotely."

Hector gaped. "Sounds like something out of a damned James Bond movie."

"Not so outlandish, though," said Perry thoughtfully. "Systems get hacked all the time by people just trying to cause mischief. But the guy would need serious computer skills."

"So we know at least one thing about this person," I concluded. "He or she is very tech-savvy."

Bonelli turned her gaze out the room's picture window, where the sun had set beyond the highway and spread molten gold over the distant mountains. Facing west from Chadwick, we could see a range of the Appalachians that formed a dramatic backdrop at this time of day; you just needed to look past all of the man-made clutter below.

The view seemed to help the detective organize her thoughts.

"Joe Pollard, the guard, was found in a stairwell at a distance from his post, which suggests he might have been pursuing someone," she said. "And the ME said he had a strange bruise on the front of his neck, near his Adam's apple."

"Strangled?" Perry asked.

"Not exactly. He could have done it when he fell, but he also could have been punched in the trachea. That's known in martial arts as a throat strike. We learned it in the academy, and it's sometimes taught as a last-ditch move in self-defense classes. It's never used in competitions, though, because it's too deadly."

Hector jerked to his feet and paced to the coffee bar. "Isn't that a little far-fetched?"

"A little," the detective admitted, "and I really hope that's not the case. I hope he was just chasing someone down the stairs when the lights went out and lost his footing in the dark. Because otherwise . . ."

I sank back in my chair. "Otherwise, this stalker isn't messing around."

"And again, it shows that this person is smart. Hit somebody with your knuckles, you don't leave fingerprints."

"Were there any suspicious prints around the stairwell where the body was found?" I asked.

Bonelli shook her head. "Not many. I suppose the guests don't use the stairs often, and even the handrails get cleaned regularly. We found a few prints that belonged to the dead guy. Also to a couple of other guards and a maintenance man, who all have good reputations and alibis for the time of the blackout."

The young cop seated at the table finally spoke up. "I did ask the IT manager who might be able to hack into a sophisticated computer system like that. He said it would have to be a coder."

"Good point, Gardiner," the detective said, though I suspected she was bluffing and had only a vague idea of what he was talking about.

As if for the benefit of the rest of us, Officer Gardiner added, "That would mean a software guy—someone who writes computer code for a living. But there could be a lot of them around."

Bonelli's lips tightened. "I think we need to call in the county prosecutor on this one. Maybe even the feds."

I saw a chance to help her save face. "Detective, you and I already know a coder."

"We do?" Being a clever woman, she took only a minute to scan her memory bank for this information. "You're right—Janos! What's his first name again, Dion?"

"Chadwick's very own IT genius." When the others

looked skeptical, I added, "The FBI now uses an encryption method that *he* invented."

"Any chance that he's the one stalking Jaki?" quipped Perry.

"I strongly doubt it, but he might be able to help us find whoever is." I asked Bonelli, "Want me to call him?"

She encouraged me with a head bob.

I searched through my phone's contacts. Fiftyish Nick Janos was my go-to handyman, but I hadn't had any reason to call his son in many months. Luckily, I did still have Dion's number. I dialed it and got a recording. But I knew he rarely left his office in the basement of his father's house, where he worked the bugs out of sophisticated computer games for a living.

"Dion, pick up," I chided him. "It's Cassie McGlone, and I'm here with Detective Bonelli."

She and I waited patiently until we finally heard Janos's live, snarky voice on the line. "Whatever happened, I didn't do it."

Dion always had a bit of attitude, and it had only gotten worse after he'd sold that encryption system to the federal government for serious money. "I'm sure you didn't," I told him. "I'll bet you never even heard of Jaki Natal."

"Who?"

I had my phone turned up loud enough that, when he said this, the singer could overhear. For the first time all day, she giggled—probably finding his ignorance refreshing.

I briefed him on what had taken place the day before at the hotel, leaving out the theft of the cat, because Dion wouldn't care about that one way or the other. "We're figuring it took a coder to hack into the hotel computer."

"Absolutely," he said. "Easy peasy."

I recalled then that his cocky style could wear on one's nerves. "If I put Detective Bonelli on, would you explain to her how that could've been done?"

"Yeah, sure."

As I started to hand over my phone, she suggested, "Put it on speaker, so Officer Gardiner can listen in."

I smiled to myself—Bonelli wasn't too proud to acknowledge that she might not be able to follow Dion's explanation without help. Soon, we all could hear his monotone tenor voice lecturing us on subversive technology.

"First, you'd have to buy malware on the Dark Web, using Bitcoin. And you'd get yourself an anonymous address with a false identity, probably from an offshore site. That way, nothing you do can be traced. You use that address to phish for the IT manager's password. Sorry to rat him out, but somewhere along the line, the hotel's guy had to have slipped up. He responded to some kind of message that he shouldn't have."

Bonelli leaned nearer to the phone with an intent look I'd seen once or twice before—like a tiger on the hunt.

"Following so far?" Dion asked us.

"Got it," said Gardiner, taking notes on his laptop.

The voice on speaker continued. "Once you've got the password, that gives you administrative privileges, and you're into the hotel's main computer. Then you just search around until you find a menu that controls the lighting and other systems for the various rooms. If the lights are already programmed to go on and off at a certain time, you can change the programming."

"Could that be done in advance?" Bonelli asked him.

"You bet. For instance, if an event was scheduled at five o'clock and you wanted to disrupt it halfway through, you'd program the lights to go off then. The fire alarm, you might have to trigger on the fly. But that could be done pretty easily, too, from just an iPad."

"Holy crap," breathed Perry.

Gardiner typed rapidly on his laptop.

"Thanks for your help, Dion," said Bonelli. "One more question: Where should we go looking for this type of person? Where would he have gotten his training, and what kind of company could he be working for?"

A laugh on the phone. "Sorry, I know this is a serious issue, but . . . Hardware guys might go that route—get a degree in engineering or computer science, then go to work for a firm. They're usually perfectionistic, methodical types." His tone carried a note of pity for such conventional souls.

"And coders?" Bonelli prompted him.

"They might get some basic knowledge in school, but after that they usually teach themselves. And they usually work for themselves, too. So basically, you're looking for someone like me—independent, hates the idea of working in an office and taking orders from a boss." Dion paused. "I guess that's not real helpful."

No, I thought. *Especially not if the stalker works out of his dad's basement, like you do.*

"Well, it doesn't make the search easy, but in the long run it might at least help us recognize the guy," Bonelli told him.

Meanwhile, I tried to picture Jaki's high-tech tormentor. Dion always looked like he'd just rolled out of bed, dressed in sloppy jeans and dirty sneakers with an assortment of tech-themed or sarcastic T-shirts.

My mind instantly went to the tall, bearded character in the *Marry me!* shirt who'd been roaming the concourse.

"If you don't need anything else from me, I gotta get back to work now," Dion told them. "Good luck, guys. Oh, and tell Janie that I'm sorry I didn't know who she was."

After he'd hung up, Bonelli passed the phone back to me. "That young man knows way too much about how to hack a security system."

"Thank God he's on our side, right?" I smiled. "Listen, I've noticed two people hanging around the expo that you might want to check out."

First I told her about the four Jak-ettes. "This one girl, Lexi, said she was planning to get a Scottish Fold cat soon, the day before Gordie disappeared. Could be a complete coincidence, but you never know. She might have a nasty boyfriend who offered to steal Jaki's cat for her."

"Have to be pretty nasty to take down the security guard," said Bonelli, but she noted the information in her vinyl-covered pad. She'd once explained to me that she didn't take notes electronically because they could be lost or hacked too easily, and besides, she was probably the only person alive who could read her own handwriting.

Then I described the *Marry me!* guy who'd been in the crowd Friday and wandering the concourse since then, always by himself.

Jaki's dark eyes widened. "I know him! I mean, I don't *know* him, but I've seen him before. At a couple of my concerts and appearances, here in the general New York area. He was close to the front at one show, wearing that shirt, so I could see him by the stage lights. He caught my eye because he did *not* look like one of my usual fans. Like you said, Cassie, he was older and had long, hippie hair. Another time, when I was passing through a crowd, he called my name and pushed through people to get near me. He made such a fuss that one of my bodyguards got worried and made him back off."

"I remember that incident," said Hector, a crease between his thick eyebrows, "but I never saw the man."

"You probably were just too far away." Jaki turned her focus back to Bonelli. "Could that be enough for the T-shirt guy to think we 'have a past' together?"

"It could be, with someone like that." After jotting a couple more lines, the detective closed her notebook with an air of determination. "Looks like we've got some more suspects to check out."

Perry leaned forward in his chair, a faint glimmer of hope in his eyes. "Now the question is—can we nail this SOB before Jaki goes onstage tomorrow night?"

Chapter 12

A little late, I made it back to my van on the plaza and, along with Becky, gave our second grooming demo of the day. We still drew maybe fifteen people, probably because it was a Saturday afternoon and beautiful spring weather for standing around outdoors. None of the Jaki fans showed up this time, and I couldn't help wondering if Lexi, the one who coveted a Scottish Fold cat, had managed to obtain one by underhanded methods. With the help of a techie boyfriend? If she had Gordie, though, Lexi probably wouldn't be demanding a ransom for him. I was sure she'd want to keep the celebrity pet, secretly, and her best reward would be bragging rights among her closest pals.

Once Becky and I had finished our session, I brought her up to speed about the situation behind the scenes of the expo. I couldn't explain the whole business about how the hotel's computer was hacked, even if I could have remembered it all. But I did tell her Jaki's concert had been postponed, and might be canceled altogether, if the police couldn't find out before Sunday evening who was making threats against her.

"Gee," Becky mused, "you'd think being a rich, successful celebrity must be so much fun. It never occurred to me that some of those fans can be dangerous. And even if her father and the cops manage to keep Jaki safe, who knows if she'll ever see her cat again?"

"She refuses to leave here without Gordie," I said. "The rest of them probably think she's crazy, but I can understand it. She knows the thief probably has him stashed somewhere and is not taking such great care of him. If she rejects this person's demand to meet with her and leaves the hotel instead, he could kill Gordie for revenge."

Easing Lady back into her carrier, Becky shuddered. "Sounds like a real psychopath. And if he does know Jaki from somewhere in her past, that makes it even creepier. She's positive it isn't Alec? He could easily have hired somebody to do his dirty work for him."

"She doesn't think so. When she told him what happened, he got mad at *her* for losing Gordie."

"Huh," said Becky. "Sounds like he at least cares about the cat, anyway."

Around five, Becky took off in her little Chevy hatchback to return Lady to her foster family and then head home. Before leaving the plaza, I phoned Mark. I knew he'd be finished with his demo, too, and I hoped we could make dinner plans.

"Babe, I wish I could," he said. "Maggie called from the clinic, and they've got an emergency—a pit bull that somebody dumped by the side of the road, beaten up and in rough shape. A good Samaritan brought him in and even offered to pay his bills. Maggie stabilized the dog, but he's going to need surgery tonight. She's been at the clinic all day, so it's only fair that I take over."

"Oh, wow, that's too bad about the dog," I said. "Sure, I understand. We can talk tomorrow. Just one more thing—did you know Jaki Natal postponed her concert?"

"Yeah, word has gotten around. What's up with that?"

"The business with Gordie has gotten creepier, and they're
not sure she'll be safe onstage. Basically, whether she performs
at all depends on how soon we can nail this catnapper."

His voice rose from baritone to tenor. "We?"

"I'm involved only as a civilian adviser," I assured him.

"This time, keep it that way," he told me. "*Please,* Cassie."

"I promise. Now go save that poor dog, and I'll see you in
the morning."

When I got home that evening, I had to drive over a steel
plate that spanned the trench in front of my shop, but at least I
was able to pull the van into my rear lot. And I wouldn't have
to worry about getting blocked in the next morning, because
it would be Sunday. Even road crews took a day of rest.

However, when I made it as far as my front sales counter, I
found a note from Sarah warning me about more complica-
tions from the construction.

*Just a heads-up—the water here has been brown all day. A guy on
the crew said the pressure is down because of something they're doing.
Supposed to be okay to drink if you boil it first, but just to be safe, I
ran out to the Quick Check, got us three gallon jugs, and put them in
the fridge. I used that water for the boarders, also. Hope by the time
you get this note, it's all running clear again. See you Monday!*

I smiled at her optimism, because neither Sarah nor I
needed any more challenges right now. Before doing anything
else, I checked the powder room at the back of the shop,
flushed the toilet, and ran the tap.

*Still brown—damn. And since the crew won't be working tomor-
row, it'll stay that way at least until Monday.*

After two sessions of grooming cats inside a warm van, I
really needed to shower and wash my hair. Well, I'd deal with
that problem after I had something to eat.

I fed my own three pets first, of course. Then I microwaved

a frozen dinner from Dawn's store, at least as healthful as anything I could whip together myself. While it nuked, I searched
through my living room bookshelves and plucked out one of
my old psych textbooks.

Yes, that actually was my major in college. Combined with
a minor in fine art, it didn't exactly bring job recruiters beating
a path to my door after graduation or promise any kind of
steady, secure income. Once I'd faced that reality, I'd decided to
explore a career working with animals. But I'd never quite
gotten over my fascination with the human mind, especially its
darker corners.

Much of my coursework had been done electronically, but
I'd hung onto a thick tome on abnormal psychology. Over
tonight's dinner, I cracked it open for the first time in a decade.
The table of contents covered the gamut of disorders from
anxiety to dissociation to mood swings to sexual compulsions
to substance abuse. After skimming a few of these, I turned to
the section I thought would be most helpful: personality disorders.

For the next half hour, I reacquainted myself with the
obsessive-compulsive, the narcissistic, the schizotypal, the avoid-
ant, the antisocial, and the borderline personality types. Their
symptoms and causes made interesting reading, and who could
say whether one or more of these neuroses helped motivate
the slimeball who had stolen Jaki's cat? But this highly clinical
material wasn't really telling me what I needed to know.

I wasn't trying to psychoanalyze a patient. I was trying to
catch a killer.

After bringing my dirty plate and cutlery to the sink and
automatically turning on the tap, I was rudely reminded that
tonight the water would only make them filthier. The same
could be said for my hair and body, if I attempted to take a
shower.

I cursed to myself again. I could think of only one solution, and phoned Dawn.

Though it was only eight p.m., she sounded drowsy—maybe from the pain pills. I apologized for disturbing her.

"No problem. I was reading a book, and even though it's pretty good, I guess I dozed off. What's up?"

"First, I need to say that I had a delicious kale, quinoa, and vegetable dish from your shop for dinner tonight, so thanks very much for that. It came in handy."

"Don't mention it. I guess working the expo doesn't leave you much energy for cooking these days."

"The state of my water doesn't help, either." I explained the problem.

"Oh, dear. Can I do anything more than just sympathize?"

"I know you usually get up pretty early, but since you're off your feet you may be sleeping later these days. . . . Any chance I can steal a shower at your place tomorrow morning?"

"Yeah, sure. My water's fine so far."

"It won't hang you up in any way?"

"Nope, I've closed the shop until Monday, when I should be limping around a bit better. I'll be up by at least seven-thirty, so pop over any time after that. In fact, you're welcome to come tonight if you want."

"I'm too tired to get it together right now," I told her. And I also didn't want to get into talking about the problems at the expo, since I shouldn't be revealing too many details, anyway. "I need to spend some quality time with my own cats. They get cranky when they haven't seen me all day."

My friend laughed. "I hear that. Even though I'm spending plenty of time with Tigger, he's going a little nuts because I can't run around and play with him the way I usually do. He keeps jumping on my lap and jostling my foot. He's trying to keep me company, and he doesn't understand when I hiss in pain."

"Ouch." Dawn had taken in the kitten as a three-month-old stray. Now he was over a year old and up to about eight pounds, but still a ball of mischievous energy. She originally had intended for Tigger to serve as a shop cat, keeping mice away from her dry goods, but I'd noticed her letting him up into her apartment more often these days. "When you first told me you broke your foot, I was afraid that he'd tripped you."

"Nope, can't blame this one on him—for a change! Right, you little monster?" I could tell from her tone that she was wrestling with the playful brown tabby.

"Sounds like your two boyfriends are taking good care of you, anyway," I said. "Okay, see you bright and early tomorrow."

Fatigue wasn't the only reason I wanted to stay home that night. My book on abnormal psychology had fired my curiosity, and I was eager to investigate that angle further.

My cleanup plans for the next day in place, I sprawled on my sofa surrounded by my three fur kids, opened my laptop, and searched under *stalker*. This brought up at least half a dozen articles by experts on various methods of stalking and types of stalkers. Different authors gave these subgroups slightly different names, but they broke down in roughly the same ways.

Most common was the "domestic" stalker, who previously had a real relationship with the victim—a former spouse or lover. This person wanted to continue the relationship against the victim's will and still tracked her every move. If she got an order of protection to keep him away from her home, he might even show up at her workplace and cause trouble.

I could testify to this from personal experience. I'd moved to Chadwick, in part, to get away from my abusive ex-boyfriend, Andy. But even though he'd shoved me into a metal bookcase hard enough to leave a massive bruise on my shoulder, once I disappeared, he hunted me down and tried to win me back. He'd left notes, like Jaki's LBH, and showed up uninvited at places where he knew I would be. Only after I'd reamed him out in a very public locale—with friends nearby to back me up—had Andy finally quit harassing me.

I realized there might be a reason why I was taking Jaki's dilemma rather personally.

The "rejected" stalker, a similar case, had some less substantial past contact with the victim. Maybe he'd flirted with her or asked her on a date and gotten turned down. He might be convinced that if she only got to know him better, she would return his love. If he was more unbalanced, he might believe that she secretly *did* return his feelings, but her cruel friends and family were keeping them apart.

To me, this description seemed to fit the person who was trying to persuade Jaki to meet with him alone. But it still didn't narrow the field of suspects that much. Statistics stated that, although seventy to eighty percent of all stalkers were men, women made up a larger percentage of rejected stalkers.

Tango, my orange tabby, had settled in next to me and began to knead my right thigh through my jeans. Talk about abusive relationships! And he purred blissfully all the while, making me feel like a killjoy for discouraging him. I tugged a fleece throw down from the back of the sofa and pulled part of it over my lap as a buffer. I really needed to make time to clip his claws, but for the moment, I plunged on with my research.

The "pretender" usually was a loner who had trouble establishing an intimate relationship with anyone. Still, he believed the victim to be his better half, the soul mate who would understand him completely and solve his emotional problems. This person often idolized someone of a higher social status, so that trait also might fit Jaki's case.

Then there was the "vengeful" stalker, who wanted to frighten the victim and take them down a peg out of envy or jealousy—a possible motive for a twisted female fan.

A woman could know martial arts. Even some of the hip-hop dancing that Jaki does in her act involves some stiff-arm punches. If this was a diehard fan, she might have studied that kind of dancing, too.

Celebrity and political stalkers were so common that they merited a category of their own. Highly visible types attracted troubled individuals who attached great importance to their target's public statements or even to roles that person had played.

Jaki had already noticed that her stalker fixated on the lyrics of some of her songs, especially "Free Me." I tried to re-member a few of the lyrics:

> *Stuck in a glass cage watching the world go by*
> *Voices of warning in my ears, strong hands reining me in*
> *Wish I could just make one real connection, someone*
>   *who loves me for me. . . .*

Those lines definitely would appeal to somebody who also felt lonely and misunderstood, and who might conclude that Jaki literally needed someone to rescue her.

Thirst finally drove me downstairs to the shop's refrigera-tor. I retrieved one of the water jugs Sarah had purchased and brought it up to my apartment to make some tea. I used as lit-tle water as possible, though, because it might have to last the boarders for a couple of days.

Sipping my brew and reviving a bit, I went back to finish my amateur profiling.

The "ultimate" stalker was the hard-core predator who often spied on a victim around the clock, memorizing her habits. His interest usually wasn't as personal as in the cases of the other types—he was more excited by the sense of power and secret control over another human being. The predator's behavior could progress to sexual assault and even murder, said the article. Most serial rapists and killers followed this pattern.

My stomach twisted. I sincerely hoped Jaki wasn't dealing with anyone who could potentially become that violent. But he already might have killed a middle-aged security guard, with a martial arts throat strike known to be lethal.

I grabbed a notebook and started jotting down certain traits that jumped out at me from my research—the ones that seemed to fit with what we already knew about Jaki's tormentor.

Rigid personality, loner, few relationships, but above-average intelligence. Low self-esteem, gains self-worth from imaginary relationship with victim. Not guilty or embarrassed over own behavior, just sees it as necessary to accomplish goal. Doesn't see how he or she is harming others. Maybe sociopathic, lacking conscience or empathy. A mean streak, and violent when frustrated. Most likely male if stalking a woman . . . though a female could be motivated by jealousy or revenge.

To that, I could add the information we'd found out today—that this person possibly had martial arts training and definitely possessed technological skills. And I would guess that, because he'd fixated on a pop star in her early twenties, he must be fairly young himself. I guessed he didn't spend quite as much time toiling over a computer in his father's basement, though, as Dion did.

Dion said the typical coder was an independent, freewheeling type. That's the only trait that doesn't seem to fit. All of this planning, maybe over years, fits better with the idea of a rigid personality. But I guess every stereotype has its exceptions.

As I wound up my research for the evening—afraid it already had doomed me to nightmares—I wondered if Bonelli also might be exploring the same material. I didn't know if her position as police detective had required training as a profiler. At any rate, she had the whole town of Chadwick, plus the surrounding area, to worry about. And lots of other crimes to solve.

I had a little more free time and all of that "wasted" education in psychology. Might as well put it to some good use.

I spent the next ten minutes crafting a cover e-mail that made light of my research and emphasized that I was not trying to second-guess anyone or step on any toes. Then I forwarded my notes to Bonelli.

The next morning, I packed shampoo, makeup, and a change of clothes into my van and drove it two blocks to Dawn's shop. In her apartment's shower, which was tiled in a cheery yellow with plants screening the small window, I finally scrubbed away the grime of the previous day and toweled off with a renewed spirit. I even repaid Dawn by cleaning out Tigger's litter box, which was difficult for her to manage while on crutches.

I dressed, borrowed her hair dryer, and just had time to share a quick cup of coffee with her before I needed to leave. I let Dawn in on the news about the stolen cat, but leaked nothing about the sabotaging of the hotel's computer or whom the police were looking at as suspects. She probably figured out that I knew more than I was revealing, but understood that Bonelli only took me into her confidence because she trusted me not to blab sensitive information all over town.

By eight o'clock, I was ready to leave. I commented to Dawn, "If it was a weekday, the backhoe would have already been digging for an hour on my block."

She groaned. "My turn will come, though. I guess if my walk-in traffic falls off, I may just have to bump up my mail-order business."

"That's an idea. Unfortunately for me, it doesn't work so well with grooming people's pets."

"Ah, but now that you've got the van, you can at least go out to your customers. Even pick up their cats and bring them in to board."

"True. And then give them little teeny earplugs!"

We wound up our short visit with that laugh, but Dawn hadn't completely forgotten the dangers that lurked at the expo. As I headed out to my van, she told me, "Good luck—and be careful."

Chapter 13

Because of the traffic lined up to enter the convention center parking garage, I decided to approach from a different direction that morning. My new route took me past the anti-cat-show demonstrators, whose numbers seemed to be holding at around half a dozen, a mix of men and women. The police must have warned them away from the hotel entrance, because they kept to a small patch of park across the street. Stopped at a light, I had more of a chance to study them and recognized a familiar tall, athletic silhouette with a thick braid down her back.

What's Grumpy Glenda doing out here? Yeah, she probably believes in their cause, but wouldn't she be better off staffing the FOCA table with Chris and actually arranging pet adoptions?

The light changed, and I had to move on. While parking on the plaza, though, I remembered Chris complaining that Glenda kept leaving her post with no explanation and spending long stretches AWOL. *Maybe to check in with the demonstrators? Even to phone them, she might want to go someplace where Chris couldn't overhear.*

And Glenda disapproved of Jaki for having a purebred cat

and carrying him around "like a fashion accessory" everywhere she went.

To minimize stress for our last demo, Becky pressed Ray back into service. While she and I prepped the Persian mix to meet his audience, I told her what I had just seen.

"I don't want to suspect a fellow animal lover," I said, "but is it possible Glenda or another protestor could have grabbed Gordie? Thinking that they were rescuing him from being 'exploited' by Jaki?"

The idea that a fellow FOCA volunteer could be involved obviously disturbed Becky, and while laying out the grooming tools, she halted with a comb in midair. "Glenda sure has been acting mysteriously ever since she came to the shelter, and I have gotten the sense that working there doesn't quite satisfy her activist urges. But even if she and her pals conspired to steal the cat, I can't see them wooing Jaki all of this time and insisting on meeting with her. What would be the point?"

"To lecture her on the error of her ways? Or even to hold *her* for ransom and make some kind of demand?"

Becky's head-shake was slow and thoughtful. "I don't know. If they were trying to shut down a lab that did animal testing or make some other big statement, maybe. But Jaki's just a singer, and Gordie's her personal pet. Seems a lot for them to go through for not much reason."

While I did not rule out the possibility of animal-rights fanaticism, I agreed that the notes and e-mails to Jaki had a more personal tone. "If the protestors took her cat, the stalker might just have heard about that and decided to exploit it to get close to her," I reasoned. "Which would mean we're dealing with two different culprits."

I told Becky about the reading I'd done the previous evening to try to understand the motives of the killer cat thief. She came to pretty much the same conclusion as I had.

"Maybe the cops should be looking further back, at people Jaki met earlier in her life," she said. "She's been performing since she was a kid. Talent shows in grade school, plays in high school. That sitcom *Too Cool for School,* when she was in her late teens . . ."

I paused in my preparations to stare at my helper. "How do you know all this? Maybe you're her stalker!"

My platinum-haired assistant laughed. "I'm not, I swear. I only had a general idea of her background up to now, but I did some research last night, too. There are lots of articles and interviews online. If the stalker says the two of them have 'a history,' it could be anybody. Even someone she beat out for the lead in some high school musical."

"That's true. But it makes finding them even harder."

"Unless they've already bothered her and her family in the past. From what Jaki and her father told you, that could be the case."

"I expect Bonelli and her guys are already looking for those kinds of connections," I said, "but I can mention it to her. If she isn't mad at me over the amateur profiling job I sent her last night."

I had ten minutes before the demo, so I gave Mark a quick call and asked how the pit bull was doing.

"I think we saved him," he said, in a tone of relief. "I was there until midnight but got him stabilized. Poor guy had a concussion, broken ribs . . . made me want to go out and do the same thing to his owner. Of course, we still have no idea who dumped him next to the highway."

A felt a fresh surge of pride and love for my significant other. "He's lucky someone brought him to the clinic and that he had you to patch him up."

"He was overdue for some luck. Hey, we had some police

action on the concourse this morning. You know anything about it?"

"Not a thing," I told him. "What happened?"

"Right after Dave and I got here, we saw the cops roust some seedy-looking guy. When he started struggling and yelling, they slapped handcuffs on him and hauled him away. I only saw it from a distance, so I've got no idea what he did."

"Very interesting! I'll check with Bonelli after our demo. See if it has anything to do with the Jaki situation."

"Let me know what you find out. Be great if they caught the guy."

"It sure would."

Hanging up, I just had time to pass this information on to Becky before we opened the van doors to greet the handful of folks clustered outside. As I'd expected, the audience was smaller on a Sunday morning and after we'd already done our "show" three times before. As usual, Ray took the public grooming more in stride than had any of the other cats. Still, I included in my talk plenty of tips on how to handle tougher customers. While addressing the group, I continued to keep my eyes peeled, but I spotted no suspicious characters or activity. Mark had the advantage over me today in that department.

Could the cops really have Jaki's stalker in custody? Would they get him to confess to killing the guard and to reveal where he'd stashed Gordie?

Halfway through our presentation, I heard my muted phone buzz. After we'd finished the demo, answered questions, and given out business cards, I finally checked on the caller's info.

Bonelli.

"Good morning," she greeted me cheerfully. "I just wanted to thank you, Cassie, for your helpful tips."

I'd been holding my breath, and at hearing her upbeat tone, I dared to let it out. "You're welcome. I was afraid you'd think I was overstepping. I'm sure you guys can do your own criminal profiling."

"Oh, that . . . Sorry, I just skimmed your e-mail, didn't have time to read it thoroughly. I'm talking about the leads you gave us during the meeting yesterday. We picked up the *Marry me!* guy this morning. Actually, he isn't wearing the shirt today, but a couple of the vendors knew who you meant and pointed him out to us. Name is Mason Reilly."

"Was he on the concourse? Mark saw someone being arrested there—said he put up a bit of a fight."

"Yeah, he mouthed off at Gardiner and LoMonaco. They started by just asking him some questions, but he demanded to know what it was about, then shoved LoMonaco. So they brought him downtown."

"You've got him at the station? Is he the guy?"

"Can't tell yet. He wants a lawyer. We've got his driver's license, though, so we should be able to find out his family situation and where he works, for starters."

Whether he has a high-tech job, for example. I thought of Dion's insight that coders tended to be eccentric and anti-authority. From both his appearance and behavior, Reilly did sound as if he fit that description.

While I'd been on the phone, Becky had been chatting with the members of our audience who'd lingered to ask questions. Now she returned Ray to the drying cage and tidied up inside the van, vacuuming up fur and throwing soiled towels in the hamper. She didn't exactly eavesdrop on my conversation with Bonelli, but I could tell she was eager to find out the latest news.

The detective continued, "As for the female Jaki fans, my guys didn't even have to go hunting for them. Dria and Ashley sashayed up to Gardiner last night and asked if he knew why the concert had been postponed."

"I assume he didn't tell them the truth," I said.

"Gave them the official lie, that Jaki was under the weather but might be recovered by tonight. He got their full names and asked if they'd been at Jaki's interview Friday. Dria claimed they'd been there, toward the back of the room, when the lights went out. She said they got scared and ran for the doors right away. Gardiner tried to steer the conversation around to Jaki's cat, to see if the girls knew he was missing without being told. Both seemed to get spooked then, and found an excuse to move on. He had no legit reason to detain them."

"He saw only two of the girls?" I asked. "I wonder if Lexi is still keeping a low profile."

"He's keeping a lookout for the two others." The detective paused. "Meanwhile, we did get an outright confession from one person."

I'd been swigging water from a bottle and almost choked. "What? And you didn't lead with that?"

"Not to the cat theft or the murder. But the hotel's IT manager figured out what he did wrong and admitted it to his bosses and to us."

Bottle in hand, I perched on a stool next to my grooming table. "This ought to be good."

"I don't know much about how all of this works, of course. But he said a couple of days before the expo, he got a very official-looking e-mail that his password had been breached and he should create a new one. He knew that sometimes hackers send out messages like that to phish for information, but he tried to verify it and said it appeared to check out. He's fairly new on the job, and for weeks now, his bosses have been stressing the need for increased vigilance and security during the expo. So he genuinely believed someone had hacked his password to make trouble for the hotel. He created a new one . . . and now he figures it automatically went back to the hacker."

"And gave that person full access to the hotel's computer system," I finished.

"I almost felt sorry for the IT guy. I sort of hope he doesn't get fired. He's in his forties, got kids in college." Bonelli wasn't normally a soft touch, but with two teenage sons herself, she probably could identify.

"Whatever happens, I'm sure it's not a mistake that he'll make again," I said.

When a beeping sounded on the line, Bonelli told me, "Oops, that's Newton. Probably wanting to know if it's safe for his guest star to go onstage tonight. As if I can guarantee that for sure."

I freed her to take the call and wished her good luck.

Becky scrutinized my face with such burning curiosity that I had to bring her up to speed. Hearing the latest, she looked relieved.

"Now if the cops can just make this Mason guy tell them where he put Gordie, we might be home free," she said.

"Here's hoping." Privately, though, I worried the case might not be solved that easily. With a nod toward the van's door, I asked, "Anything suspicious happening out there?"

"Suspicious, no. But a nice middle-aged couple acted very interested in adopting our boy Ray." She smiled. "I told them they could drop by the FOCA shelter any time to start the process, and they promised they would."

"Fantastic," I said. "After all, that was our whole purpose in being here, originally. To find homes for some of these critters."

"Yeah, with all the other drama, we shouldn't lose sight of that. I just hope they don't come by on a day when Glenda is there—she might scare them away." Becky opened the cage door and stroked Ray's soft, golden fur. "Since he's been such a good boy, guess I should get him back to the shelter now, so he can relax. I may come back here for lunch, though, just to see how things are going."

"Okay. I'll try to meet up with you, Mark, and Chris," I told her. "First, I'm going to go check on Mom and Harry. See if Looli is still racking up the ribbons."

I locked up the van, crossed the plaza, and entered the hotel lobby. I'd just passed through the automatic doors when my phone rang again. I stopped to check it, and I got a start.

Jaki Natal herself was calling me on her private line. Things must either be very good . . . or very bad.

"Hi, Jaki, what's up?" So cool, like we were BFFs from way back.

She spoke in a low, rather breathless voice. "Cassie, everyone wants me to give up on finding Gordie. They're insisting I leave the hotel and fly back to LA. I can't do that—I know he's still in danger. Please, you've gotta help me. You're the only one who understands!"

Chapter 14

This time, the towering bodyguard had to knock on the door of Jaki's suite and ask if I was expected. But Mira let me in and steered me toward the bar near the door. Jaki, Hector, and Perry sat around the big table by the window, deep in a serious confab. I got the idea that we needed to leave them alone for a while to hash things out.

"Can I get you anything to drink?" Mira asked. "Last time, you said you like chamomile tea."

I guessed that a good personal assistant needed to remember such things. "I'll take coffee this time, thanks. With milk and sweetener."

"Stevia okay?"

Figured that the Bradburne—or at least Jaki—would have a choice of sugar-free options on hand. "Perfect."

Mira made herself a cup, too, and I complimented her on her oh-so-chic haircut. We speculated for a minute on whether I could pull off something similar, skirting the issue of what it would cost in a top-notch salon.

"Being self-employed, I generally groom my own fur," I told her with a laugh.

She shrugged her thin shoulders. "You could splurge once. Since you've got the skills, you might be able to figure out how the stylist cut it and maintain it yourself after that."

I remembered that Mira had been the source of a lot of inside info for Becky and Chris, and decided to take advantage of this opportunity. "So, how did you come to be Jaki's assistant?"

"I just kind of fell into it, in high school when she first started getting a lot of gigs. I was one year ahead of her and thought of going into theater myself. But not as a performer—I was more interested in costumes, props, the behind-the-scenes stuff. Of course, even those jobs are hard to get, and they pay peanuts."

I nodded. I'd heard that live theater, even on Broadway, wasn't exactly a gold mine for anyone in terms of employment.

"So I started helping Jaki with her costumes and makeup, just for fun, and running errands she was too busy to do," Mira explained. "We always got along well, and the arrangement just worked for both of us. When she went to LA, she asked me to come along as a paid assistant." The lady in black slid onto the bar stool next to mine and leaned confidentially closer. "Frankly, almost everyone else around her—even Hector, sometimes—deals with her as Jaki Natal the performer. They want to make sure that she gets to the next gig on time, that she's physically ready to go onstage, that kind of stuff."

"More of a business relationship," I said.

"Exactly. But she also needs a *friend* who's more on her level. Somebody to be supportive when she doesn't feel so well, or needs to gripe and let her hair down. She counts on me for that." Mira dropped her gaze to her half-empty mug of coffee. "Might sound silly, but she counted on Gordie for that, too. He was almost like . . . What do they call it? Her emotional support animal."

"Yes, I got that feeling," I said.

"Heck, I miss the little guy, too. I took care of him as much as she did. I don't mean that as a criticism. Jaki *liked* taking care of him, but she was just so busy that I usually ended up feeding him at least once a day, cleaning his pan, keeping track of his carrier, and brushing him if he was going somewhere that he'd be photographed." Mira's face and tone saddened again. "I still feel awful that I let her down on Friday. I should have kept track of where that guy went with the carrier, maybe even chased after him."

"And maybe he would have dealt with you the same way he did with the security guard!" I pointed out. "It might be lucky that you *didn't* get in his way."

Mira frowned, as if she hadn't considered that before. With a glance toward the table where the other three still quietly wrangled, she told me, "It's just that I understand why this is driving Jaki so crazy. Gordie was—*is*—a really sweet, lovable cat. I just hope this guy hasn't done anything to hurt him."

I broached what I supposed might be a sensitive subject. "Last time, when Hector suggested she take something to calm her down, Jaki said she didn't want to 'go down that road again.' Has she had a problem in the past?" When Mira stiffened defensively, I assured her, "I'm not sniffing around for gossip—I'll keep it confidential. I'm just trying to figure out if anyone has a hold like that over her."

"It was nothing. When all this fame first hit, she was getting offers from everywhere and going crazy trying to accept them all. Trying to please everybody. She got stressed, so of

course somebody offered her some pills to keep her energy up
for a concert, then another pill to help her sleep. . . . She got
kind of dependent on that routine for a while. But Jaki's got a
good head on her shoulders. She saw what was happening, so
she spent a couple of weeks at a clinic and got back on track."
Mira's tone grew emphatic. "It was all prescription medicine,
no street drugs, and she took it for just a little while. So, no,
there isn't anybody who'd 'have a hold on her' from those
days."

Now I felt a little embarrassed for asking. "I just wondered, because it sounds, from some of the notes she's gotten,
like this person thinks she's under a lot of pressure and wants
to rescue her."

Mira made a face. "People believe all kinds of trash they
read or hear in the media. Like, a year ago, Jaki caught a cold
that turned into really bad laryngitis, and she had to cancel a
few concerts. Some blogger started a rumor that she'd over-
dosed and was going into rehab. Not a word of truth in it,
and Rose put out denials to the press. But once something
like that gets in the wind, some folks still want to believe the
worst."

Hoping to change the subject, I noticed that a credenza
against the wall had been heaped with fruit baskets and other
gifts, some professionally decorated and others with a home-
made appearance. "What's all this? Courtesy of the hotel?"

The assistant rolled her eyes. "The biggest basket is, but the
rest are from fans. Some of the messages are nice and thoughtful, but others . . . Well, I think that's why everybody wanted
to talk with you again this morning."

At that point, the secretive discussion around the oval table
broke up. Hector acknowledged me with a grouchy nod and

got himself a cup of coffee; Perry just waved and retreated to his favorite side chair to make a phone call.

Only Jaki looked pleased to see me. She crossed the room, wearing a fitted red sweater and slim black pants, and looking more alert and pulled-together than the day before. "Really sorry, Cassie, to be taking so much of your time."

"Not at all. I know you're dealing with a crisis." Tilting my head toward the pile of gifts, I added, "Mira was just telling me that most of this stuff is from fans. Do they know that Gordie is missing?"

"No, no. Rose and Perry put out the word that I wasn't feeling well, so I got all of these packages sent to the suite. Flowers, candy, cough drops, vitamin C, echinacea . . ." She shook her head, with a crooked half-smile. "No one actually said what was supposed to be wrong with me. Guess I should be glad people didn't send Pepto-Bismol . . . or Midol!"

I smiled, too. "But I gather not all of the gifts were thoughtful."

"No, unfortunately." Her sweet face turning grim, Jaki opened a folded cloth table napkin to reveal one small, white gift box, the kind you'd use for a short necklace or a bracelet. The lid sat loosely on top, and next to it rested what looked like a blue-and-green plaid ribbon with a small bow. Closer up, though, I realized it was a pet collar accented with a miniature bow tie; wisps of silvery fur still clung to the inside.

"I called Detective Bonelli, and she told me not to handle this any more than I did already," Jaki said. With shaking fingers, as if defusing a small bomb, she used one of the hotel's ballpoint pens to nudge the lid of the box aside.

A heart-shaped silver tag rested on a square of white cotton wool. It was engraved with the name GORDIE and what looked like a California phone number.

"This is the note that came with it." She pointed to a folded piece of postcard stock that lay next to the box; still using the pen, she flattened it so I could read the electronically printed message: *Your cat really misses you, Jaki. You can have him back tonight if you'll meet with me privately after your show. I'll text you the time and place. Meanwhile, Gordie sends you his heart.*

The message raised hairs on the back of my neck, and the pet being held hostage wasn't even mine.

"I can't tell you how I felt when I read that," Jaki said, her voice thick. "I was shaking so bad, I thought I was going to throw up. It felt as if . . . as if he could just as easily have sent me . . . a piece of Gordie." Tears coursed down her face again.

I put an arm around her slim shoulders, feeling protective as a big sister. The note definitely carried a veiled threat. This slimeball was clever, all right. And forget the business about his wanting to be "friends" with Jaki. No one with a decent motive would stoop to terrifying her like this.

Hector wandered up and tried to reassure his daughter. "Honey, the cops already arrested this guy."

I started to have my doubts. "When was the box delivered?"

"About an hour ago." Perry joined us, tucking his phone into his jacket pocket. "But he could have arranged the delivery just before they nailed him."

"Bonelli is sending someone for the box—they're going to try to get fingerprints from it, anyway." With the ballpoint, Jaki nudged the lid back into place. Her gaze lingering for a moment on the little plaid collar with the bow tie before she folded the napkin over everything again. "I can't leave here, though, without Gordie. This monster will kill him, I know he will."

"Well, you sure as hell can't meet with him alone, and take the chance that he might kill *you*," her father declared.

The suite's phone rang. Perry picked up the handset, then passed it on to Hector. "It's Detective Bonelli."

The stocky man settled on the wide arm of the ivory sofa, as if poised for action, to take the call. He mainly listened, and I couldn't deduce much from his brief responses, but below his mustache his frown grew deeper and deeper. When the call ended, he stood up with a jerk, crossed the room, and slapped the handset back into its base.

"She doesn't think it's the right guy," he said. "The one they've got, I mean. This one's the songwriter—the one who wanted Jaki to pass his stuff on to her agent. When he heard the cat was missing, he saw a chance to make a deal with us. Even if the cat turned up in the meantime, he says, at least he'd have made a connection to help his career."

"So he doesn't have Gordie?" I asked.

"He swears he doesn't, and Bonelli can't see why he'd lie about it. He's already blown his chance to get what he wanted, and things would go easier for him if he cooperated. She said he's got no record besides a minor drug bust. And when he's not playing guitar in dives, he works as a short-order cook. No technology background."

"As far as he's telling them," Perry muttered.

Meanwhile, Jaki had gone back into a funk. She slumped in one of the dining chairs near the gift-laden credenza, brushing fingers over the screen of her phone.

"Any new messages?" I asked her.

"No. . . ." But something in her voice invited me to come and look over her shoulder.

The small screen displayed a selfie of Jaki kissing Gordie on his furry cheek, the cat's eyes half-closed as if in bliss. She scrolled to another shot of herself in a roomy airplane seat, her young face bare of makeup; she peered out the window at golden sunset clouds while Gordie sprawled across her lap in sleep. His curved paws seemed to hug the top of her leg.

Scroll to another shot: Jaki arriving for a personal appearance, beautifully dressed and coiffed, with the unflappable silver tabby tucked under her arm. In the next, she watched TV in a darkened room while wearing a T-shirt with pajama bottoms in a funky, tropical print; Gordie sat upright next to her on the sofa, his hind legs stretched in front of him like a person. Finally, a short video showed the cat manically chasing a windup toy around a living room, with Jaki giggling and a male voice laughing in the background.

"Alec's right," she told me in a dull tone. "We got careless. We should never, ever have trusted Gordie to a stranger."

"You and Mira were both frightened," I reminded her, "and you were set up by someone very smart and calculating. Don't blame yourselves."

Perry crossed the room and also tried to console her. "Yeah, look what happened with the hotel's IT guy. He's an expert, but that phishing e-mail even fooled him."

I remembered Becky's theory of that morning, and asked Jaki, "You said some of the e-mails you've gotten lately were similar to notes that have been left for your family over the years. So it sounds as if this creep might live around here. Is there anybody, way back in your past, who could be behind this? Somebody you turned down for a date, or even another girl you beat out for a role?"

She sighed deeply and shook her head. "I've tried to think, but . . . I've been performing since I was about ten. I'd sure hate to think somebody from my grade school talent show could hold a grudge for that long!"

Hector also snorted. "Yeah, that's ridiculous."

"Boys in high school, maybe? Ones you broke up with, or never dated at all because they acted too weird?"

She scrunched her face. "Don't all boys in high school act weird? I didn't even date that much, because I was so busy with dancing and singing lessons and rehearsals for plays and other school shows. Then I blew off senior year to go to LA and work on the series."

"There wasn't anybody who stands out?" I pressed her.

"Just one dude I went out with a couple of times, who was really obnoxious—Larry Vanderveer. Super good-looking but with a huge ego, y'know? I figured we might get along because he was in a band, but he was used to girls doing anything he wanted and got pretty steamed when I told him no. After that he spread rumors around school that I was slutty, to get even."

"I remember him." Hector scowled. "He just came to the house once, but there was something about him I didn't trust. Acted real polite to my face, but like it was—how do you say it?—a put-on. Jaki always told me I overprotected her, so I tried not to interfere. But I was glad when she stopped seeing him."

"Any idea where the guy is now," Perry asked, "or what he's up to?"

"I did a search," Mira said, "but I couldn't find him online. Not around here, anyway."

"By now, he could have moved out of the area," Jaki guessed. "Maybe he even changed his name. After all, if you're a rocker, *Larry Vanderveer* doesn't sound very badass." She cracked a sly smile.

Hector, though, looked as if he'd begun to take my approach seriously. "It might be somebody else, though. Some

guy you hardly noticed, or some incident you don't even remember. We should ask your mama."

"Or your brother and sister," I suggested. "Did they go to
the same school? They might have known about someone
who had a crush on you, or a beef against you, that you
weren't even aware of."

Jaki straightened, and the spark came back into her dark
eyes. "Might be worth it. Better than doing nothing!"

Perry let out a sigh and slapped his knees. "Well, if the
killer cat thief is still at large, I guess I'd better cancel tonight's
show, too. We'll have to refund a lot of three-hundred-dollar
tickets, but at least we'll save on all of that extra security."

"No," Jaki told him. "Don't."

Her father swung toward her in alarm. "We've got to, for
your safety."

"As long as you have all that security, I'm going to go on. I
came here to support a cause, and those ticket sales are going
to help homeless animals."

"You want to be a *martyr* to the cause?" Hector scoffed.
"Out of the question!"

"This guy wants to meet me after the show. If I agree to
that, he has no reason to harm me while I'm performing."

She's got a point there, I thought, but I didn't intend to interfere. This was between Jaki and her father.

"When he texts me, we'll set it up," Jaki went on. "Then
we'll tell Detective Bonelli. See if she can lay a trap. I'll lure
this . . . person into the open, make him or her tell me where
Gordie is, and then the cops can nab him."

"He's bound to be expecting that," Perry protested. "He'll
have a Plan B in place, for sure."

"Then we can have a Plan C and a Plan D." Jaki turned to
me. "Do you think Detective Bonelli can keep me safe?"

"I do—she's really sharp. And if she doesn't honestly feel she can, she'll tell you that, too."

I could see Hector relenting. "*Might* be worth a try. After all, until we catch this guy, nobody in the family will really feel safe. I'll give the detective a call."

That sounded like my cue to leave, because I knew Bonelli would not appreciate my becoming any more involved in the case than I was already. Amid thanks from Jaki and Perry, I started for the door of the suite.

Hector offered, "I'll walk you out, Ms. McGlone."

This surprised me a little, and I half-wondered if he wanted a chance to tell me to stop interfering in their affairs. But his demeanor was gentler than that.

In the foyer of the suite, he took me aside. "You're probably wondering, at this point, why I don't just insist that my daughter leave here now, for her own safety."

"I can tell you'd prefer that," I said. "I'm sure Jaki knows, too. I guess you realize she's a grown woman, and it's her career and her choice to make." I did not add that Jaki was the one making the millions and probably paying all of their salaries. That gave them reason to respect her decisions, but also to protect her from danger.

"All of those things are true," Hector agreed, "but still, I'm her father as well as her manager. If I absolutely forbade her to go onstage this weekend, she'd have to honor my wishes. After all, she needs the rest of us to make the concert happen."

I could see the truth of this. If Hector dismissed the musicians and Perry put out the word that the show would not take place, Jaki couldn't exactly perform a cappella to an empty theater.

"The trouble is," he continued, "I know how much that cat means to her. I'm sure Jaki gets lonely on the road for company besides her cousin and her papa. It's not a natural life for a beautiful young girl. It's hard for her to even make true friends, much less to meet a good, steady man. Too many people are dazzled by her fame or want to use her in some way, you know? But she trusts me, she trusts Mira . . . and she trusts that damned cat."

I nodded. "She showed me videos of her and Gordie hanging out together in the plane and the hotel room."

"That's how it is. To me, that animal was just a reminder of no-good Alec, who ran around on her, but Jaki loves Gordie. If I force her to leave here now and that *bastardo* does kill her cat, my daughter will never forgive me. So it has to be her decision."

"And if she chooses to leave, and that happens, she'll never forgive herself."

Hector bowed his head, understanding. "So please, do whatever you can to find him?"

It was nothing I hadn't committed myself to already. "I promise, Mr. Natal."

I stepped out into the hall again and wished the bodyguard a good evening.

Speaking of parents, it had been a while since I'd heard from my mom. I needed to make sure she and Harry still were okay down at the cat show.

"Looli got Best of Breed—that means she's in the running for Best in Show!" my mother gushed. She didn't gush often and had never even come close to gushing about a cat before. I could only take this as more evidence that she was, as the old song went, wild about Harry. That still felt weird to me, but I guessed if she could let me make my own decisions about my love life, I could return the favor.

At least he didn't have a passion for NASCAR races. Or even worse, hunting.

"Cassie, could you take a picture of us with her ribbons?" Harry requested. "We were going to ask our pal Steve again, but he doesn't seem to be around."

It took me a second to remember that Steve was the young staffer they'd been talking to the day before. "Sure, glad to oblige."

Harry handed me his cell phone, then he and Mom sat on metal folding chairs pulled close together and held the good-natured Sphynx between them. This time I was impressed that my mother actually laid a fond hand against the cat's hairless rib cage. I'd heard that, with enough motivation, people could be desensitized against a phobia. If Mom could overcome hers, I supposed I could try to get over my aversion to Harry.

It wasn't so much that I *disliked* Harry, I just had a really hard time imagining him in place of my father. Dad, a periodontist who painted watercolors on the side and loved jazz, had been a warm, relaxed kind of guy. He'd died of a heart attack at fifty, not due to stress but mostly because of a congenital problem. Since I was an only child, we'd been very close, and I'd considered him the fun parent, with my mother the practical taskmaster.

I'd gotten over the shock of losing Dad so young and past the deepest stage of mourning him, but he still occupied a room in my heart that no one else could fill. For three years, my mother had seemed to feel the same and showed no interest in finding another man. It had been coincidence—an effort to solve a problem for me—that resulted in her meeting and hitting it off with Harry. That was fine. I certainly didn't expect her to sit home alone with no social life. But the idea of their relationship becoming serious gave me the twitches. Like a naïve eight-year-old, I preferred to go on thinking of Harry as just my mother's "friend."

As I took a second shot of them with the cat for good measure, I saw Steve enter the benching area through a side door. I'd noticed a few other official-looking types roaming the floor today, too. Nice at least to know the hotel had made good on its promise to beef up staffing and security.

Giving Harry back his phone, I asked both of them quietly, "I don't suppose you've seen anything suspicious while you've been down here."

Mom leaned toward me and also dropped her voice. "Just one thing that I wanted to tell you about. There's been a man wandering about, ever since the first day, who doesn't seem to have any real business here. He just looks out of place, y'know?"

"In what way?" I asked.

"He's maybe in his forties," said Harry. "Tall, with a shaved head but beard stubble and glasses. Yesterday he was wearing some kind of cat-themed sweatshirt. Today he's got on a sweater and jeans, and he's carrying one of the show tote bags that you get for free when you buy a ticket."

Give him credit—Harry had a good eye for detail when it came to people as well as buildings. "None of that sounds too strange, though."

"It's more his behavior that's odd," Mom explained. "He doesn't seem to have a cat in the show, and he never sits to watch the judging for very long. He just walks slowly down all the rows of cages as if he's looking for a particular cat or type of cat. And even though he looks a little frumpy—can you say that about a man?—he's got a strong build and an athletic way of moving."

If her description made sinewy Harry jealous, he didn't show it. My mother shared my love of mystery novels, and even though she didn't consume them at the rate that I did, it seemed to be having an effect on her imagination.

I interpreted. "In other words, he doesn't seem the type to spend his evenings reading poetry with a calico purring on his lap?"

Harry nodded. "Exactly. Sometimes he just stands back against the far wall and takes pictures with his phone. As if he's trying to get the lay of the whole room."

"And he stops and talks to people at random," said Mom. "Not to us, but I heard him asking a lady down the row, who has Maine Coons, about how far she traveled to the show and whether she breeds her own cats."

"Maybe he's just doing research because he's interested in the hobby," I suggested.

"Well, that's what I supposed, too," Harry told me. "But it was just odd enough that Barbara thought we should mention it to you."

Funny to hear him refer to my mother by her first name, when talking to me. But I was hypersensitive to all of these little nuances, I supposed.

"By the way, Cassie, have you heard anything more about the concert tonight?" Mom asked. "Will there be one? Is that girl Jaki feeling any better?"

Right, she and Harry would have heard the official explanation, that Jaki was ailing. "Last I heard, she's doing better and wants to go on. Her father and Perry tried to talk her out of it, but . . ."

I cut myself off, because across the ballroom I spotted a figure who exactly fit their description. Over six feet, wearing dark-rimmed glasses, a button-down shirt with a gray cable-knit cardigan, well-worn jeans, running shoes. But the low-key outfit felt out of sync with his cue-ball head, granite jaw, five o'clock shadow, broad shoulders, and slow, almost prowling stride.

Whether he might be the high-tech wiz who'd hacked the hotel computer, I couldn't say. And Jaki's stalker? That someone his age, and with such hard-edged good looks, would be obsessed with a twenty-three-year-old pop singer seemed unlikely.

But he sure did look like he could kill a security guard with one quick punch to the throat.

Chapter 15

"I see the guy," I whispered to my mother and Harry. "I'm going to follow him."

"No!" Mom looked alarmed.

Harry's warning was less dramatic. "Just be careful, Cassie."

I stayed about ten paces behind the tall man, doubting that on the cat show's crowded floor I'd attract his attention. Still, I played it cool, because even though he moved at a relaxed pace, the tall man did seem to be scanning his surroundings.

For cops or security guards? Was he up to something he didn't want anyone to see? Poised to bolt at any minute?

He left the cat show/ballroom area and headed out to the main concourse. Fine, I was going there to meet my friends, anyway. As he strode out I noticed that, although he had a fit, V-shaped torso, his buttoned sweater bunched a little at the waist in back.

On the upper concourse, he halted and took the sort of casual stance that Harry had described. Back to the wall, he set down his tote bag, unbuttoned his cardigan, tucked his hands casually into his pockets, and just watched people pass.

I stopped nearby at a vendor's booth that sold specialized cat beds and carriers and pretended to browse while keeping an eye on him.

After a few minutes, the tall man pulled out his phone and made a call. I was much too far away, and the concourse was too noisy, for me to overhear anything. I just noticed that his eyes kept roaming in an alert way during his whole conversation. But when he lowered them to type something on the phone—E-mailing Jaki? Texting a co-conspirator? Hacking into the computer again?—I pulled my own cell from my purse and snapped a long-distance picture of him.

Finally he tucked his phone back into the rear pocket of his jeans. Doing so, he briefly pushed up the lower edge of the cardigan, and my heart froze at what I thought I saw.

Along the waist of his jeans, toward the back, the dark edge of a holster.

Yeah, that would explain the bulge under his sweater.

The mystery man picked up his colorful advertising tote bag and strolled farther down the concourse. I let him get some distance away before I found a quiet alcove and also made a call.

Angela Bonelli wasn't picking up, so I left her a message. I included my photo of the guy, described him in more detail, and told her which way he was headed.

"I don't know who he is or what he's up to," I added, "but he's got a gun."

After pocketing my phone again, I trailed the man in the sweater for a few more minutes. Finally he paused by a door that said AUTHORIZED PERSONNEL ONLY, looked both ways, tried it, and then slipped inside.

That surprised me, and I wondered how that door remained unsecured. And if it was, how did the tall guy know about it? Dion had said the hacker would be able to make changes in the computer's coding on the fly by using an iPad.

The mystery man surely had room to hide one of those in his tote bag.

I'm no fool, though, and having no idea what lay beyond that "authorized-only" door, I did not intend to follow him. I just left another quick message for Bonelli to tell her what I'd seen. I gave her the exact location where the guy had disappeared and even sent her another photo, of the door.

At that point, I felt as if I'd put in a full morning as an amateur sleuth. Technically my participation in the expo was finished, and my only reason to hang around was to see whether Jaki's concert went off as planned. In the meantime, I hoped to finally grab some lunch with Mark.

I stopped by the FOCA table to visit the dozen or so kittens and adult cats up for adoption. Becky had returned from her trip to the shelter with a stack of fresh flyers. Having finished her stint as my grooming assistant, she was helping Chris to talk up the group's services.

"No Glenda?" I asked them.

"She left early," Becky said, "but at least she asked permission first. I told Chris about your theory."

He gave me a tight smile. "It certainly would explain the way she's been skulking around since she got here. And any time someone even mentions Jaki Natal, Glenda puts her nose in the air like one of the cats just took a dump, and says spoiled celebrities like Jaki set a bad example for their young fans. But honestly, Cassie, I'm acquainted with some of the folks who are protesting, and I don't think they include any high-tech geniuses."

"There's always the chance that a person who hasn't got the skills could have recruited someone who has," I reminded him.

"Yes, we can't rule that out," Becky put in.

"Otherwise, how are things going for FOCA?" I asked them.

"Pretty darn good," Chris said. "We've had a couple of people interested in the calico kittens, and somebody else asked about their mom."

"Not too surprising." Becky arranged the new batch of flyers in a stand-up Plexiglas holder. "Calicos are usually popular, being so colorful."

Her partner held up a finger. "But one lady also asked about Jasper, the black cat. He's about eight years old, too, so I consider that a jackpot. Both black cats and older cats are usually hard to place."

"This calls for a round of . . . cold water." Becky pulled three bottles from a cooler behind the table. We all twisted them open and drank as if we'd been stranded in the desert for a month.

Once my thirst was quenched, I told them, "I got one of my cats, Cole, during a special black cat adoption event at a shelter in Morristown. It was held right before Halloween, and the organizers mentioned that black animals are at risk during that season from people who think they're evil or who want to play at being devil-worshippers."

"It's true." Becky visibly shuddered. "Personally, I think black animals are beautiful."

I glanced at their sign-up sheet, which had about a dozen names. "You have commitments from all of these people?"

"They'll have to come down to the shelter, be interviewed and sign papers," said Chris. "We just have to hope they stay enthusiastic and don't have second thoughts after they get home."

Closing the lid of the cooler, while dodging my eyes, Becky asked, "I guess you're going to the concert tonight?"

"I guess. Don't know whether it's a kind of payment for

services rendered, or if I'll still be in a semiofficial capacity." I sensed her disappointment. "Just between you and me, with it being held Sunday instead of Saturday, there could be some seats available."

She shrugged. "They'd probably still want three hundred dollars for them. At those prices, I don't think our volunteer credentials will be enough to get us in."

"I can ask Perry about it," I offered. "I can't promise anything, though. If they're still sold out . . ."

Becky lit up. "Oh, I understand, absolutely. But would you try?"

"I will, as long as he's not too harried. Things in the Jaki Natal camp are a little nuts right now."

Chris threw his partner a sideways look. "Yeah, Becky, and if we do get in, we might be sorry. There could be another blackout . . . or worse."

"Don't even think it!" I warned him. "Anyway, I'm going to check in with Mark. He and Dave should be all finished by now."

"Give them our regards." Becky sounded much cheerier than a moment ago.

Continuing down the concourse, I wondered if it would be wise for me to even ask about getting the two FOCA volunteers into the evening's concert. At the very least, Perry and the others might feel I was taking advantage of my access to Jaki. At worst, something bad *could* happen during her performance, and instead of enjoying a fun evening Becky might witness something violent and traumatic.

I was so preoccupied as I hurried through the crowd that I didn't even notice Dria approaching from the opposite direction until she deliberately slammed into my shoulder. The rangy blonde nearly knocked me off my feet.

"Hey, sister," she snarled at me, "what're you tryin' to pull? Tryin' to get me and my friends in trouble?"

Since she was almost a head taller than me—and I'm no shrimp—I thought it best to pretend ignorance. "Ow! What're you talking about?"

"Damn, a person tries to have a friendly conversation, about *cats,* for God's sake. Next thing she knows, the cops are asking her all kinds of personal questions! It had to be you who tipped them off. I didn't talk to anybody else about that."

I hoped I could keep up the innocent act a little longer. "About what?"

"That Lexi likes Scottish Fold cats. That she wanted to get one. So what the hell's going on? Is one missing? Like, from the cat show?"

"Something like that." I figured I'd better tell a harmless version of the truth. "And because I know cats, the police asked me to keep a look out for anything suspicious."

"Me and my friends are *suspicious*? You gotta be kidding." Dria still vibrated with outrage. "They questioned Lexi, too. Such a farce! Her folks could afford to buy her a hundred of those cats. Why the hell would she steal one?"

Dria fisted her hands, and I prepared to duck if she took a swing at me. "I'm sorry. I was just doing what I'd been asked to do. I'm sure it must have embarrassed her."

"Effin' right, it did. You'll be lucky if she doesn't sue you."

I couldn't take that too seriously. "For giving the police information that they requested?"

Even Dria seemed to realize that wouldn't wash. She unclenched her fists, probably at the reminder that I had contacts with the cops and could accuse her of assault. Still, she fired off one last threat. "Maybe we'll just tell everybody that you suck, that your shop sucks. That you abuse the cats and . . . and give them bad haircuts."

I stifled the urge to laugh at her last insult, figuring then she really would hit me. She'd started to retreat, so I just took the opportunity to continue on my way at a brisk pace. "Please give Lexi my apologies, and have a nice day."

Whew! Dria had really bought into the image of the tough-as-nails Jersey girl, it seemed, and was doing her best to live up to it.

She didn't follow me, though, and when I finally reached the veterinary clinic's booth, I exhaled with a sense of safety. Mark and Dave had wrapped up their last demo of the day and were packing up. I gladly pitched in to help them collapse the examining table, fold up their signs, and roll up their banner. The hotel had provided a standard six-foot table for promotional materials, so Mark left behind brochures about the clinic and various aspects of cat care.

"Pizza?" He pointed down the concourse to our left. "There's a really good place down thataway."

"Lead on," I said. "Does Dave want to join us?"

We glanced back, but the vet tech already was headed in the opposite direction, smiling and laughing with another cute guy of about the same age.

Mark shrugged. "He's probably got plans with Carlo. Guess it's just you and me."

I slipped my arm through his. "I'll never complain about that. Anyway, I've got some news that probably should stay just between the two of us."

"Oh?"

We shared a Neapolitan pizza. Not at all bad for something from a concession, probably because it was operated by one of our favorite Chadwick restaurants, Slice of Heaven. Meanwhile, I summed up for Mark the key points of my morning: Jaki refused to leave the hotel without knowing her cat was safe and had decided to perform as a way of flushing out her stalker. I also told him about Dria's outrage over the fact that I'd caused the Chadwick cops to target her and her friends.

Mark asked if I'd heard anything about the seedy-looking guy whom he had seen arrested. I told him the man's name was Mason Reilly and he was an aspiring songwriter; the cops were still questioning him but didn't think he'd stolen the cat or attacked the guard.

"So the real bad guy probably is still out there." He looked grim. "If Jaki got a box with the cat's collar and tag, how does she even know if Gordie's still alive? She said he had health problems. . . ."

I hadn't considered that, maybe because I knew Jaki wouldn't want to consider it. "She doesn't, I suppose. Guess she should ask to see a live video for proof. That's something you'd do if it were a human hostage situation."

"Maybe they should start treating it like one." Mark pondered a moment longer. "Jaki could tell the cat-napper about Gordie's health issues and ask if she could drop off his medicine and prescription food at some prearranged spot. After all, this creep probably doesn't want the cat to die, at least not before he's met with Jaki. He'd lose his only bargaining chip."

"Not a bad idea. And arranging a drop-off might give the cops an extra chance to nab the guy before her concert. At this point, they might even know who to look for."

After mulling whether or not to do so, I finally told Mark about the man my mother and Harry considered suspicious, and how I'd watched him for a while and then passed the information on to Bonelli.

The last part upset him, as I'd been afraid it would. "You actually tailed that character? God, Cassie, what'm I gonna do with you?"

I figured this was not the moment to make any jokey, off-color suggestions. "I stayed well off his radar. I guarantee, he never noticed me."

"You can't be sure of that. This stalker sounds very slimy. He's sending Jaki e-mails and gifts that can't be traced and he seems to know her every move. If he decides now that *you're* a threat . . ." Mark rumpled his short, dark hair with one hand. "Just keep in mind, you don't travel with bodyguards!"

"I handed the ball off to Bonelli, as any private citizen should. I did brainstorm with Jaki and her father about how the stalker might be someone out of her past, though they probably would have figured that out eventually on their own. As far as I can see, I've done all I could to help. From now on, I sit back and let the cops take over."

"Great resolution," he told me, with just a hint of sarcasm. "Please stick to it!"

He had just finished lecturing me when my phone rang and I saw Bonelli's number. As soon as I answered, her emphatic alto voice scolded me, "Cassie, never, *ever* tail a possible suspect on your own again!"

"Hey, how was I to know he was even a potential suspect unless I watched him for a while? I didn't want to sic your guys on a perfectly innocent, cat-loving citizen. So, did you find him?"

"We found him. Right in that restricted area you saw him enter." A beat of silence. "Dead."

"What?"

"He'd been shot. Probably with his own gun, because you were right, he was wearing a holster. The killer took the gun, I guess, so now he won't have to fall back on his martial arts skills anymore."

Bonelli's sarcasm could beat Mark's any day. "Sounds like you don't think this guy was the stalker, either."

"He had a PI license from California, and his phone contacts included Alec MacMasters. We're trying to reach the TV star himself now."

My head spun. Well, at least it didn't sound as if Alec had hired the guy to steal Jaki's cat. That would have been my suspicion if the PI himself hadn't been shot.

Suddenly, I began to worry about my mom, too. I'd thought she was pretty safe down there among the cat show crowd. But the dead guy *had* been chatting with the lady down the row from them, just yesterday. That was too close for comfort.

Angela signed off then to attend to urgent matters, and I relayed her news to Mark.

"Unbelievable!" he said. "What could possibly be worth all this bloodshed? It's not as if Gordie's worth a trillion dollars, even in ransom money."

"Besides, the stalker told Jaki he's not interested in her money," I pointed out.

"He can't possibly expect that she's going to fall in love with him after he's put her and her family through this hell," Mark said. "Either there's some hidden payoff for him, in terms of money or his career . . ."

"Or he's nuts," I finished quietly. "I really think that's the only explanation. A sane person would know this approach isn't going to get him what he wants, but a deluded person might not."

"And yet he's been able to keep one step ahead of everybody who's been chasing him."

"An organized sociopath." I remembered the terminology from my research. "He's convinced that Jaki is the answer to everything that's wrong with his life, and nothing's going to stand in his way. The rest of us are all just obstacles to be removed if we cause him too much trouble, and by any means necessary. He feels no shame, no embarrassment, no remorse."

Mark stared at me. "I know Bonelli has teased you about joining the Chadwick PD, but you sound more like you're training for the FBI."

I winked. "Bet you thought those psych books in my apartment were just to class up the décor."

"I just hope that, if you admit this guy could be crazy, you'll stay as far out of his orbit as possible from now on. I'm serious, Cassie. He sounds more dangerous than anyone you've ever dealt with before. Most of the others had something to lose, so they couldn't afford to be too reckless. This guy could be living in a fantasy world where he thinks he's invincible."

I couldn't argue—as usual, Mark was making perfect sense. "I don't plan to take any more chances. As I said, from now on it's up to Bonelli, her officers, and the convention security to keep Jaki safe. I'm backing away." I glanced at my watch; it was after one. "Right now, I'm literally fleeing the scene. Since I don't need the van anymore, I think I'll drive it back to the shop and pick up my CR-V."

"You're coming back here?" He raised one eyebrow. "I thought you were staying far away."

"Mark, I have to at least see if Jaki performs tonight and whether they flush out the killer. Besides, I might get a free pass into a show that's costing other folks three hundred dollars a ticket. Wanna be my date?"

He frowned crookedly. "I think I'd better, if only to make sure you don't take any more crazy risks."

Since he and Dave still had to pack their equipment into a pet ambulance and run it back to the clinic, we agreed to meet back at The Grove around six.

A slightly melancholy mood had descended by now upon

the wide concourse as the vendors dismantled their booths and packed up their cat-themed T-shirts, baseball caps, artworks, and home accessories. Back into crates went any unsold cat trees, beds, toys, fancy carriers, litter boxes, and cage drapery. I even spotted one of the "mascots" strolling off, still wearing most of her tuxedo-cat costume but carrying the head and paws. I guessed that they might hamper her driving home, and in case of an accident she probably didn't want to have to explain her getup to a traffic cop.

Though I still felt sorry for Jaki and concerned about the fate of Gordie, I made my way back to my gaudy grooming van with a little more spring in my stride. I *had* done everything possible to help, and to go any further might hamper Bonelli's official investigation. She, like Mark, had told me in the strongest terms to stay out of trouble, and from here on that was what I intended to do. No matter what happened tonight, with all the security presence, Jaki ought to remain safe. Hector would never allow her to place herself in danger.

If something bad happens to Gordie, it will be in spite of my best efforts. At least I think I got Bonelli and the others to take his peril seriously. They believe now that it's important to keep him alive, if only as a bargaining chip that could be crucial to Jaki's safety.

Closer to the van, I spotted a folded sheet of white paper tucked under one windshield wiper. Jeez, I knew my time volunteering at the expo was technically over, but was security nagging me already to vacate the plaza? Well, with all the craziness going on, anything was possible.

I yanked the paper free and unfolded it.

STICK TO GROOMING CATS AND STOP
PLAYING COP.
IT BACKFIRED FOR TWO PEOPLE ALREADY.
THINK YOU GOT NINE LIVES?

THERE'S MORE THAN ONE WAY TO SKIN A CAT.
WHAT HURTS MORE THAN LOSING SOMEONE
YOU CARE ABOUT?
A PET.
A LOVER.
A PARENT.

Chapter 16

The garlicky taste of the pizza rose again in my throat, and for a second I thought I'd vomit right there on the sidewalk. I hung onto the van's rearview mirror until the plaza and its pedestrians stopped whirling around me. I wanted to crush the hateful note or tear it to smithereens.

But no, that wouldn't be smart.

I glanced up. There didn't seem to be any security cameras pointing in the direction of this plaza. With so many strangers milling around out here, there would be no point in asking if anyone noticed someone leaving a note on my windshield any time within that past two hours. But in at least one way, luck was on my side; Bonelli stood conferring with a couple of her officers about ten yards away. I hurried over.

I waited at a polite distance for her to finish her conversation, but when she noticed me, she seemed to cut it short. Maybe my wide-eyed pallor caught her attention.

"Yes, Cassie?"

"I just found this on the windshield of my van." I passed her the sheet of paper.

She scanned it and cursed under her breath.

"Looks like it came off a standard printer," I commented. "I don't know if it would be any good for fingerprints."

"Unfortunately, this bastard hasn't left prints on anything he's handled so far," she said. "But we'll check it. Are you going home now?"

I nodded. It wasn't a lie.

"Good. Where's your mother and Harry?"

"Still down at the cat show. Looli's got a shot at Best in Show."

Bonelli wrinkled her nose, as if she had no idea who Looli was and doubted the prize was worth the two of them risking their lives. "Tell them to leave as soon as the show's over and not to take any chances in the meantime."

"Listen," I told her, "Mark and I had one more idea. Could Jaki reply to one of the stalker's e-mails, and tell him that Gordie has a health problem and needs special food and medicine? If she could set up a time and place for the guy to pick them up, it might give you a chance to nab him."

The detective sounded skeptical. "Possibly . . . if the cat's even still alive at this point."

Her statement chilled my blood. If anything had happened to Gordie, the stalker might well go on pretending he was still fine. "Jaki could ask to see a video, for proof. That might even give you a hint as to where he's hiding out. And meanwhile, you'd be buying time."

"Could be worth a try," Bonelli said. "I'll mention it to Jaki, though we don't have much time left before her show."

We sat on the plaza's brick retaining wall to talk more confidentially. "Did you ever make contact with Alec MacMasters?" I asked.

"We did. He admitted hiring the PI. Said he figured we'd be concentrating on the dead guard, and he hoped in the meantime his man could find Gordie. He knew how upset Jaki was about the cat—guess he really does still care about her. He told the detective not to get in the way of the cops, just look for the cat. Guess that was enough, though, for our stalker to see him as a threat."

Maybe he was getting too close, I thought. *Without Gordie, the stalker has no leverage.*

I thought aloud. "How was that PI able to get into that restricted area? And were there any security cameras inside that might have recorded what happened?"

"Both the door lock and the nearest camera had been disabled. Electronically, so the tampering wouldn't have been obvious to anybody passing through."

"Yikes." I sagged back against the retaining wall. "This guy thinks of everything."

"He does," Bonelli agreed. "And unfortunately, now he's got a gun, which ups the stakes. Hector Natal and I have been trying for the past hour to talk Jaki out of performing tonight. If this guy happens to be a good shot, he could pick her off from anywhere."

"But he doesn't want to kill her," I argued. "Not as long as he still has any hope of meeting her. Don't you see? He thinks this will be the high point of his life, that she'll realize they're soul mates and it will all have been worth it."

Not for the first time, Bonelli eyed me suspiciously. "You sound like you know this creep."

"I absolutely don't, but he fits a certain profile all the way down the line. Well, except in one way—he doesn't sound like the typical freewheeling coder. But I'm sure there are exceptions to every rule."

"Yeah, don't get too cocky. You *don't* know what this guy is capable of, and neither do we. We've got to be prepared for anything, especially if our prima donna insists on giving that concert tonight." The detective laid a firm hand on my shoulder.

I shook my head, feeling helpless. "I was going home to change, but how can I possibly leave here when my mother could be in danger?"

The detective frowned in sympathy and pulled out her radio. "I'll send one of my guys down right now to keep an eye on her. How can he find her?"

By now I knew the number of Looli's booth, and although Bonelli had met my mother, I gave her a full description of both Mom and Harry. She got one of her officers on the radio and passed all of this information on to him.

"He'll stick close to them for the rest of the show," she promised me, after signing off. "Now you should take your van, go home, and lay low until all of this is over!"

Again, I only nodded. No sense making any promises I might have to break. Especially not to the police.

I did drive home, feeling reasonably sure that, other than brown water in my pipes, I wouldn't find any nasty surprises there. Unless the killer cat thief had an accomplice, I doubted that he would go out of his way to harass me when the chief object of his obsession remained holed up at the Bradburne Hotel. To keep track of her every move and leave her notes, he couldn't leave the premises for very long.

Did he have a room in the hotel? Live nearby? Or maybe he'd found a secret hiding place of some kind. I thought of the door that I'd seen the PI enter. It sounded as if his body had been discovered somewhere on the other side. How far had the cops searched after finding him? Maybe not quite far enough to find the killer's lair. . . .

In spite of Bonelli's warning, I had to go back to the Bradburne tonight. First, I needed to be sure my mother was safe, and second, I had to find out if Jaki's plan worked and her stalker finally got caught. So I parked my van on the street. At least the road crew had not left anything too obstructive in

front of my shop, though a ditch now ran along the curb and
I'd still have to drive over a steel plate to get into my rear lot.

As I unlocked the shop and turned on the lights, I told myself that I needed to get my mind off the killer-cat-thief case,
which really wasn't mine to solve. Right now I had to tend to
four boarders and my own three cats. I'd told Mark I would
meet him at The Grove at six, and I intended to keep that
date.

I had gotten away from setting my alarm system every time
I left the shop, but I sure as hell would do that tonight.

I'd just scooped out the last boarder's litter pan when my
cell phone rang. I stuck the pan back into the cat's condo,
peeled off my vinyl work gloves, and answered the call.

Perry, sounding apologetic. "Cassie, I hate to bother you
again. Are you still at the hotel?"

"I came home to take care of a few things, but I was planning to go back tonight. Why?"

"Jaki's going to have a brief rehearsal for her show at five,
and before that she wants to talk to you again. You put an idea
in her head today, when you asked about people from her past
who might still have issues with her. She and Mira have been
on the phone since then with her mother and her brother, and
I guess they want to run a few things by you."

I glanced at my watch. I'd have to give my cats very slap-
dash attention if I was going to get back out to the hotel by
five. "Can't they brainstorm with Bonelli?"

"Yeah, I asked that, too. But the detective's off running
down some leads of her own. Anyway, you know how Jaki
is—she wants to bat around ideas with somebody who's sim-
patico before she takes anything to the cops."

I sighed. I could have used a shower before dinner, but
right now my pipes offered only water that might have come
from the muddy Mississippi, and I hated to impose on Dawn

twice in one day. Maybe just a change of clothes and a spritz of cologne would be enough. "Yeah, I can do that. When does she want to see me?"

"Can you meet us in the convention center theater, about four-thirty? Know where that is?"

"I think so. Big double doors, halfway down the concourse from the hotel?"

"That's it. There'll be a guard at the door, but he'll have your name." Perry paused again. "Cassie, I realize this is asking a lot. None of this is your affair, and if you told me to forget it, I would completely understand. But Jaki trusts you. She seems to think you're the only one besides her who cares what happens to Gordie."

"It's okay," I told him. "How are you holding up? You sound beat."

A strained chuckle. "I'll survive, but it's been a rough afternoon for everybody. I finally got MacMasters on the phone this afternoon, and he is one unhappy spaceman."

"Over what happened to his private eye?"

"Can't really blame the guy. He hears Jaki's cat was stolen, so he hires a PI to look for it. Trying to do this hush-hush, so she won't blow up at him for interfering. But of course Alec didn't know about the dead security guard. So he's outraged that his guy walked into a much more dangerous situation than he was prepared for, and got killed, too. Now Alec is joining the chorus of people trying to persuade Jaki to get out of Dodge while she's still in one piece. But our darling diva won't budge."

Sounded like chaos, and I almost dreaded stepping back into the midst of it. "She's a very strong-willed lady and very loyal to her pet. I can't promise, Perry, that even I can change her mind."

"That's all right, Cassie. I don't expect miracles. Just do what you can, okay?"

"I will," I promised him. "See you at four-thirty."

I was gauging how much time I had to get ready for the evening, and how best to manage it, when I heard a knock on my glass front door. I'd locked it behind me and kept the sign turned to CLOSED—plus it was Sunday—so I doubted that it would be a customer.

Bonelli? Dawn?

I crossed the playroom and, through the screened wall, glimpsed a chubby apparition with a halo of pink hair. Adele Kryznansky refused to gray gracefully, which was fine, but whatever dye she used didn't penetrate very well, so it came out a sickly salmon. I briefly hoped that the semitransparent walls of the playroom might have been enough to keep her from spotting me, but when she waved through the front window, I knew I wouldn't get that kind of a break.

Oh, well, my neighbor's eagle eyes had helped me monitor suspicious activity around my shop on more than one occasion, so I guess I owed her a few minutes of my time—whatever it was that she wanted.

I unlocked the door, and she toddled briskly in without waiting for an invitation. I guess she'd been chilly out there in her pilling wrap cardigan, gray sweatpants, and fluffy bedroom slippers. Close up, I smelled a taint of cigarettes on her breath. I subtly retreated behind the sales counter.

"Sorry to bother you, Cassie," she said, at least. "I saw your van was back, and I figured you might not be busy on a Sunday afternoon."

"Actually," I said, "I've got to go out again at four. I need to clean up a little, and I'm wondering how I'm going to do it, with our water issue."

"Isn't it *awful*?" Adele squinted behind her gold-rimmed glasses, as if in real pain, and her thin lips scowled. "I don't know how much more of this they expect us to take! I've had a migraine almost continuously since they started. First it was the jackhammers, not just the noise but those damned *vibrations*. And now they're dropping those big chunks of concrete into the Dumpster. . . . I jump out of my skin at every bang!"

"Tell me about it. I've got a shop full of other people's cats—luckily, only four right now—but it's making them restless and off their feed. That isn't going to please my customers."

Uninvited, she hopped onto one of the stools in front of my sales counter. Since Adele is barely five feet tall, it took quite a spring on her part. "The folks downstairs from me in the insurance office are at their wits' end. Some days their clients can't get into their parking lot, or else can't get out of it, or have to park way down the street. And when they do get inside the office, I guess they can't have a sensible business discussion with all of the noise going on."

"Yes, I'm sure it's difficult for them, too." I stole a glance at my wall clock, aware of the minutes ticking by.

"I phoned you yesterday, but you were out in the van, I guess. Your assistant took a message, though. Sarah, isn't she? Lovely woman! Anyhow, I know you're friendly with the police, with the things that've gone on since you opened your business. Isn't there something you can do about this, someone you can talk to—?"

"I doubt the police can help, Mrs. Kryznansky. Nobody's doing anything illegal. You'd probably have to contact the town hall, maybe Public Works."

"I tried that, but they just brushed me off. The fella I spoke to was very rude and said if they didn't take care of this now, soon we'd have the water lines failing all over town, so I'd just have to put up with a little inconvenience. I'd call this brown water more than a little inconvenience!"

Adele looked like she was settling in for a nice, long bitching session, which made me shift nervously on my feet. I had visions of Mom and Harry at the cat show, unaware of the danger, probably packing up by now to leave. Maybe Bonelli's guard would look away, for just a second. . . .

"Mrs. Kryznansky, I don't mean to be abrupt. But I really need to go upstairs now and get changed as best I can. I'm involved in that weekend cat expo out at the Bradburne, and the big windup is tonight."

"Oh, I'm sorry." The little woman slid off her stool, a move in the right direction, but her tone was a bit sulky. "I guess I'm holding you up."

"Well, it's not going to be easy for me to get ready under the circumstances, but I have to try."

This wrested a smile from Adele and she jerked her head toward my front window. "That's ironic, huh? Too bad you can't groom yourself as easy as you groom those cats! Anyway, thanks for listening to my gripes, and have a nice evening."

Through the front window, I watched her return next door—partly to make sure she kept going. After that, my gaze came to rest on the oversized cartoon of the preening cat on the side of my van, and I realized Adele had given me the answer to my dilemma.

That monster still has almost a full tank of clean water that won't be needed any time soon. It also has a deep sink, sponges, soap, and even a hair dryer!

I fed all the cats, downstairs and up. Then I grabbed some black pants, a silky top suitable for the concert, low-heeled black shoes, and my travel bag of toiletries and makeup.

I had to drape the van's windows to wash up, and I felt a little like Superman changing in a phone booth. But twenty minutes later I stepped out of the grooming van and slipped behind the wheel of my CR-V—clean, presentable, and ready for whatever the evening might bring.

Or so I thought.

Chapter 17

At the theater door, my volunteer credentials plus my name got me past the sturdy female security guard, who looked like she could hold her own even against a martial arts expert. I found myself studying her ID tag up close; something about it surprised me, though I couldn't quite say why. Maybe because it was laminated, while my temporary tag was a card that slipped into a plastic holder. She must have been on the permanent staff at the convention center.

I walked down the long aisle of raked, empty seats to the good-sized stage. An electronic keyboard, a set of drums, and some amps already stood in place, so I guessed that Bonelli still had not persuaded Jaki to cancel. The star stood among the instruments, conferring with her father and a mature, sharp-nosed woman I hadn't seen before; meanwhile, Perry huddled with Rose, the publicist, at stage left. He broke off to welcome me and gestured for me to come up and join them.

"You look nice, Cassie," he told me.

"Thanks." I felt tickled by the compliment, and wondered what he'd say if I admitted how I'd managed to pull myself together.

"Jaki's working out the songs for tonight with our stage manager," Perry explained. "She'll just be a minute. Can I get you something in the meantime? Water?"

"No, thanks." I turned to Rose, who tonight wore a chic plum-colored skirt suit with low black pumps, an outfit that still would let her dash around the hotel and convention center as necessary. Her makeup also struck the same professional note, flattering but understated. Nevertheless, her dark eyes had taken on the same expression of near panic that I'd noticed in Perry's. "This situation must be so hard for both of you."

"It's personal for me," Rose admitted. "I've worked with Jaki for ten years. Oh, she has her temperamental moments, like most celebrities—and most young people. But overall, she's a terrific talent and a real trouper. Loves performing, doesn't make a lot of crazy demands. But this business with her cat really has sent her around the bend."

I nodded. "I think the worst part for her is not knowing if Gordie is okay. She said yesterday that if Alec had taken him, at least she'd feel the cat was safe. This jerk is hinting that if Jaki doesn't cooperate, Gordie could pay the price. Has she heard anything more so far? About when this guy wants to meet with her, and where?"

Perry shook his head. "Not that I know of. I really hope she's not keeping any secrets from us . . . or from the cops."

By then, Jaki had noticed my presence and crossed the stage to join us. "Cassie, thanks so much for coming . . . again. I keep imposing on you and dragging you back into this mess."

"It's okay." I resolved not to tell her about the threatening note that I'd gotten. Why add to her worries? "What did you want to talk to me about?"

"Excuse us," she told Rose and Perry, and led me to the lip

of the stage. We both sat with our legs dangling over the empty orchestra pit, out of earshot from the others.

"I tried out the approach you suggested to Bonelli," Jaki said. "First I asked LBH if I could see a video, just to be reassured that Gordie was okay. He or she got pissy about that and wrote back, *It sounds like you don't trust me.* So I explained I was only worried because Gordie needed special food and medicine to stay healthy. I offered to have someone leave those things at whatever place LBH suggested, to be picked up."

She seemed to be handling this well, I thought. "And?"

"LBH replied that Gordie is fine for now, and when I come to our meeting place after the show, I can bring along anything he might need. So he or she isn't falling for it, and maybe suspects that we're planning to set a trap."

I figured that ruse had been a long shot, anyway. "He might be desperate, but he's also smart."

"Or she," Jaki reminded me.

I'd backed off my suspicions about Grumpy Glenda and the animal-rights protestors, though. I didn't think any of them would threaten Gordie or risk his health, much less kill a second person and steal his gun. This had to be someone who had a personal issue with Jaki . . . and was more than a little deranged.

"What you asked me earlier," she continued, "made me wonder about people in my past who might have some kind of grudge against me. I was on speakerphone for an hour this afternoon, brainstorming with Mira, my mom, and my sister Carmel, asking them if they could remember anyone like that. Turns out, they thought of a few. Some I knew about, but others I had totally forgotten until Mom or Carmel reminded me."

"Any that stood out?" I asked.

"Well, when I was thirteen, I got the role of Belle in my high school production of *Beauty and the Beast*. I beat out this redheaded girl, Alexis. She was a year older and had played all the starring roles until I came along. For that production, she only got the part of Babette—that's a maid who turns into a singing, dancing feather duster—which really ticked her off. In any scenes we had together, she'd play little tricks to upstage or distract me. I mostly just rolled with it. But Carmel said today that Alexis used to badmouth me all the time behind my back, saying I was 'too ethnic' for the part. She even suggested I'd 'done some favors' for the director, who was a married, middle-aged guy, to get the role. I didn't even know about all this at the time, and Carmel never told me because she didn't want to upset me."

Interesting, I thought. "Does this Alexis still live around here?"

"I have no idea, and neither does Carmel. Neither of us can even remember her last name. Why?"

"Just that one of the four girls I mentioned to you, the Jakettes, was called Lexi. Becky and I saw her with the group on Friday, but never again. Lexi said she was hoping to get a Scottish Fold cat and had 'a plan.' I think the cops already questioned two of the girls, but Lexi wasn't with them, and they haven't been able to track her down."

Jaki looked keen. "Do you know if she had red hair? Not that it means much these days, the way people change their hair color, but . . ."

I remembered that I actually had photographed the Jakettes, and pulled out my phone. "I had a sense that they all were younger than you—late teens, I mean—but I could have been wrong about that." I scrolled back to the shot of the four young women in their J-A-K-I shirts. I had taken it from the van, shooting into the sun, so their faces were shadowed. Showing it to Jaki, I said, "The taller blonde is Dria, and the brunette is Ashley. . . . I forget which one was Lexi, but there *is* a redhead in the bunch. Look at all familiar?"

Jaki squinted hard at the small screen and finally shook her head. "Sorry. Like you said, they're kind of far away, and their faces are a little too dark."

Mira had emerged from the wings, and at that point she joined us in our speculations. "Remember, there's always Larry Vanderveer. I didn't have any luck tracking him down, but maybe the cops would."

Jaki made a face. "Even though I didn't like the guy, I'd feel kind of bad to sic the police on him for no real reason. There's no evidence that he's involved. And honestly, I don't think all this sneaky business of sending me notes and gifts would be Larry's style at all. He was more of an in-your-face bully."

I wondered about that. My ex-boyfriend, Andy, had been hot-tempered and physically abusive to me in person. But after I'd moved to Chadwick to get away from him, he'd sent me plaintive and rather self-pitying notes and e-mails trying to persuade me to get back together. I didn't mention this to Jaki, not wanting to sound like a know-it-all on the subject of stalkers, but privately I reflected that her Larry could have a similar Jekyll/Hyde personality.

Somebody that full of himself didn't sound like he'd have gone on carrying a torch, for years, over one girl who'd turned him down in high school. You never could tell, though. Lately, Larry would have heard Jaki on the radio and seen her on TV, maybe in concert. He could have become obsessed with "the one that got away," or just jealous of her success. But if Vanderveer no longer lived around Chadwick and didn't have much of an online presence, he could be hard even for the cops to track down.

Perry, frowning, dropped by to interrupt us. "Jaki, I just got a call from the front desk. Alec is here."

It took her a second to register this. "Alec . . . *MacMasters*? What do you mean, *here*?"

"He just checked in to the hotel."

Her jaw dropped in outrage, and her cheeks flushed. "Perfect—we were just talking about big egos! I can't believe it. He's going to make this all about him, right? That grandstanding . . ."

"Couldn't agree more," said Bonelli, showing up behind Perry. "Now I've got two major celebrities to protect."

"I'm so sorry," Jaki told her. "I never dreamed he'd do anything like this."

With a thin smile, Perry observed, "Guess he must really love . . . that cat."

Jaki's phone sounded—I recognized a couple of bouncy bars from her hip-hop number "Bits and Pieces." She pulled it out, faced away from us, and, for a couple of minutes, stared at the screen in silence.

"Something wrong?" I asked.

"Another e-mail. From him."

"Alec?" Mira asked, but Jaki shook her head and passed the phone to Bonelli. When the detective muttered a bad word, I knew the stalker had made contact again. I asked Jaki about the message.

"Sounds like he's going to give me the directions to our meeting place in stages. He says right after my show ends, he'll send me to the first location. Once I arrive there, I'll find a note that will lead me a little farther, and so on. I guess he wants to make sure I'm not followed, and that no one can get there before I do and bust him. Oh, and he said after I get the first message, I have to leave my cell phone behind."

"So you can't call for help, and so we won't be able to trace you that way." The grim-faced detective jotted a few notes and returned the celebrity's phone to her. "Don't worry, we'll give you a small tracking device to wear. If it even gets that far. I'm still hoping to smoke this guy out before you even leave the stage."

The young singer squared her shoulders and put on a brave face. "I have confidence in you."

Bonelli, in her navy pantsuit again tonight, squatted next to where Jaki sat, still on the edge of the stage. "I'm asking you one more time—cancel this concert. We still have no idea who's stalking you, but he or she now has a Smith & Wesson semiautomatic. Whether or not this person knows how to use it, we need to be prepared for the worst. We can do our best to keep you safe, but if this nutcase smells a trap or panics for any other reason, you'll be up there under the spotlight for him to get a clear shot. You're only twenty-three, kid. Do you really want to risk that?"

Her words obviously impacted Jaki, who drew a deep breath and tilted her face to the ceiling as if asking for divine guidance. She seemed to seriously consider Bonelli's advice, but her answer remained the same. "If I worried about every threat I get from a crank, I'd never go onstage at all. I still think if I play along with him, I'll be safe . . . at least until after the show. And meanwhile, he might tip his hand and give you a chance to bring him down. Right?"

"I think you watch too many crime shows on TV," the detective complained. "Got that in common with your new friend Cassie." She straightened. "Okay, if you're on in two hours, we'll do our best to track down this bozo before then. Meanwhile, you'd better respond to his message."

"Oh, God." Jaki squeezed her eyes shut, as if the prospect frightened and revolted her. "What the heck do I say?"

Mira silently passed an arm around her cousin's shoulders in support.

"Say you're looking forward to meeting him," I advised. A sharp glance from Bonelli told me I'd overstepped. "Sorry."

"I *was* about to recommend almost the same thing," the detective told Jaki. "You might even act excited that he's making it all so mysterious, and tell him you can't wait to find out who your 'secret admirer' really is."

Obviously, Bonelli didn't need any help from me in psyching out the stalker. She'd probably had actual training in profiling criminals.

Jaki typed several lines, let the detective read over her shoulder to approve them, and hit send. Then she let out a long breath as if she'd just jumped off the edge of a high cliff. It was a good thing, I thought, that she had acting talent and experience. She'd need them to keep up this façade, especially if she ended up talking to the creep face-to-face.

Mira disappeared into the wings and returned with a fresh bottle of water for her cousin. Bonelli had just stepped away to answer a question from one of her officers when my phone rang. I didn't like the timing and worried that the stalker had somehow gotten my number, too.

The sight of Mom's name on my screen sparked a different set of worries, but she sounded carefree, almost bubbly. "Looli didn't get Best in Show, but she got third! Can you imagine, with so many entries? Harry is over the moon."

"Wow, congratulations, guys! Couldn't be happier for you. We all knew Looli was a champ." After a pause, I added, "You really seemed to enjoy yourself this weekend, too."

"I did, isn't it funny? I'm getting over my lifelong fear of cats," she said.

"Yes, Harry certainly has helped you on that score."

Mom picked up on the arch tone of my voice. "Cassie, I know you still feel uncomfortable around him, probably because he gave you so much trouble a few months back about Looli's mystery rash. But even though Harry can be a little high-strung at times, he really is a nice man."

"I'm starting to see that, Mom. And the important thing is that you like him."

"I do. I guess because he's a gentleman. He's intelligent and well-read, he has an interesting job along with some hobbies, and he's nice-looking. You don't know how rare it is to find all of those qualities in a single man of my age! And maybe because of everything he went through with his ex-wife, he really seems to appreciate *me*."

That last comment endeared Harry to me more than any of his other traits. "Then he's got good taste, too. I'm glad he makes you happy." I noticed a policeman stride past with a walkie-talkie, and suddenly remembered the stalker's not-so-veiled threat against my "parent." "So, is the cat show over?" I asked Mom. "Are you guys leaving now?"

"Pretty soon. We'll stop in at the restaurant and have a nice dinner to celebrate. Can you join us?"

I hesitated. "I may wait. . . . Mark said something about getting together for dinner later." I lowered my voice, out of paranoia that the stalker might somehow be within earshot. "Listen, Mom, it really would be best if you didn't hang around here too long tonight. There's a lot of crazy stuff going on."

Her tone grew hushed, also. "Is there? I thought I was seeing more security around. One policewoman has been hanging out at the end of our aisle for the last fifteen minutes, which seems kind of strange. Does she expect people to riot if their cats don't get the top prizes?"

I had to smile at the image, but the reality was serious. Should I tell Mom the truth—that the athletically built man she'd pointed out to me had been murdered with his own gun by someone who was still at large? That someone, probably the same person, had left a note on my windshield that all but threatened *her* life? My mother has a tendency to be nervous under the best of circumstances, so I couldn't see that scaring the wits out of her would do any good. Especially when she was being subtly guarded and was about to leave the hotel, anyway.

Instead I told her, "I think it's because Alec MacMasters, Jaki's ex-boyfriend, showed up here this afternoon."

"Alec who?"

Okay, Mom's age group wasn't exactly the target audience for a show like *Galaxy Wars*. "He's a big star on a hot new TV series. He's probably just here to offer her moral support over her missing cat, but it was really unexpected, which just makes it harder for the hotel to cope. So really, you two . . . sorry, you three . . . should start for home as soon as you can."

"Well, I'll tell Harry, though I'm sure he'll at least want to get something to eat first. Are *you* going to be all right?"

"Yeah, I'll wait until things settle down before I leave. And I'll probably meet up with Mark."

"Okay, dear. If I don't see you before we go, talk to you to-morrow."

"Love you. Be careful."

When I signed off, I found Jaki eyeing me in curiosity. "That's right, I forgot," she said. "Your mother was down at the cat show."

"Her . . . boyfriend's cat came in third for Best in Show." It was the first time I'd actually used that term to refer to Harry Bock. I tried to describe Looli to Jaki, but she apparently had never seen a Sphynx and couldn't picture one. I went into my phone and pulled up the last, clearest shot I'd taken of Mom and Harry posing with the cat.

"Oooh, that is weird-looking," said Jaki. "'Course, I should talk—my cat's got folded-down ears."

I laughed. "It's personality that counts, isn't it? Looli's very sweet, which also helps in a show."

"Your mom's pretty. She looks like you, but I guess her hair's wavier and redder, huh?" Jaki handed back my phone. "My mom's been wanting to come here and help with all that's going on. But Dad thinks she's better off staying home to keep an eye on Carmel."

"There's a patrol car watching their house," Mira told us, "so the two of them might be safer there, anyway."

Jaki's mention of her mother and sister reminded me of something. "When we got interrupted earlier, you were telling me about people you might have had problems with when you were a kid. You said your family might remember better than you did. Were they able to think of any more?" I directed the last question to Mira, also.

Jaki thought. "Maybe just one other . . . a guy Carmel reminded me about. *Reminded* isn't even the right word, because he was hardly on my radar at all. Stefan Dumas."

"Another jerk?"

"No, at least not like Larry. Just a very shy, nerdy guy who kind of dogged after me in high school. I never exchanged more than a few words with him."

Mira chimed in. "I remember him, too, but not well. Carmel said your brother might know more."

"Teo works for a travel agency in Jersey City," Jaki said, "but by now he should be done for the day. Maybe I should call him."

She dialed and caught her older brother relaxing in his apartment. After she'd explained the reason for her call and he agreed to help, she asked, "Can I Skype you in?"

Soon the image of Teo Natal, as good-looking in his own way as Jaki, filled the small screen of her phone. "Stefan Dumas? Man, I haven't thought of him in years. Whad'ya want to know?"

"Carmel said he had kind of a thing for me," Jaki told him.

"Oh, God, did he ever! Poor schlub. He kept begging me to fix the two of you up because he was too shy to ask you himself. But I knew you wouldn't be interested, and anyhow, you were dating Larry. He would've pulverized Dum-ass."

Mira winced. "That's right, everybody called him that, didn't they? But he wasn't *really* dumb."

"Naw, he got terrific grades. In math and science, anyway. Only made the jocks hate him more. Boy, he used to get the tar beaten out of him after school."

"Teo!" Jaki scolded. "I certainly hope *you* never did any of that."

"No, I didn't, but I heard about it. His mother even came to talk with the principal once. But I guess she was such a b— . . . such a nasty person that she didn't do Stefan any favors. Anyhow, the school never made much effort to track down the bullies or discipline them."

"And this went on all through high school?" I asked.

"Almost. Until senior year." A dry chuckle from Teo. "Then Dum-ass finally turned the tables."

"How?"

"Again, I just heard this secondhand. One of the regular bullies, a guy from the football team, jumped him after school. Huge guy, but he ended up with a broken collarbone. Turned out that Stefan had taken up a new hobby, mixed martial arts."

I held my tongue, but Mira said it for me. "Oh. My. God."

"Yeah, right? Couldn't blame him—he needed to defend himself. But I'll bet that big kid never saw it coming."

"Teo, did you ever hear what happened to Stefan?" I asked. "Does he still live around here?"

"Don't know. He did mention, junior year, that he was applying to colleges. Wanted to study electrical engineering. So he might have gone out of state and stayed away."

Did we have time, I wondered, to do an Internet search for Stefan Dumas?

"Is that it?" Teo asked us.

"Yes." Jaki sounded distracted as she signed off. "Thanks, bro. Love you."

Afterward, I commented to her, "An awful lot of coincidences."

"Maybe even more than you think. Can I see that picture you showed me on your phone, again?"

"The one of the Jak-ettes?"

She shook her dark head. "Of your mom and Looli."

I pulled it up again, and Jaki peered closely. Then used the zoom feature to isolate a background figure. "Damn, I think that's him."

My heart gave a thud. "No, can't be. . . . Really?"

"Mira, whad'ya think?"

Jaki's cousin studied the image, and her sharp chin dropped. "Yeah, could be!"

"I thought he looked kind of familiar, but I never would have made the connection," Jaki said. "Of course, I can't be sure after so many years. I'd need to see him walk and talk. . . . But this guy is wearing a tag. He's Bradburne staff?"

I nodded. "Though maybe his ID is as fake as his name. If it *is* your old admirer, he's not Stefan 'Dum-ass' anymore. He's calling himself Steve Rickert."

Chapter 18

Jaki spread the word of our discovery to Detective Bonelli. Meanwhile, I called my mother. She wasn't picking up, which concerned me a little. I left her a message.

"Mom, please don't hang around the hotel tonight. Go straight home with Harry and Looli, right now. And on your way out, if you see that hotel staffer, Steve? Don't talk to him. Avoid him completely if you can. As they say on the cop shows, he's a 'person of interest' in this whole mess. Call me when you're on your way home, okay?"

Bonelli showed up at my elbow. "You talked to this guy, Cassie. He was dressed like Bradburne staff? With an ID tag?"

"I noticed today that the security guard at the theater door had a laminated tag. Steve's is in one of these plastic sleeves on a lanyard"—I held up my own volunteer tag—"which you can get in any office supply store. It looked like the others, though, and even had his photo. . . ."

"The Bradburne hired a bunch of extra guys a couple of weeks before the expo. Who knows how well they vetted them. . . . He's going by the name Steve Rickert? We'll see if he's actually on their roster."

I had a troubling thought. "This might explain how the stalker knew I had a parent involved in the expo. I wonder, though, how he found out I was helping Jaki. Unless Mom or Harry let it slip, or he overheard them talking about it."

Bonelli nodded. "Or there's another possibility. If he's been able to switch off some of the security cameras, maybe he also can hack into some of them. He might be able to monitor the hall outside Jaki's suite to see who's coming and going."

I hoped in vain that she might be kidding, but her troubled expression told me she was dead serious. No wonder this guy always seemed to keep one step ahead of us!

Jaki started her rehearsal then, a bit later than scheduled. Accompanied by just a keyboard player, a guitarist, and a drummer, she launched into another of her hits, "Shady Lady." I'd heard the sassy pop-rock number before, on the radio. By comparison, Jaki's performance tonight sounded a little anemic, and not just because of the spare accompaniment. Big surprise, though. I couldn't imagine how she would keep it together during a ballad, much less a high-energy dance number, with all she had hanging over her head. If there was even the slightest chance that crazy Stefan might be somewhere out there in the audience, waiting to take a shot at her . . .

Time for me to quit the edge of the stage for a more appropriate seat in the mostly vacant front row. The things I'd learned that afternoon left my mind spinning. I couldn't believe that the seemingly nice, helpful, self-effacing guy who'd called Harry "sir" could possibly be the monster behind this scheme. But no one else fit the profile so well.

Unless . . . could both Jaki and Mira possibly have misidentified him as Dumas?

With a start, I remembered that we'd first run in to Steve

when we were scoping out the convention center in advance. *And so was he!* He'd been wandering in and out of doors, some of which probably led to stairwells, and making notes on his iPad. He could have been planning how to hack the computer that afternoon, right in front of us, and we'd never have suspected.

As far as I could remember, he'd been dressed like a worker but not wearing an ID tag that day. Other staffers already were wearing them, though. How hard would it have been for him to notice how they were designed and what information they included, then print a facsimile for himself? Who was likely to examine it really closely unless they had reason to suspect a problem?

And low-key, boring Steve Rickert didn't look like a guy who'd be a problem.

My stomach rumbled, and I checked my watch. Five of six. Ages ago, it seemed, I'd promised to meet Mark at the restaurant at six for dinner. Before the rest of us knew . . . what we at least thought we knew now.

No reason I shouldn't go meet him. Bonelli and her cops are on the case. Jaki's got protection around her, and nothing dangerous should happen until after she performs.

Besides, it worried me that Mom hadn't returned my last call. On the way to the restaurant, I'd stop by the cat show, which ought to be breaking up by now. Look in on her and Harry and make sure they were planning to head home, as I'd told them to.

Would Steve be there? If he was the stalker, probably not. He had a big reunion planned with Jaki later on, and was probably off somewhere getting ready for it.

I saw no sign of Mom or Harry on the cat show floor, and

many of the competitors and their animals already had cleared out. On a hunch, I moved on to The Grove and found the two of them seated at a table, sharing a plate of hors d'oeuvres.

When I asked Mom why she hadn't answered her phone, she apologized. "It's so noisy in here, I guess I didn't hear the ringer."

"Where's our prizewinning 'pearl'?" I asked Harry.

"I couldn't bring her in here, of course," he said, but with a proud smile. "She's tucked away safely in a friend's hotel room, having her own supper."

That put me on alert. "What friend?"

"Nancy, the woman down our row who had the Maine Coons. She's staying over another night, and said she'd be glad to keep an eye on Looli until Barbara and I had some dinner."

Mom must have noticed me eyeing the hors d'oeuvres they were sharing, stuffed mushroom caps the size of cupcakes. "Won't you join us, Cassie? Pull up another chair—there's an extra at that table."

I glanced around the crowded restaurant. "I'll probably get flack if I do that. Actually, I was supposed to meet Mark here...."

"Oh, yes, he stopped by a few minutes ago. Said to tell you there was a problem at the clinic, some dog had a setback." Mom's temporarily unfocused gaze told me she was trying to remember his message exactly. "He hopes to make it back later for Jaki's show, though, and he'll call you."

By now I was starving, so I meekly asked the party of three at the next table if I could grab their extra chair. They gestured for me to take it, and I joined Mom and Harry.

Half of the mushroom caps were stuffed with Parmesan cheese, the others with sausage. Combined with the hearty Italian bread in the basket, I hardly needed anything more. Which was just as well, I thought, because I might need to stay on my toes tonight.

Mom told me, "I did listen to that very agitated message you left on my phone about half an hour ago. What was all that, about Steve—?"

I cut her off with a wave of my hand. This noisy environment, where we had to raise our voices just to be heard by each other, was no place to discuss police business. "Not here, Mom. I'll explain later. But do me a favor, both of you. As *soon* as you finish dinner, get Looli from Nancy, head for your car, and get out of here."

"Yes, you said that, but why—"

I needed a creative fib. "There have been some more security issues because of that actor showing up, and they might affect the concert tonight. If there's another blackout or alarm malfunction while Jaki's performing, things could get dicey. Detective Bonelli herself told me that you two would be better off away from the hotel."

"And what about you?" Harry asked.

I appreciated his concern; he wasn't so bad, after all. "I'm going to stick close to Bonelli and her people, who are prepared to deal with whatever happens. Anyhow, I don't have a prizewinning cat to worry about, and you do! If there is trouble, I may call Mark and also warn him off."

Harry sipped his white wine, then shook his head. "I don't understand how this place could still be having so many electronic and security problems. The hotel has been in business for a year, so any bugs should have been worked out by now. Unless the new convention center has put more stress on the system. That did add another hundred thousand square feet . . . if you count the catering kitchen, though that isn't even functional yet."

The catering kitchen, right!

Did the cops think to search there? Did they even know about it?

Trying to sound casual, I asked Harry, "Where's that sup-posed to be located, anyway?"

"I believe it's somewhere at the south end of the conven-tion center." He chuckled. "I studied the layout of this whole place before we came, but since then I've spent most of my time at the cat show. You've probably seen more of the con-vention center and the concourse than I ever have."

It wasn't possible, was it, that Bonelli's crew had missed the unfinished area? If the complex was completely wired, wouldn't some blip in the network let guards know if anyone unauthorized was going in and out of a space?

Unless "Steve" figured out how to bypass those security cameras, too.

Trying to be subtle, I glanced at my phone. No new mes-sages, but it was nearly six-thirty. Just half an hour until Jaki would go onstage. I patted my lips with the sage green cloth napkin and pushed back my chair.

"Thanks so much for sharing your appetizers with me, folks," I said. "I need to get back and see if everything's still on for tonight. Please do as I said, okay, and leave soon? I'll explain everything tomorrow."

"You be careful, too, Cassie," my mother called after me. "Don't take any of your crazy chances!"

I waved my hand as if this were nonsense, but had to admit that she knew me too well.

Starting to feel a bit footsore in my dress shoes, even though they were flats, I crossed the hotel lobby, passed through the tall, automatic glass doors, and hoofed it back down the long con-course. Aside from the fund-raising concert, the cat expo had pretty much ended and most of the concessioners had cleared out. They and their customers had left behind just enough debris to make work for the maintenance staff, who efficiently pushed brooms and emptied trash cans. I thought it seemed a little early, but they probably had orders to make the concourse look clean and welcoming for the concert crowd.

At a brisk pace, I passed the closed doors of the theater and kept going. *Harry said the catering kitchen was to the south. How the heck can anyone figure out south when they're inside a complex this big? But he did make it sound like it was away from the busier areas.*

I headed for the most remote corner, where it seemed no one would have any good reason to go.

There, I passed one solid single door marked UTILITY CLOSET, then another labeled STORAGE, each with keypads below their latches. This looked like some type of service corridor, which might make a sensible location for the kitchen.

At the very end stood a double-door entrance with no identification. The passage looked wide enough to roll out, say, a large rack or serving cart. Each door had a square window near the top, but both were covered from the inside with what looked like cardboard. The entrance had been blocked off by a sawhorse that bore a sign lettered in bold black on orange:

WARNING
CONSTRUCTION SITE
NO ADMITTANCE

Bingo.

The tiled floor just in front of the door wore a fine covering of dust, as if the cleaning crew didn't bother to sweep behind the sawhorse. This let me know a couple of things:

There probably hadn't been a lot of construction workers tromping through there in a few days. But someone *had* come through, more stealthily, because the sawhorse had been shifted and replaced.

A keypad on the wall to the right of the double doors nearly discouraged me. If it took a numerical code to enter, I wouldn't know it, and I didn't dare spend too much time trying various combinations. As I got closer, though, I saw that luck was still in my favor. Someone had stuck a rubber wedge in between the two doors to defeat the security system.

I hesitated, knowing I might blunder into a dangerous situation. The covered windows prevented me from seeing if anyone was inside the space, and through the slim gap between the doors I glimpsed a dull glow. On the other hand, if the killer cat thief were already inside, he wouldn't have had to prop the doors open. He would probably only do that if he'd stepped out and wanted get back in quickly. . . .

Or if he's expecting someone else who doesn't know the combination. Someone like Jaki.

I pulled out my phone but didn't want to make a call that might be overheard. Instead I texted Bonelli; I told her I'd been passing by the kitchen-under-construction and wondered if her guys had checked it, because the door was jammed open. I waited a minute but got no response. She probably was busy tracking down some other lead.

Maybe she'd already caught up with Steven/Stefan and was questioning him. That idea boosted my nerve.

Holding my breath, I pushed one door inward just a little. The space that yawned beyond it was faintly lit by ceiling panels—probably some type of energy-saving, off-hours lighting. In its unfinished state, the area resembled a state-of-the-art hospital emergency room as much as a kitchen.

Stainless steel gleamed on all sides. The long central worktable looked scrubbed for surgery. Mammoth industrial sinks lined the right wall, their tall sprayers curved downward at rest, like the necks of robotic swans. The professional-grade appliances arrayed on the left still bore neon-red or acid-green labels from the factory. Even the gray porcelain tile of the floor threw off a hard, reflective shine, except in a few areas probably scuffed up by the workers.

I did not see or hear any sign of another person in this space, so I dared to keep exploring. Farther toward the back of the main room, the ceiling panels still gaped in some places, and capped-off electrical wires dangled from the openings like jungle snakes. A tall ladder slanted against one wall bore a thin film of dust that again showed it hadn't seen much use recently. Nearby, a rolling rack of open shelves, the kind that could move many trays of hot meals at once, stood empty.

Behind the rack, I glimpsed a low, white-draped form, and crept nearer. A round, room service–type table stood shoved up oddly against a closed, windowless door. In sharp contrast to the rest of the sterile, lifeless environment, the table had been spread with a neat linen cloth and set with two of the hotel's dessert plates. An unopened bottle of red wine stood between two stemmed glasses, near a small, unopened Valentine box of "assorted chocolates." Across the center of the table lay a florist's bouquet of red roses mixed with baby's breath and tied with a white ribbon.

For a second, I tried to rationalize all this. The tableau looked so carefully assembled—could it be a genuine room service delivery that had been parked here for some reason? But my sixth sense didn't buy that explanation. I remembered the tidy presentation of Gordie's heart-shaped silver tag nestled in the small white gift box, which had been tied shut with the cat's plaid collar.

My flesh prickled.

I would have backed away that instant, except for the faint scratching noise that came from the other side of the half-hidden door.

That could have sent my mind to all kinds of lurid places if it hadn't been so familiar to me. It soon was followed by another sound that I'd both hoped and dreaded to hear.

A long-drawn, mournful meow.

Chapter 19

I lost my sense of caution and rolled the dinner cart out of the way. The single door had no keypad, and when I tested the latch, it gave.

The small room behind also was dim, but as soon as I cracked open the door, a silver tabby cat pressed himself into the gap. I blocked his escape—a move I'd perfected with my own cats as well as on the job—pushed into the room, and shut the door behind both of us. Gordie rubbed against my shins and purred loudly, starved for attention.

Or just starved? I scanned the space, which was outfitted with shelves like a storage room or pantry. On the floor, I spotted a cheap plastic double bowl with hollows for food and water. The food side was empty, but a bag of inexpensive dry stuff sat on a shelf above; not the special diet that Gordie needed, though. A shimmer in the other bowl told me that he at least had been left with some water. One sniff let me know there also was a used litter pan somewhere in the room.

Most important—off to the right, I spied Gordie's distinctive aqua-blue carrier.

My heart pounded with fresh excitement. Here was a

chance to solve a big part of everyone's problem. Grab the cat, return him to Jaki, and she'd have no need to risk her neck by meeting her stalker in person. Steve/Stefan might even lose his nerve when he realized he no longer had the perfect bait to reel in his dream woman.

And with the expo winding down, no one would think it odd for me to be walking down the concourse at this hour with a fancy cat carrier.

Definitely worth the risk.

Since the Scottish Fold was playing up to me anyhow, I scooped him into my arms, crossed the narrow room, and tucked him into his carrier. I whispered to him to be quiet and closed it up. Toting the bag, I tiptoed back to the storeroom door and eased it open.

I pushed it shut behind us and carefully rolled the room service cart back to where it had been. I had left the double doors exactly as I'd found them, about half an inch ajar with the rubber doorstop wedged in between. Gordie and I should be able to make a quick and quiet getaway.

Out in the main kitchen area, with a little more light, I checked my phone again for the time. Six forty-five; Jaki would be about to start her show. Would she feel better if she knew her cat was safe? I set down the carrier for a second and typed a text to Bonelli: *Found Gordie! Tell Jaki he's okay. I'm*

Bad move to take my eye off the door, even for a second. My clever exit plan also let Steve make a quick and quiet entrance.

Before I could even glance up again, he was inside. He still wore his "uniform" of a gray polo shirt and dark dress slacks, topped by a black windbreaker.

At least he turned away from me to shut the door. I ducked behind the end of the long worktable and pushed the cat carrier behind me. Before pocketing my phone, just in case it would do any good, I hit send.

In the stillness of the empty kitchen, Steve/Stefan must have heard the shuffling sounds, because he spun around. I worried that the gap between the tabletop and its lower shelf might not do much to hide my crouching silhouette.

"Who's there?" He sounded neither as frightened nor as angry as I'd have expected. Also a little . . . hopeful? Did he actually think that Jaki might have figured out his hiding place and come to meet him ahead of schedule?

That did seem to be the way his thoughts were trending, because his voice turned gentle and wheedling. "I know you're in here. It's okay, you can come out. Don't be afraid."

Figuring it was only a matter of time before he spotted me anyhow, I stood up slowly. It wouldn't be the first time I'd disappointed a guy, but until now the consequences hadn't been fatal.

"You!" His bland, Boy Scout face spasmed; I almost expected him to stamp his foot and throw a tantrum. "How did *you* find this place?"

For the time being, I tried to forget that this unimpressive-looking young guy might have killed two men who'd had, presumably, better self-defense skills than mine. Stefan stood only an inch or two taller, and the couple of times we'd met before, I'd thought of him as having a slight build. Now I noticed that he actually looked pretty fit, maybe from all of those hours in the dojo.

I tried desperately to think of an approach that would defuse the situation, from his point of view. I kept my tone calm and quiet, as if handling a rabid wildcat that might slash me to ribbons.

Use the name he gave himself.

"It's okay, Steve. I just want to help you," I said. "To keep you from making a bad mistake."

"The worst mistake I could make now is letting you walk out of here." He jabbed a hand inside his windbreaker and whipped out the stolen semiautomatic.

Oh, crap. All blood rushed from my brain to my feet, and the pistol's barrel, though fairly small and half a room away, loomed gigantic in my mind. This was not even the first time I'd been held at gunpoint, but trust me, that sense of barely controlled hysteria never gets old.

Somehow, though, I managed to keep talking in a way that I hoped would make sense to Mr. Dumas/Rickert. "That's where you're wrong. See, Jaki and I have gotten to be friends. The security guard, the private eye . . . those guys didn't mean anything to her. And if you killed them in self-defense, Jaki will understand that. But if you shoot me in cold blood, she'll be really upset. She could never forgive you, and it would ruin your whole plan."

This sounded like pure BS even to me, but at least it made Steve stop and think. He must already know that I'd had contact with Jaki, since he'd left the ominous note on my windshield.

"You're interfering!" he accused. "If all of you just stopped *interfering,* none of this had to happen."

"I know, Steve. The others don't understand. They think you're trying to hurt Jaki, but you'd never do that, would you?" I nodded toward the alcove with the room service table. "I saw the nice surprise you set up for her. That's lovely. I'm sure she'll appreciate it."

"Sh-she's still coming?"

I nodded. "She has to do her show first, of course. So she probably can't make it until after eight. And I know she's waiting for the last few clues from you about how to get here. I just

stumbled onto this place because I'd heard there was an unfinished wing and got curious about it. I never would have
guessed this was your meeting spot. Very smart!"

His eyes hardened behind their dark-rimmed glasses, and
his grip on the pistol steadied. "You're making fun of me."

"No, not at all. You've handled everything very cleverly
from the beginning. Even Jaki can't believe how much trouble
you went to, just to arrange it all."

Showing at least some fleeting grasp of reality, he snorted.
"She probably doesn't even remember me."

"Oh, she does. I was showing her pictures I took at the cat
show, and one of them had you in the background. Right
away, Jaki said, 'Hey, I know that guy. It's Stefan' "—I thought
it better to leave off his last name—" 'from high school!' After
that, she figured it must've been you leaving the notes and
sending the e-mails, the past couple of years."

He looked truly confused now. Because I had my facts
straight, he couldn't accuse me of just making stuff up. "She
really recognized me?"

"She did. She said, of course, that you've matured a lot
since she last saw you." I decided the best approach from here
on out was to lie my head off. "She told me she felt sorry that
the two of you never got together back then. She was so busy
with all of her lessons, and then the TV show, that she hardly
had time to date anybody. Anyway, she's glad for this chance to
make things right. She's looking forward to seeing you later, so
you two can catch up and finally get to know each other, the
way you should have years ago."

I might have overdone it, I realized, when I saw tears running down the guy's face. For a second, I did feel some com-
passion for Stefan: brilliant but oddball teenager with a
difficult mother, regularly taunted and even beaten up by the
school jocks. Eventually, though, he'd developed two areas of

expertise—electronics and martial arts. The day he'd broken that bully's collarbone and left him howling in the schoolyard must have been a tipping point.

A secret superhero in his own mind, Stefan—now Steve—would not be cowed anymore. He would go after what he wanted in life.

And the prize he wanted most was Jaki.

If she had graduated and simply moved elsewhere, he might have forgotten about his crush on her. But she became a star, so he could watch her on TV, find pictures of her all over the Internet, listen to her albums, and maybe get a ticket now and then to one of her concerts. This continued their relation-ship, if only in Stefan's head. She became the goddess who would finally give meaning to his lonely life. He just needed to get her to return his feelings.

Helpful as it was for me to understand his thought processes, I warned myself not to let my sympathies get the better of me. Stefan seemed to be wavering now, but I still needed some ex-cuse to get past him and out that door to safety.

"The only thing Jaki's still concerned about," I told him, "is Gordie. She understands why you took him, but the thing is, he's not as healthy as he looks. He has a kidney condition and needs a special diet. I'm sure you didn't know about that, but if he doesn't get the right kind of food soon . . ." I frowned in the direction of the carrier. "Jaki loves Gordie, and she'd be heartbroken if anything happened to him. Why don't you let me take him to her now, while she's onstage, so she can see that he's still okay?"

He stiffened again. "Then she won't come later on."

"Sure she will. Like I told you, she *wants* to, now that she realizes it's you she'll be meeting. But if I bring the cat back, it will help. She'll know for sure that you don't mean her any harm."

"*I* don't mean her harm?" Stefan's cheeks reddened. "*They're* the ones who are destroying her! Her family, her agent, her record company . . . To them, she's just a property, a money-making machine. I heard they got her hooked on drugs just to keep her going even when she was exhausted. Then last year that stupid playboy actor broke her heart." Tearing up again, he wiped his nose on the sleeve of his windbreaker. "That song she wrote, 'Free Me'? That was the *real* Jaki, calling out for someone to take her away from it all, to love her for herself. That's what I'm going to do! Once she realizes that, she'll be happy to go away with me."

I knew better than to argue with him about his delusions. Obviously Stefan had kept up with, and believed, every bit of exaggerated gossip about Jaki's career, her brief episode of abusing prescription drugs, and her rocky love life. And he interpreted her moody pop ballad about longing for escape, adventure, and romance as a desperate cry for help that only he could answer. There was no way I, a stranger, could hope to talk him out of all those fantasies.

Stefan calmed a little, and his gaze roamed around the gleaming, antiseptic surfaces of the dormant kitchen as dreamily as if it were a romantic rooftop garden. "This place was supposed to be our secret, hers and mine." His hazel eyes, behind the rectangular glasses, locked onto me again. "If you go back now, the cops will want to know where to find me. And you'll tell them, won't you?"

"No, Steve. I promise—"

"You were on your phone to somebody when I came in!"

Damn, I hadn't thought he saw that. "To Jaki. I texted her that I'd found Gordie. That was all I had time to write."

"Great, just *great*." His eyes darted around now, as if he might find some escape from his dilemma among the rows of stainless-steel shelving. "The cops can trace your freakin' phone. Think I don't know that?"

I hung my head in a show of humility. "I'm sure you do, Steve. You know a lot about electronics, that's for sure."

"Stop it!" he screamed. "You're just screwin' with me, aren't you? I bet none of it's true. Jaki didn't remember me, and she's not coming, is she?"

Afraid to string him along any further, I shut up and hyperfocused once more on the gun. But so far, in all of this time, Stefan hadn't used it. If he had no practice with one, he could be a lousy shot. He'd nailed the PI at close range, but it would take more skill to hit me from about twenty feet away, especially if I ducked.

Or was it one thing for him to use lethal force in self-defense, but another to kill an unarmed woman in cold blood? If he shot me now, he wouldn't be able to rationalize it away.

No question, he'd be a murderer.

During our mutual silence, I thought I heard faint sounds from the concourse outside. Wishful thinking? If I screamed for help, Stefan might just panic and shoot. And if the noises came from an unsuspecting maintenance worker who'd noticed the door left ajar, I could get another innocent person killed along with me.

All I could do was delay as long as possible. Going back to my calm, cool voice, I asked, "What time is it now?"

He blinked, as if wondering what new trick I was up to. But after all, I didn't pose much of a threat. I didn't have a gun of my own, and I was too far away to rush him. In the barren kitchen, there wasn't even anything handy that I could throw at him—unless I wanted to hurl the carrier and sacrifice Gordie. He probably guessed that wasn't going to happen.

Still, he didn't trust me long enough to look away for an instant. "You tell me."

I checked my phone. "Five after seven. Jaki will have started her show. A shame you can't be there to see it."

In a brittle voice, he told me, "You won't see it, either."

I put the phone away carefully, still keeping one eye on his gun. But my pulse rate slowed just a little from full panic mode. While checking the small screen, I'd seen Bonelli's recent answer to my text of fifteen minutes earlier: *Sit tight, we're right outside.*

Guess I just needed to get myself out of the line of fire. Right on cue, another pathetic meow issued from the cat carrier on the floor, still tucked safely behind the steel table.

"Aww, poor Gordie." I glanced down to let Steve know what I was up to, then squatted to comfort the cat. "It's okay, boy. You'll be back with your mommy again soon—"

"Freeze! Hands up!"

As the double doors burst open, I dove to the floor next to Gordie, behind the steel table. The hard linoleum burned the palms of my hands, and I shut my eyes, braced for the shootout.

When a minute passed and it never came, I dared to peer from my hiding place. It looked as if, surprised from behind, Dumas had been too stunned to even fire his weapon. Officer Gardiner, the young one with the flattop, quickly removed the pistol from Stefan's raised hand and cuffed him, while reading him his rights.

Chapter 20

Once handcuffed, Stefan Dumas stood still and mute, his normally pale face beet red. Embarrassed that he'd lost his battle of wits with the cops? Furious that I'd conspired in his capture? He did shoot me a venomous glare, as if he wished he'd killed me when he had the chance.

I really hoped they'd send him away to someplace secure where he'd never escape. I sensed Stefan would be very good at plotting revenge.

Once I could see the situation was under control, I rose unsteadily back to my feet. My legs felt as cramped as if I'd been huddled behind the steel worktable for hours instead of just minutes. I hugged Gordie's carrier to my chest, feeling bonded to him by our shared near-death experience.

The sight made Bonelli smile, and she asked me, "How's our hostage doing?"

"Probably better than I am. How'd you find me, by my phone?"

"Yeah, and it helped that you'd already mentioned checking out this kitchen. You took a hell of a chance, though, lady."

I shook my head. "I didn't mean to, but once I realized Gordie was in that pantry, I thought I'd have time to whisk him away before Stefan came back." I stuck a finger through the mesh of the carrier, and the tabby rubbed against it. "I'm sure he has no idea what a close call we both had. Can I get him out of here? Maybe take him to Jaki?"

The detective considered. "She's onstage now. Besides, the cat may be evidence."

"Well, you don't need to dust the carrier for prints to know that Dumas took the cat and was keeping him down here."

"No, I suppose not," she relented.

"Can I at least tell Jaki's people that Gordie's safe? Maybe e-mail her cousin?"

Bonelli nodded permission, and I fired off a message to Mira. I hoped she would get a chance at some point to pass on the good news about Gordie and put Jaki's mind at ease.

As Officers Gardiner and Waller hustled Dumas out of the unfinished kitchen, a couple of other cops filed in to give the place a going-over, probably for more evidence. I pointed them toward the room service cart and the storage room beyond it, explaining that Gordie must have been shut up in there ever since he disappeared.

My phone played "Stray Cat Strut" as Mira got back to me. "Cassie, you're an angel! If you bring Gordie backstage, I can show him to Jaki and then take him up to the suite. Your boyfriend's here, too, looking for you."

When I relayed all of this information to Bonelli, she finally agreed to let me go. "Come downtown tomorrow and give us your official statement. We already heard enough tonight to tack unlawful restraint and terroristic threats onto Dumas's charges."

She told blond Officer Waller to escort me to the backstage of the theater. As I picked up Gordie's carrier and headed for the door, Bonelli added, "And Cassie . . . nice work."

That floored me, since the detective usually warned or scolded me about sticking my nose too far into police business. Her rare compliment almost—maybe not quite—made up for everything I'd gone through over the past half hour.

I certainly felt safer than I had all weekend, now that I was escorted by the youthful, broad-chested, and square-jawed Officer Chris Waller in his full uniform. We'd met once before, under similar hair-raising circumstances. After we got beyond earshot of Bonelli, he threw me a sideways look and cracked, "The department needs to form a special unit for cat crimes and put you in charge."

"It's insane, isn't it? The first time, I did poke my nose into a situation that I could have left alone. But now I've gotten such a rep that people actually try to recruit me, and it's hard to say no."

"Especially when they're as famous as Jaki Natal."

"And Alec MacMasters," I reminded him, with a wink.

Waller grinned. "None of that fazes Bonelli, though. She'll grill a TV star the same as she would a gangbanger. But she's one reason things stay lively around here. When she gets hold of a case and thinks there's more beneath the surface, she doesn't give up. She makes us work hard, but she always works harder."

"That's what I figured." It made me happy to hear one of the officers praise Angela so highly. She'd always come through for me and my friends, and it was good to know the rest of the squad appreciated her, too.

As Waller, Gordie, and I entered the back of the theater by a side door, we could hear Jaki belting out "Shady Lady" with far more smolder and strut than she'd shown earlier at the rehearsal. I wondered if Mira had managed to tell her cousin that I'd found Gordie safe and well—the news might have raised Jaki's spirits. At least she sounded in such good voice that her audience of well-heeled patrons should feel they were getting their money's worth.

I reached the wings, where Perry caught a glimpse of me and the aqua cat carrier. Grinning broadly with those spectacular teeth, he gave me a double thumbs-up. I guessed that Bonelli had kept him posted on Dumas's capture.

Mira dashed over to give me a hug and let out a muffled squeal. "I can't believe you actually did it—tracked down Gordie *and* the stalker. That lady detective wasn't lying, you really are amazing!"

I felt myself blush and wondered if the restrained Bonelli had actually used such a word to describe my talents. "Just stubborn and more than a little crazy, I think. But very happy to be able to return this guy to you."

I handed over the carrier, and Mira fussed for a minute over the frightened cat. As the strains of Jaki's amplified voice almost drowned us out, her cousin stage-whispered, "I can't interrupt her now, but as soon as there's a break, I'll try to catch her eye."

She set the carrier down close to her foot, where I also could keep watch over it. Neither of us wanted to take the chance that anyone could make off with the cat again. So it spooked me a little, a second later, when I heard a male voice crooning softly, "How are ye, Gordie, m'boy? Been through a lot, have you?"

I whipped around and saw some guy with wavy bronze hair squatting near the carrier. Wondering where Officer Waller had gone, I prepared to yank Jaki's pet out of danger, until Gordie's admirer smiled up at me.

I'd only seen one episode of the *Galaxy Wars* TV series— while unwinding with Mark at his apartment on a quiet

weekday evening—but that was enough for me to recognize
Alec MacMasters. His thick hair dipped over his forehead, his
eyes crinkled at the corners when he smiled, and his choppers
gleamed even whiter than Perry's, almost glow-in-the-dark.

Despite the shock, I managed down-to-earth conversation.
"Got to him in time, I think. He seems a little thin, but not too
rattled."

"Well, the doc can give him a quick checkup, right?" He
glanced over his shoulder at Mark, who was walking quickly in
our direction. Worried about my safety? Or about my expo-
sure to the hunky male TV star?

"Cassie, are you all right?" he asked. "Bonelli said—"

"I'm fine, and she's got the stalker in custody."

Mark wrapped me in a protective hug; until that moment,
I hadn't realized how badly I needed one. I hesitated to tell
him any more and risk making him really upset with me.
Luckily, at that point Jaki finished her number, and for a couple of minutes the audience's applause made any conversation
backstage impossible.

While nodding her appreciation, Jaki glanced toward the
wings. Mira waved to her, lifted the cat carrier, and pointed to
it dramatically. Relief and affection swept over the singer's face,
giving it a glow beyond the effects of her stage makeup. She
blew Gordie a kiss and, intentionally misinterpreting, Alec
blew her one back. She responded with a wry shake of her
head.

Clasping the microphone against her modest cleavage with
both hands, she spoke to the crowd again. "I was going to finish up tonight with 'I Need My Space' "—people started clap-
ping again, and she gave them time to settle down—"but I'd
rather end with a song I wrote not long ago for someone who
means a lot to me. I made a dumb mistake and let him down. I

was afraid I'd lost him forever, but now I'm sure we've still got a lot of good years ahead of us, together."

She smiled brightly, and most of her audience would have been too far away to see the tears that glistened in her eyes. The pianist began a quiet ballad as Jaki sang.

> *Another love affair gone sour, another night so far from*
> * home*
> *I'm by myself in my hotel room, at least I know I'm not*
> * alone*
> *You're always happy just to listen to my sorrow or my*
> * joys*
> *You sit with me in wordless comfort, a welcome change*
> * from all the noise*
> *You give me strength to face the challenges of life*
> *And when I break, you help me mend*
> *I promise that just like you're always there for me*
> *I will be there for you, my friend.*

I wondered if some in the audience, who might know that MacMasters had shown up at the hotel to help Jaki deal with some kind of crisis, assumed the song was dedicated to him. But the TV star himself was humble enough to know better. He bent down next to the carrier and whispered to the silver tabby, "How about that, Gordie? Your mum's singing a song she wrote just for you!"

After the show ended, I learned that Becky and Chris had indeed been allowed to slip in and grab two unoccupied seats. Their efforts to get backstage for autographs were almost thwarted by a security guard, though, until I spotted them and vouched for them. I even got to bring them along when Mark and I were invited to the after-party up in the Presidential Suite. At least for that evening, any friends of mine appeared to be welcome.

Becky gushed over Jaki while the singer graciously signed her program, and Chris requested the same favor from Alec. Then both FOCA volunteers turned to me, wanting to know how we'd snared the stalker. I gave them only a superficial recap, throwing most of the credit to Bonelli, and promised to fill in more details another time. Because they knew no one else at the gathering, the two slipped away shortly after that.

The closing cocktail party brought together everyone in Jaki's entourage, as well as folks I hadn't met before from the hotel's promotional team and top management. Everyone seemed in high spirits, not totally fueled by trips to the bar.

Once Jaki and Gordie had their joyful reunion, she introduced him to a few guests, then shut him away in the bedroom of her suite to finally give him some of his prescription food. That area was as large as a decent studio apartment, though, so it must have felt like cat heaven compared to the storage closet where he'd spent the last few days. While drinks and food were going around in the living/dining area, Mark took Gordie into the suite's spacious bathroom to give him a quick check-over.

Jaki's reunion with Alec seemed on the warm side, too, considering that when she'd first heard about his arrival at the hotel she'd accused him of staging a publicity stunt. With a soft Scottish burr that he didn't use on his TV show, Alec told Jaki, Hector, Mira, and me how he'd hired the PI.

"My bodyguard recommended him, and he had great credentials, a military background," he said. "But somehow this kid Dumas still must have gotten the drop on him. All of that still blows my mind!"

"Having dealt with Stefan face-to-face, I have a theory," I said. "Ordinarily, he didn't look or act the least bit threatening.

Even someone with all that training could have let their guard down around him."

Hector shook his head in wonder. "He told that lady detective he used some kind of tai chi move to get the guy's gun, and 'had to shoot him' in self-defense. Said the same thing about the security guard, who caught him sneaking around in the stairwell with an iPad."

"So cold." Mira shuddered and took another sip of her cocktail. "It's one thing to murder someone you hate, in a rage, but just to eliminate any stranger who gets in your way . . ."

But it totally fit the profile of a psychopath, I thought. "The only thing that mattered to him was getting to Jaki."

A shadow seemed to pass over the singer's face, still beautiful as a china doll's in her stage makeup. "I'm sure if I'd disappointed him in any way, I would have been eliminated, too."

Alec pulled her close in a one-armed hug that still let him hang onto his beer. "Well, that didn't happen, because you had a lot of good people around who love you and went the extra mile to keep you safe."

Perry and Rose circulated among everyone at the party, including Bradburne management. Because the event had made decent money, all stresses over how closely they had skirted disaster seemed forgotten, or at least forgiven. Since in the end Jaki did perform, very few concert tickets had to be refunded, and some people who couldn't make the Sunday night show had donated their ticket prices to the animal charities, anyway.

So by tonight the sun-kissed color had returned to Perry's face. When we met in the buffet line, he pulled me aside for a second. "Cassie, I know you don't want too much made of your part in all this, especially in the press. But Bonelli told me how that guy cornered you in his hideout and you kept him talking until the cops arrived. That took guts, girl! I don't know if I could have been that cool-headed."

Self-consciously, I chuckled. "Let's just say that my BA in psychology never came in handier."

He swiped a hand through his artfully rumpled haircut. "You'll probably never forgive me for involving you in such a dangerous mess, when you signed on just to give grooming demonstrations—for free, yet!"

"I don't blame you, Perry, or Jaki. I could have said no at any point, but I really wanted to help her get her cat back and end the threats against her and her family. She's a brave lady, too, though I doubt that she'll ever want her fans to know the whole story."

"Rose is cooperating with the police to play down the whole crisis as much as possible. The media will know that Jaki had a stalker, which was the reason for delaying her concert and for Alec flying in. They'll also know that, with the help of the local cops and some expo volunteers, Stefan was located and arrested, so Jaki's Sunday show went off as scheduled."

"Sounds smart," I told him.

Just then, my favorite vet emerged from the bedroom suite with his report on Gordie. He told Jaki that the cat had dropped a couple of pounds and showed a few other signs of stress, but nothing that a return to her usual TLC shouldn't cure. "When you get back to LA, just have your regular vet run a blood test to make sure his kidney values are still okay."

The star offered to pay Mark for his trouble, but he waved that off. "All this excitement has definitely been a break from my routine. But there is one favor *Alec* can do for me. . . ."

Jaki gestured with her whole arm for the movie star to join them. "Name it, I promise he'll do it!"

From the sideboard, Mark picked up a small notepad and a pen, both with the Bradburne logo. "My younger brother,

Artie, is a huge fan of *Galaxy Wars*. If I can get your autograph, he'll probably frame it."

MacMasters laughed and signed. "No problem, man."

No doubt he imagined Mark's brother to be a teenager, and would have been surprised to know that Artie was in his mid-twenties. When I'd visited their family on holidays, his conversation had revolved mostly around sci-fi and fantasy video games, movies, and TV shows. It made sense that he also followed Alec's series.

While Mark and the TV star chatted, I took Jaki aside and quietly explained what I'd found in the unfinished catering kitchen. "In this stark, isolated space, Stefan had a whole table set up for the two of you. I can't imagine how he thought you were going to react."

She shivered. "That's so creepy! Well, I can't ever thank you enough. I'll feel so much safer now, traveling and going onstage. There are still other weirdos out there, but I don't think very many are as determined and deadly as this guy was." When her father passed by, Jaki caught his arm. "Dad, we owe Cassie some kind of reward for all of her help!"

My cheeks warmed. "Oh, no, please. I was only too glad to do it. And as Mark said, it brought a little showbiz glamour into our lives." Afraid she would insist on some extravagant gift, I glanced at the suite's electronic clock. "Anyway, I should be getting back to my shop and my apartment. No telling what new catastrophe might be waiting for me." I explained about the road work, the brown water, and the emergency methods I had used to get cleaned up for that evening. "Guess I'll be showering in the van again tomorrow morning."

Mark draped an arm over my shoulders. "You could stay at my place, but you'd still have a drive back to town."

As Jaki listened to this, a gleam came into her dark eyes.

"Cassie, do you have someone checking on your shop and your cats while you're here?"

"I usually rely on my friend Dawn, but she's laid up with a broken foot." Because I sensed the singer was hatching some kind of plan, I added, "Possibly her boyfriend, Keith, could sub for her. . . ."

"Find out if he can. We booked this whole floor, and there's at least one room still empty. Why don't you and Mark stay the night here, on us? Then you'll both be well rested—and showered—for work tomorrow."

That did sound tempting. I'd had a bit more than usual to drink, and from Mark's festive glow, I suspected he had, too. The outfit I'd changed into for the concert would last through the next morning. . . .

And besides, Mark and I hadn't had time to spend the night together in . . . a while.

From his grin, I knew he found the invitation welcome, too.

"Thanks, Jaki," I told her. "That reward, I might just accept!"

I called Dawn, hating to bother her after ten p.m. She'd already gone to bed, but Keith answered.

"Sure, I'd be glad to pop over and feed the cats," he said. "But what's going on? Are you okay?"

"Everybody's fine: me, Mark, my mom, Harry, Jaki, and Gordie. The only one who's not okay is a guy named Stefan Dumas, an old high school classmate of Jaki's. He's in the custody of the Chadwick PD."

"Sounds like a hell of a story," Keith said.

"It is. I'll tell you and Dawn all about it tomorrow."

Neither Mark nor I had any luggage, but our room provided us with spa bath products, white terry robes and slippers, and fresh cotton sheets that felt like silk. Those things helped us both forget the stresses of the day—my actual life-and-death confrontation, and Mark's concern over where I was and what kind of mess I'd gotten myself into this time.

He still didn't know that I'd actually faced down an armed Stefan Dumas one-on-one, and I wasn't about to tell him that night. We were in high spirits, and I didn't want to provoke another session where he would moan about me taking terrible risks and I would promise, really meaning it at the time, that I'd never, ever do such a thing again.

Much better to keep dialogue to a minimum and communicate nonverbally. We both deserved to savor this rare taste of the good life.

Tomorrow it would be back to reality.

Chapter 21

By the time I got back to my shop Monday morning, Sarah already had opened for business and greeted me with a big smile. "I guess you folks had a wild time last night. Detective Bonelli already called, said to get back to her when you can."

"Thanks," I told her. "I'll just run upstairs first, change my clothes, and feed my own cats."

In spite of Keith's visit the previous night, Matisse, Cole, and Tango still managed to convince me they all were starving. I gave them breakfast, then headed back downstairs to assume my fair share of responsibility for the shop's boarders.

When I gave Sarah the Persian cat cell phone cover, she squealed—which she doesn't do often—in appreciation. "It looks just like my Harpo!"

We didn't have any pickups, drop-offs, or special grooming sessions scheduled for that day, so we let the first of our three restless boarders out into the playroom. A Russian Blue named Igor squirmed the whole time I was carrying him. Once free, he bounded around the stepped series of floating shelves as if his tail were on fire.

I also returned a phone call from my mother, who had heard on the news about the arrest of her supposed friend "Steve" for stealing Jaki's cat. I repeated the official explanation of how he'd been captured, downplaying my involvement. Mom didn't need to know how close I'd come to being a cadaver on the steel carving table of a half-finished industrial kitchen.

Bonelli already had given Sarah a condensed summary of the night before. While we worked now, I elaborated a bit more for my assistant, and she had the good sense to gasp at the risks I'd taken.

"Didn't I predict," she said, "that when you finally got that van fixed up and on the road, it would just get you into more trouble? One of these days, girl, your luck is going to run out."

I tried to laugh it off. "Nine lives, right? I should still have maybe four or five left."

"On the other hand, you're a hero! So how come they didn't give you more credit in the news?"

"Because I asked them not to. Honestly, I don't need that kind of publicity."

"I guess not," Sarah agreed. "You could end up with stalkers of your own."

"Exactly. Believe me, after the stress I saw Jaki going through, I really wouldn't want to be famous."

By the time I finally returned Bonelli's call, the digging and dumping outside had begun again, so I took my cell phone to the rear of the shop.

"I know I need to come by and give a statement today," I told the detective. "Mark and I were stuck at the hotel late last night, so we got a room. Well, Jaki got us one."

"Really! Got friends in high places now, have you?"

"We spent the night in luxury, which I'm sure is more than Stefan Dumas can say."

"I guarantee that. Have to admit, I've never had a collar quite like him before."

"I can imagine. He and I had a very spacey conversation. One minute he had me feeling sorry for him, and then that cold, ruthless side would pop out. From what Jaki and her brother told me, though, the guy's childhood and teen years must have been horrible."

"We did find out that his mother died last year, of a brain aneurism," Bonelli told me. "I have a feeling that sent him off the rails. Even though he was always obsessed with Ms. Natal, at that point it took over his whole life."

"Was he holding down a job, at least?"

"He worked as an electrical engineer for Martison Technical Services, out on Route 10, for about three years. But he got fired recently from that, too. His boss said Dumas started out polite and conscientious but lately developed a snarky attitude and took too much time off."

I remembered what Dion had told us, about methodical hardware types versus the freewheeling software guys. "Then Stefan wasn't a coder."

"Nope, but he was friends with one, another guy at the company. After Dumas got fired, he told his buddy that he wanted to get back at Martison, screw with their office's lights and the alarm system. It sounded pretty harmless, and his pal didn't like the management much, either, so he had no problem helping out. It was just like Dion Janos told us—they bought malware, came up with a fake identity, et cetera."

"And as an electrical engineer, Stefan probably would've had no trouble figuring out the hotel's grid, once he'd hacked into the system."

"True." After a pause, Bonelli added, "You gotta wonder about some of these perps who really are smart. Why they can't put it to some better use than causing mayhem."

"He had too many problems," I guessed. "I suspected as much, even before I went into that kitchen and saw the table he'd set for himself and Jaki. He was terribly lonely . . . but terribly angry, too. Will he get any kind of psychological help?"

"Remains to be seen. I doubt very much that he'll get off on an insanity plea—he knew killing the guard and the PI was wrong. On the other hand, the way he planned that meeting with Jaki wasn't very clearheaded. How could he hope not to get caught?"

I saw her point—coming after all his careful planning, that part was almost self-destructive. "Maybe he figured if only she returned his feelings, it would all be worth it."

Just then, a shovelful of pavement hit the Dumpster out front with a crash that reverberated through the whole shop. Poor Igor bolted down from the playroom shelves and dashed for a carpeted tunnel at the back of the space.

"What's that—?" Bonelli started to ask. "Oh, right, the new water line."

"Yes, and my neighbor dropped in on me personally yesterday to ask why I couldn't use my 'pull' with the police department to make it magically go away. I'm resigned to the drop-off in my business, but you have to admit, seven to seven is a big chunk of the day to have to listen to this."

"The longer they work each day, the faster they'll get done," the detective pointed out, with her trademark rationality. "But since I'm sure your nerves don't need any more stress at this point, I'll see what I can do. Maybe at least to shorten the hours."

"I'd be grateful," I told her, "and so would Mrs. Kryznansky."

The rest of my first day back was blessedly uneventful, with few drop-ins because of the construction mess. At least by two o'clock the water in my taps and toilet began to run clear again. I took a break then to stroll to the police station and dictate and sign my official statement.

That evening, I finally had time to pop over and visit Dawn. She met me downstairs and let me in by her shop door. She still wore the soft boot but was hopping around pretty nimbly on her crutches. As we stepped together into the rough-hewn freight elevator to go upstairs, I commented, "I guess this thing has been working okay for you? Nick did a good job on it."

"Sure did," she agreed. "It's never let me down yet—except when I wanted it to."

While we rose, slowly but surely, I told her how Nick's son Dion had helped in the police investigation at the expo. The elevator jolted to a stop at Dawn's second-floor living space, and the old iron door slid open. Kind of cool, in an artsy-urban-loft way.

Soon we both relaxed in her living room, me with a glass of white wine and my friend with an herbal tea that wouldn't fight with her painkillers. She settled back on her sofa, her soft-booted foot resting on one batik throw pillow and several others propping her up in back. I gave her the small gift bag from the expo, and Dawn enthused over the brass cat hair clip. Working blindly but expertly, she pulled back a handful of her long, thick auburn hair and fastened it with the ornament.

Tigger sprang up on the sofa back to have a look.

Dawn laughed. "He's a fool for anything shiny. I'll have to watch out or he'll grab it for himself."

"Check the bag again," I said.

She found the striped catnip mouse and tossed it across the room to divert the kitten's attention.

"So tell me," she said. "How did you really nail this Dumas guy? I got the feeling the news reports left an awful lot out."

"Okay, but you're only the third person—besides Bonelli and Sarah—that I'm telling about this." I described my confrontation with Jaki's stalker in detail. "So far, neither Mark nor my mother knows the whole story, and I may want to keep it that way."

Dawn, who already had shared a couple of narrow escapes with me, could empathize. "Yes, you may. Unless you want a lot of scolding, hand-wringing, and warnings about not taking crazy chances. Sounds like you did a great job, though, of talking him down."

I recalled Stefan's anguished face. "I just hope however the trial goes, and wherever they send him, he gets the help he needs. Hard time in a regular prison would destroy him. He's been bullied all his life."

Dawn looked at me with a tilted head and an odd little smile. "Honestly, Cassie. Always worried about the underdog, even one that was ready to kill you!"

The next day, a follow-up news story about Stefan's arrest outed me as the expo volunteer who'd noticed suspicious activity in a restricted area and tipped off the cops. Jaki was quoted as thanking "the Chadwick PD, Bradburne management, Cassie McGlone, my friends and family, and all the fans and cat lovers who offered their support for me and Gordie during this stressful time."

I got a mention and Alec didn't. Maybe he was still on probation?

The news article triggered a surprise phone call from Dria Mason, the rangy spokeswoman of the Jak-ettes. She actually apologized for giving me such a hard time, now that she and her friends knew I was only trying to help their idol find her stolen cat. Dria promised that, rather than blackening my reputation, they would spread the word that I was a dedicated friend of felines.

Whether or not that helped my business any, at least my demonstrations at the expo brought a spate of new requests for the mobile grooming service. Sometimes, if the client wanted me to come out early in the morning or late in the afternoon, Sarah rode along to assist me. But I soon realized that if I was going keep the shop open at the same time, I would need a third pair of hands.

My first choice, of course, was Becky. It would still be only a part-time position for her, but at least a paying one. Combined with her pet-sitting, it might help her to make ends meet and stay in the area.

A week after the expo, I checked in with her by phone. She was delighted to report that the animal shelter had seen a sharp uptick in visitors and pet adoptions. Rocket, the mini pinscher, had found a home with a family who had picked up a brochure at the FOCA table. A local retirement community had expressed interest in adopting Ray, the older cat I'd used for my demo, as a mascot.

"As for Glenda, we asked her what the heck she'd been up to, hanging out with the protestors," Becky said. "I told her that it looked so suspicious, Chris and I began to wonder if she had something to do with the cat being kidnapped."

"After all," I said, "she was pretty vocal in criticizing Jaki for 'exploiting' Gordie by toting him around to photo ops."

"Exactly. Glenda was shocked and angry at the accusation, but later she came to see how we might think that. She's been a little mellower and easier to get along with ever since."

"Good." It seemed the perfect time for me to pitch Becky the idea of helping me groom cats for customers on the road.

"With the street work in front of my shop, I've started going out on more house calls, so I could use the help."

"Wow, Cassie, I'd love to. How big an area do you think you'll be covering?"

"I've already had several calls from outside Chadwick, but I'll keep it within about a ten-mile radius, for starters. I've also been asked to do a groom-a-thon for charity this summer."

Becky chuckled. "I'm guessing that one won't be as glamorous as the expo."

"No, but with any luck it won't be as dangerous, either."

Our conversation reminded me that Perry originally hoped to make the North Jersey Cat Expo an annual event. But even though it was a financial success, it also had turned into a public relations nightmare. If I'd been Perry, I would never have wanted to put myself through such an ordeal again.

Of course, I wasn't Perry.

One afternoon, as Sarah and I worked at the shop in relative peace and quiet, he called, sounding just as enthusiastic as the first time he'd dropped by in person.

"How's the Chadwick PD's best secret weapon?" he teased me.

"I don't know if they'd agree with you on that," I volleyed back. "They probably consider me their biggest pain in the butt."

"Nonsense. Anyhow, I'm not calling on you for any more sleuthing. I just want to know if I can count on you to do your mobile-grooming thing again at the Second Annual North Jersey Cat Expo."

The man really was a glutton for punishment. "The Bradburne's actually holding it again? After all of this year's drama?"

My assistant perched on the stool next to mine and raised her eyebrows. I told him, "Sarah wants to hear. I'm going to put you on speaker."

"Sure, go ahead," Perry said. "Hey, the event made money and got a lot of media attention. The animal shelters are happy, and the sponsors are happy. In the end, even Jaki was happy. Only one person I know who isn't happy, and he's behind bars."

And, of course, two guys *had* been killed. But I supposed neither Perry nor the Bradburne could be held responsible for those tragedies.

"Maybe I'm speaking too soon," he went on. "I'm guessing you got a bump in business after your appearance, Cassie, but maybe even that wasn't enough to make up for everything you went through."

I admitted, "I just have a penchant for sticking my neck out a little too far."

"Well, your grooming demos were such a success that I really hope we can count on you for next year. I swear there will be no stalkers, no cats in jeopardy, no gunplay of any kind."

I still hesitated to make even a verbal commitment. "And no guest stars?"

"Now, Cassie, we *have* to have a guest star to bring in more than just the hard-core cat lovers. No guarantee yet, but we do have somebody in the pipeline. Again, he's big and he's local."

"Who?" I noticed Sarah leaning closer, out of curiosity.

"Like I said, not a sure thing yet, but . . . we're talking to Marty Blatt."

Sarah groaned. "That jerk from the radio?"

I asked, "C'mon, Perry. For real?"

"I know, I know." He tried to placate us. "Blatt's got this reputation as a shock jock. He's controversial, and he offends some people—once in a while, even me. But he *is* funny, and he'll bring out an audience. He was born and bred in Jersey, and believe it or not, he's also a total cat guy! He and his wife have a dozen rescues. Think of the headlines: 'Marty Blatt—Just a Big Pussycat.'"

By now I could hear that Perry was almost lampooning himself. Sarah wore a crooked smile but also shook her curly, graying head.

"Sarah looks doubtful," I told him, "and I always respect her judgment."

"Well, it is almost a whole year away. Just know that I'll be checking back with you. Meanwhile, we'll keep your parking space open on the plaza, okay?"

"Great, Perry. Thanks for thinking of me."

When I'd hung up, Sarah said primly, "In a year, maybe he'll have found a more *appropriate* guest star."

"Let's hope," I agreed. "A local guy whose radio show ticks off just about everybody! Gee, what could possibly go wrong?"